EL PASO SUNSET

El Paso SUNSET

A NOVEL

LOUIS BODNAR

NEW YORK

LONDON • NASHVILLE • MELBOURNE • VANCOUVER

El Paso Sunset

A Novel

Published in New York, New York, by Morgan James Publishing. Morgan James is a trademark of Morgan James, LLC. www.MorganJamesPublishing.com

ISBN 9781631952548 paperback
ISBN 9781631952555 eBook
Library of Congress Control Number: 2020939932

Cover Design by:
Rachel Lopez
www.r2cdesign.com

Interior Design by:
Chris Treccani
www.3dogcreative.net

Morgan James is a proud partner of Habitat for Humanity Peninsula and Greater Williamsburg. Partners in building since 2006.

Get involved today! Visit
MorganJamesPublishing.com/giving-back

To my Lord and Savior, Jesus Christ and to the forever
and always love of my life, Joan Bodnar.

"We were together. I forget the rest."
—Walt Whitman

"The ultimate of human freedoms is the freedom of choice."
—The author

"The farther backward you may look . . . the farther forward you are likely to see." This is an anonymous saying that I once heard or saw long ago that is better said by Saint Augustine: "Trust the past to God's mercy, the present to God's love, and the future to God's providence." For it has been written, "No eye has seen, no ear has heard, and no human mind has conceived the things God has prepared for those who love Him"
(1 Cor. 2:9).

With God's grace freely given, the completion of the intimacy between a man and a woman in a relationship completely **depends** *on each, by their own God-given choice, coming to know and understand themselves fully. And this only actually happens the moment that the woman forgives her own father, lets him go, and lets her son go to another woman of his own . . . and the man forgives his own mother, lets her go, and lets his daughter go to another man of her own.*
—The author

CAST OF CHARACTERS
(In Order of Appearance)

The Good Guys

Steven Vandorol—El Paso attorney and special prosecutor

Chief Judge Kathy Carbon—El Paso County chief district judge

Rommel—Steven's Great Dane dog

Eddie Egen—El Paso Police Department chief and Steven's best friend

Ernesto Luis Martinez—El Paso County district attorney

Vanessa Carson—Steven's attorney friend from Washington, DC

Christina Ortega—Steven's law office receptionist and legal assistant

Ray Ortega—Steven's private investigator and Christina's father

Marce—Steven's law office legal assistant

Beth Barker—Member of the special prosecution (Francisco Montes, her husband)

Jacob Warren

Emily Blankenship—Jacob's girlfriend

North Anderson—Member of the special prosecution team

Captain G. Jack Reacher—US Army Special Forces, Ft. Bliss (Joan Reacher, his wife)

The Bad Guys

"Gravelly Voice" —just a voice on a speaker of a burner cell phone

Colonel Stanislav Lemev—Spetsnaz Russian Special Forces

General Wang Xiangsui—Communist Chinese Peoples' Liberation Army

Colonel Qiao Liang—Communist Chinese Peoples' Liberation Army

Major Ward Powell—Spetsnaz Russian Special Forces

Ubiytsa—Ward's dog, a Russian Ovcharka (Ubiytsa being the Russian word for "Killer")

Muhammed Atta—Muslim Islamist terrorist

PROLOGUE

She was simply beautiful.

She had honey-blonde hair, cut in a long bob style above her narrow shoulders, beautiful high cheekbones, and makeup so perfect it seemed like she wasn't wearing any at all. Her perfectly shaped eyebrows and long black eyelashes curling upward complemented a small, pert nose. Her lips were painted with pale pink lip gloss. She had the shapely body of a mermaid.

The man watched her closely, getting very excited.

She was wearing a spaghetti-strap camisole, very modest, hiding her ample breasts. He continued to stare at this gorgeous woman sitting alone at the bar in the Hilton Inn in Lubbock, Texas.

He continued to stare. She was having a glass of wine and reading a paperback. She looked tired after a long day taking the Professional Responsibility portion of the Texas Bar Exam that he himself had just taken as well. She was wearing jeans over what he pictured to be shapely long legs, with white sandals and toes painted with red nail polish.

His gaze traveled back to her small bottom sitting on the bar stool and up to her bare shoulders. He was feeling sexual excitement, lust, and desire just looking at her shapely rear from afar.

This man was on a mission—an evil mission, a mission to humiliate and debase the beautiful woman sitting at the bar.

He wore jeans, cowboy boots, a black Stetson, and a cowboy shirt, open at the collar, with long sleeves to hide a small vial of Rohypnol. He had been watching her since his contact called him to let him know that she had left her room after most likely freshening up. His contact, another cowboy, his best friend and mentor sitting off to the side, touched his own Stetson, signaling the man and smiling broadly. His friend was also looking forward to some real fun himself.

The man signaled back, smiling as well. This was going to be a tandem rape. *The haughty wench is in for a real surprise,* he thought. *When she wakes up, that is.* He almost laughed out loud as he walked toward the bar.

"How about another white zin?" the bartender asked the beautiful woman sitting at the bar totally engrossed in her paperback book.

She looked up. "Oh, why not?" She paused, smiled brightly, and asked, "Is the restaurant here pretty good?"

The bartender grimaced and, whispering, said, "It's garbage, but the Rib Crib, just two blocks away, has the best barbeque in town!"

"Thank you . . . I'll probably take that suggestion!"

This woman had a wide, beautiful smile: sparkling with snow white, straight teeth and sunshine in her eyes. The bartender couldn't help but notice these features as he put another glass in front of her. "Ma'am, I hope you don't mind me saying, but you have the most radiant smile I've ever seen in my life!"

"Thank you," she replied softly, as a man sat down beside her, lightly brushing against her side.

"I agree with you, bartender!" the man said, taking off his hat and putting it on the seat beside him. "Let me have a glass of merlot."

She turned toward the man. He was a handsome guy and looked vaguely familiar. She knew him from somewhere, this cowboy in jeans with a thick snakeskin belt, massive ornamental belt buckle, and boots. "Thank you as well! Have we met?"

"I'm from El Paso, and I'm here taking the Professional Responsibility portion of the Texas Bar Exam," he replied. "I saw you in the exam room earlier today." There, he had tried to catch her attention several times, but she had ignored him completely, angering him further each time. *I guess she doesn't remember me at all, from DC,* he thought. *The fake mustache and glasses must be working.*

She nodded. "I guess that's where I've seen you. Do you practice law in El Paso?" She was now smiling brightly.

"No, I don't. I just moved there from Alaska a couple of months ago." He was smiling at her as well. "Can I buy you a drink?"

"No, thanks. I just got one," she said, pointing at her wine glass. "Anyway, I'm leaving after I finish this one." She was no longer smiling. She suddenly had a bad feeling about this really handsome guy, a gut feeling she didn't like. She shivered slightly.

He stuck out his hand. "My name is Bob Le Mont," he lied as he thought she might remember him by his real name. "What's your name?" His hand grazed her wine glass, knocking it over and spilling the wine on the bar. "Oh, gosh! I'm so sorry . . . bartender, get her another one. I'm so sorry."

"That's okay. Don't worry about it. I was just leaving anyway." She tried to stand.

"No, please don't. Let me make it up to you . . . my bad." The bartender immediately put another glass in front of her. "Please," he said, pleading softly yet very respectfully.

"Oh, okay," she relented. "But then I've got to get something to eat. I'm real tired . . . and very hungry."

"I'll buy you dinner. It's the least I can do." He put his left arm around her soft shoulder.

She jerked back, surprised, and, like a magician, he passed his right hand over her drink, dropping the dose of Rohypnol right into her glass of wine.

He pulled his hand away and immediately said, "I'm so sorry, really. I meant no disrespect." His tone was contrite and humble.

She relented again. "No problem. I'm just tired."

She took a long swallow of her wine and set the glass back down on the bar.

"Are you sure I can't buy you dinner?"

"No, thanks."

"Where are you from?" he asked her, although he knew exactly where she was from.

She suddenly wasn't feeling very well. "I'm from Washington, DC, but I've just moved to El Paso myself. I'm going to practice law there." The room was starting to spin.

"Really? Well, maybe we can have dinner there when we get back, okay?" he said gently, noticing that she was getting dizzy and drowsy.

"Yeah, maybe." She was slurring her words. "I don't know. I think I'm going to throw up." She almost slid off the stool.

He grabbed her and signaled his contact, who came in a flash. With the woman carried between them, the two walked out of the lounge area, passing the distracted bartender counting twenties in an envelope.

———————

She was in a haze, on a bed, and completely naked, arms and legs tied to the bed with white nylon chords. She could make out two men standing over her, both naked as well. The whole room was spinning, swimming, turning. The lights were dim. She felt like she was in a helicopter, rotors circling, whuump, whuump, whuump. She felt sick, nauseated. Her head hurt, and the whole room was spinning wildly.

"Man, she's got a great body," she heard one man say to the other.

And she screamed in pain as she lost consciousness.

CHAPTER 1

She was parked on the corner of Wilmot and Parkland Street in the west El Paso Walmart Supercenter parking lot. It was packed with almost a thousand cars of all shapes, sizes, and colors, but the majority were white, the norm in El Paso as citizens sought that color's protection against the burning sun.

It was early afternoon in the unusually hot late December day. People were coming and going, shopping for New Year's Day festivities and imminent football-watching parties.

Her targets were in a neighborhood three blocks away. She had scouted the home and the neighborhood near Coronado High School several times in the evenings. She was ready to carry out her assignment as a professional who did all her jobs very well. She enjoyed her work immensely and derived great satisfaction from it. She was a killer.

She was in a nondescript white Nissan Sentra with darkly tinted windows, gray interior, its engine idling, and the air conditioning on full blast—right in the middle of the parking lot next to cars almost identical to hers. She glanced at the car's digital clock. 1:10 p.m. It was time. She had allotted one hour for her job. She was a very thorough professional.

She turned off the engine, stepped out of the car, locked the doors, and started walking toward Wilmot Street.

She could have easily passed for a high school senior. Her long, dark hair was pulled back into a ponytail, and she wore mirror-dark black sunglasses, their large lenses hiding most of her face, and a Dallas Cowboys hat. With no makeup on except for lip gloss, she was gorgeous. She wore a Coronado High School Thunderbird football jersey, sweatpants, and black Nike running shoes. A 9mm Beretta M9 semiautomatic, with silencer, was tucked against the small of her back on a belt, hidden by the jersey.

1

She also had a North Face backpack containing a nylon face mask, lip gloss, surgical gloves, and two extra clips of ammo. She was ready and getting a little excited as she always did before an assignment.

The sun was straight up in the sky, brilliant and white hot. Its glare made it hard to see in the burning haze.

She slowly walked across the parking lot, passing cars radiating and reflecting the sun. She couldn't ignore the acrid smell of hot asphalt and gasoline. She seemed to be walking in a sun-city hell until she reached Wilmot Street. Looking both ways, she saw no cars coming, so she walked across to Parkland Street. She walked slowly to the right and continued down the block. All appeared deserted except for an occasional tricycle or other toys in the driveways. No one was braving the oppressive midday heat.

These streets had large, well-kept homes with long driveways and sprawling, landscaped lawns filled with desert plants, succulents, and silvery rock, which was, again, the norm in El Paso. Mesquite and acacia trees, plentiful all-around, gave shady respite from the searing sun.

The homes were large, mostly white and gray stucco with large windows, many with boxlike sun-reflecting awnings. Spanish modern architecture was prevalent in this expensive and ostentatious part of west El Paso.

She casually turned up on Vista del Sol and walked to number 1055, her final destination. She stopped and looked all around, turning slowly and scanning the nearby homes and the entire neighborhood. She checked the mailbox, opening it with the back of her hand. The mail had apparently been delivered as the box had a few envelopes. As she closed it back again the same way, she looked across the street. All window blinds were down. She could see the heat rising from the rooftops, the sun still blinding. She shaded her eyes to check again: all deserted, all garage doors down. She was completely alone.

She followed the cement walkway to the side of the house, took out the gloves from the backpack, put them on, and went through the gate to the backyard. As she closed the rough, cedar gate behind her, she noticed the backyard was completely surrounded by an eight-foot privacy wooden fence.

The backyard was large and ran the entire length of the house. It had two large, old elm trees that canopied most of the yard, lowering the temperature by twenty degrees at least. The landscaping was exquisite, with brick flower beds full of succulents and cacti, all professionally arranged. A huge rainbow playset sat between the trees. With its plastic slides and swings and a wooden playhouse on top, she thought it was probably very expensive.

The patio was to the right and was covered with a huge Sunshade retractable awning. She also noticed a massive built-in barbeque grill, two tables, chairs, two chaise lounges, and a small, plastic kiddie pool half full of water.

She walked to the glass patio doors, which had heavy, light tan curtains drawn, and tried the sliding glass door. It was unlocked, so she slid it open. All was dark and cool inside. She stepped in and was shrouded by the curtain. She stood behind it and waited. She knew no one was home. After a few seconds, she backed to an opening and was inside the family den.

She took out the sheer nylon mask, hesitated a moment, then put it back in the backpack. *I won't be needing a mask,* she thought and smiled. She walked into the kitchen. Getting a glass from a cabinet, she filled it with water from the dispenser on the fridge, opened the door, got out a pear, and sat down on a bar stool. She took out the Beretta, tightened the screw-on silencer, chambered a round, put the weapon on the counter, took a drink, bit into the pear, and chewed as she waited.

At half past one, she heard the garage door rambling open, car doors closing, a long pause, and then the door into the kitchen opening. "Close the garage door, Michelle." An overweight but pretty woman in a nurse's uniform stepped in and saw her standing right in front of her, the gun mere inches from her face. The nurse stuttered, eyes wide with terror, "Who . . .?"

And she shot her right between the eyes. Pop, pop.

The woman teetered for an instant and fell dead to the right, helped along by a slight shove. The assassin heard the garage door rambling down as the little girl came to the door, pushing her way in. "Mommy, can I have a peanut butter and jelly . . ." She saw the woman and screamed, shrieking, as the gun fired—pop, pop—right into her small face. The girl crumpled to the floor like a rag doll and died instantly.

She dragged the girl by her feet and left her beside her dead mother.

She walked back to the bar, put the Beretta on the counter, and finished eating the pear. She drank the rest of the water, put the glass in the sink, took out her cell phone, set it on the counter as well, and waited.

The cell phone rang. "Yes?" She listened, pushed *end*, and continued looking around, enjoying the cool air conditioning.

In fifteen minutes, she heard the garage door open again and recognized the distinct purring of the now-familiar Porsche. She got off the stool, picked up the Beretta, slowly walked to the door, and stood with her back against the wall to wait.

The door opened. "Michelle, my belle, Daddy is home!" a big man with eyebrows raised in anticipation yelled and stepped into the kitchen, with a bright, wide smile on his face. He heard a noise and turned.

And she shot him right between the eyes as well, one muffled pop. The big man absorbed the shot with eyes wide open. He stood for an instant, swayed gently, and then collapsed straight down as if his legs had disappeared from under him.

She watched the blood pool around his head for a few seconds, raised the gun again, and shot him in the chest twice—pop, pop. The muzzle stayed open; the gun was empty.

She picked up the shell casings, put them in her pocket, reloaded, chambered a round, and put the weapon in her belt against the small of her back. She stepped over the dead man and out into the garage where she pressed the door button and watched the door ramble down.

She came back in, closed and locked the inside door, glanced at the thermostat to make sure that the air conditioning was as cold as possible. It wasn't, so she set it lower. Back in the kitchen, she finished eating the pear. As she threw the core into the garbage disposal, she turned on the tap, flipped the switch, and after a few seconds turned both off. After carefully touching up her lip gloss, she eased out through the curtain and went out the same way she came in. Walking to the side and out the gate, she removed her gloves, stuffed them in her pockets, walked down the driveway to the street and looked around again. Judging it safe, she turned left on the still deserted street and walked slowly back to her car, smiling brightly, seemingly just a teenage cheerleader walking through the neighborhood and on to Walmart.

CHAPTER 2

"Come on in, Judge. Really nice to see you on this fine El Paso evening." Steven Vandorol was smiling warmly as he held the front door open for Judge Kathy Carbon, 65th District chief judge. She looked very beautiful and was *the second most beautiful woman to have crossed my threshold this December,* Steven thought.

Kathy was tiny, under five feet, Steven guessed, and probably weighed less than a hundred pounds. Her black, shiny hair, speckled with gray, was complimented by her makeup, a tiny nose, and small mouth. *She doesn't look like a judge at all on this New Year's Eve, but just a very pretty woman,* he thought.

Steven knew her very well professionally, had been in her court hundreds of times; she had even appointed Steven to the municipal bench when there had been an opening. She also had been instrumental in recommending Steven to District Attorney Ernie Martinez last August to head the special prosecution team in a major fraud and conspiracy case.

Kathy and Steven had become good friends, professionally. Steven admired and liked her very much. He had been surprised but pleased when, during a call to his law office, she had asked him out for New Year's Eve dinner and reception afterward.

"Thank you, Mr. Vandorol, but tonight I am a civilian. Please call me Kathy," she said, smiling brightly. Then she hugged Steven warmly.

Steven hugged her right back. "I guess, then, I can say, Kathy, you look positively gorgeous this evening. Happy New Year!"

"Thank you, Steven. Happy New Year to you. You look very nice yourself."

Steven had on a starched white shirt, paisley tie, tan slacks with razor-sharp pleat, and his favorite maroon sea turtle boots, shined to a high gloss. A little over six feet tall, broad shouldered, and weighing in at one eighty,

Steven Vandorol was back to his high-school-football-playing physique, maintained by early morning five-mile runs with his dog.

He was clean shaven, Hungarian dark, with a wide forehead and receding hairline. His prominent nose was crooked, having been broken many times in childhood brawls. It was the only facial feature that embarrassed him. High cheekbones accented large, dark brown, piercing, sometimes slightly violent and even cruel eyes—eyes with just a hint of a slant, evident in the race coming from the Mongol and Hun hordes that began the Hungarian bloodlines. His hair was perfect—brown, now graying at the temples and sideburns, razor edged.

His eyes reflected his soul. Previously turbulent, after recovery from the evil of Washington, DC, they now reflected a serenity and calm he was proud to have earned by his own choice. *Free at last from most of my evil ways,* Steven always thought when he now looked at himself in the mirror.

"Nice boots, Steven! I've seen you wearing them before in my court . . . I couldn't compliment you on them in court."

Steven laughed, "Yes, they are my favorites!"

"Alligator?"

"No, sea turtle. El Paso's very own Tony Lama!"

She came in and Steven closed the front door. "Can I take your jacket?"

"Sure, thanks." She shrugged off her coat and handed it to Steven, who hung it in the closet.

"Gosh, Steven," she said, awed by the magnificent view out the large glass window. "This is the most amazing view of El Paso Juarez that I've ever seen, and I'm El Paso born and have lived here all my life."

Outside, the setting sun had just barely dipped between the Santo Cristo Mountains of Mexico. The lights below in El Paso and Juarez were just starting to twinkle and shine in the dusk, gleaming and shimmering in the twilight.

She paused, briefly admiring the breathtaking view, then looked around. "And you have a very nice place, by the way."

"Thank you, Kathy, it's my oasis . . . my favorite place in the world. Can I get you some wine?"

Steven's huge Great Dane Rommel was sitting by the couch watching the woman intently, ears standing tall, black eyes shining.

"That would be grand," she said as she nonchalantly walked up to Rommel and gently patted his head. Rommel was almost purring.

"Well, that's interesting," Steven said, remembering his date with Beth Barker, one of the attorneys Ernie Martinez, the El Paso County district attorney and Steven's boss, had assigned to the special prosecution Steven now led. That particular date hadn't ended well at all.

"What is?" Kathy asked, stroking Rommel's head. "He's just a gentle pussy cat!"

"Rommel didn't want anything to do with the last woman who visited here." He paused, smiling at the little love fest. "My dog avoided *her* like the plague from the first moment she walked in here."

"I guess dogs can sense good and evil . . . in both male and female," Kathy said, still stroking the dog and smiling beautifully.

"Rommel's pretty perceptive, and he's sure *not* shy tonight. He usually takes his time in warming up to people."

Steven poured two glasses of chianti, walked over, and handed a glass to Kathy. "Chianti okay?"

"Perfect." Kathy took the glass and sat down on the couch right next to Rommel's huge head. She raised her glass: "Happy New Year again."

Steven raised his glass and said, "And to you, Kathy." Rommel gently laid his huge snout right in her lap. Steven laughed, "Rommel!"

Kathy interrupted, "He's fine." She scratched behind his ear and added, "He's a beautiful dog, Steven." She paused, took a sip of her wine, and asked, "Ernie told me . . . in confidence . . . about the attack on your home during Thanksgiving. Are you alright?" She locked eyes with him.

Ever since Steven had been appointed as special prosecutor, he felt like he had a big red bullseye on his back.

The case of the state of Texas against the Alvarados—father, Alberto, and son, Ricardo Alvarado—El Paso Power and Electric Company, Kemper and Smith law firm, Henderson and Lane law firm, and other defendants, both named and unnamed co-conspirators, was a special prosecution and indictment that had national implications looking forward to the November 2016 presidential elections. It was initially a prosecution of the Alvarados, their lawyers, and the El Paso Power and Electric Company for the sale of fraudulent annuities, a giant Ponzi scheme, and was the largest fraud prosecution in Texas to that time.

The indictment was later amended and expanded by the joint action of the governors of four states to include widespread border corruption, mass illegal emigration forced on the border states by the president's unconstitutional executive orders, and a vast conspiracy to stack the federal government with Muslim radicals.

The indictment was already in place and had been for well over a year, all before Steven—a lawyer with no ties to any faction, business or political—was appointed by the district attorney.

All the pervasive and ongoing corruption, both on the border and nationwide, was apparently financed by the Alvarados, huge donors to both the president and the National Democratic Party.

Even before his appointment as special prosecutor, the continuing investigation of the Alvarados by Texas Rangers and the El Paso Police Department found the federal government complicit and the border corruption was just the tip of the iceberg. The Alvarados, both billionaires, were at the origin of pervasive fraud, their hooks reaching deeply into the Democratic Party, all the way into the current administration and the White House, and directly to the president's inner circle of Muslim Brotherhood appointees.

It was widely suspected that the assassination contract on Steven and his entire prosecution team of Beth Barker, heading the drug unit; North Anderson, the DA's first assistant; and Eddie Egen, El Paso police chief, was contracted by the Alvarados, especially Ricardo Alvarado, who was also suspected to be a ruthless drug lord and head of the Sinaloa Cartel.

As the investigation into the Alvarados widened, more and more corruption and crimes were discovered, including white slavery, drug and weapons smuggling, all in collusion with a corrupt federal government and its corrupt leftist radical political appointees.

Since his appointment as special prosecutor, there had been an attempt on Steven's best friend, El Paso Police Chief Eddie Egen, and an attempt on Steven's own life by a well-organized assassination team that almost destroyed his home. Steven was saved by the grace of God and Eddie and Andi, his wife, as the couple had invited Steven and his children, visiting from Oklahoma, on a rafting trip in Big Bend on the Rio Grande over Thanksgiving break.

There was also an attempt on Steven's life just recently during the Christmas holidays at his law office. Steven had discovered, and the El Paso Police Department had defused, a bomb wired to the entrance of his law office.

But the attempt that angered Steven the most was the near killing of his beloved dog, Rommel, by shots from a high-powered sniper rifle fired from the scenic lookout on Franklin Mountain high above his Golden Hill Terrace home.

"I'm almost sorry I got you involved, Steven," Kathy said. Besides appointing Steven to an associate municipal judge when there was an opening, she had been instrumental in recommending Steven to the district attorney, to be the special prosecutor.

"Don't be, Kathy!" Steven said and sat down in the wingback chair. "I'm fine. I've got my dog and my oasis. I'm fine, really . . . Eddie's got me and my dog covered with 24/7 security. We're being watched as we speak. I'm really okay!" He took a drink and changed the subject. "Thank you for this invitation. I've been looking forward to our date. Are you okay with it?"

"You mean going public with our friendship?" She smiled at Steven. "I'll answer that . . . no problem whatsoever. You're a good-looking guy, Steven, and a darn fine lawyer as well. No, no problem at all."

"Thank you, Kathy. You're a dear, a very beautiful dear." Steven was smiling warmly. "What's your future look like?"

"I'm in my own oasis, Steven." She smiled at Steven and raised her glass again. "Here's to each of us finding our happiness."

Steven raised his glass. "As my daughter once told me, 'Happiness is like a butterfly; you can chase it and chase it and never catch it. But when you sit down to take a rest, it alights on your shoulder.'"

"Amen." She clicked her glass with her friend, took a sip, paused for a moment, and said, "How is the amended indictment coming along?"

Taking a sip of his wine, he cleared his throat and said, "I'm working on it when I can. It's been tough in November and December, but I've almost caught up." He took another sip of wine and continued, "I'm still looking to hire an experienced young lawyer to help me with my practice so I can devote my time fully to the special prosecution. I'll try to have the amended and superseded indictment ready for filing probably in late July." Kathy nodded with a small smile as he spoke. "And there's good news there as well. A lawyer in DC, whom I worked with—she's still a good friend—is coming to El Paso the first week in January to check it out and maybe work with me." He finished by grinning ear-to-ear.

"Who's that?" Kathy asked.

"Her name is Vanessa Moore."

"That's really good! I'll look forward to meeting her. I can then call for the secret and closed grand jury to be empaneled. And after you present your entire case, all the evidence, especially of high treason against all the corrupt federal government officials, and the grand jury issues and certifies the true bill of indictment—"

Steven finished her thought: "Then you, Kathy . . . can issue warrants for the arrest of all the criminals."

After dining at Café Central, attending a subdued New Year's Eve party, and dropping Judge Carbon off, Steven sat at home in the dark, drinking a glass of Courvoisier and stroking Rommel's head, his large black eyes shining in the brilliance of outside lights streaming into the room.

Before the two lay the El Paso-Juarez panorama of a billion sparkling jewels—emeralds, diamonds, rubies, gold, and silver—all lying on a jet-black velvet ocean before a completely black void of infinite sky, shimmering, blinking, pulsating, and piercing the blackness of the gloomy nighttime.

As he marveled at this spectacle, Steven rose to set down his glass and walked onto the balcony where the entire world of El Paso-Juarez stretched into eternity before him. Rommel followed and sat down beside him.

Both man and dog marveled at the vividness of the light show below and the eternal, infinite black void above. It was as if the two were all alone in the magnificent outdoor theater of God. It was as if an immense outdoor movie screen was laid before them in a technicolor IMAX theater.

Steven and Rommel gazed in complete wonderment and awe at God's nighttime creation. The sky above the panorama of brilliant lights and sparkling colors was an ominous, totally black void, standing out in silent contrast.

Steven was thoughtful. He was pensive. He was serene and peaceful as he thought of one of his favorite sayings: *the farther backward you may look . . . the farther forward you are likely to see.* He felt he was in the pause of that saying, between looking backward and seeing forward. He looked down at Rommel, who again cocked his head. Steven thought he saw him smile.

"So, what do you think, Rommel? What's our future like?"

Rommel grunted as if answering.

"You're right. I—we—have much to be thankful for. We—I—have faith in God and Jesus Christ. I have my kids, and I have good friends . . . and you and Pegasus."

And there before all of El Paso, Texas, and Juarez, Mexico, with the good Lord and Jesus Christ in his heart, Steven Vandorol kneeled, bowed his head, and with Rommel beside him, prayed out loud:

Dear Lord and Jesus Christ, I love you with all my heart and soul and thank you for all you have done for me. I'm so very grateful for all the help, all the blessings and miracles, the guidance, and blessed assurance. And I'm so grateful that you are with me and for me, guiding me, comforting me, and being in my heart and soul, protecting me and comforting me with your grace, every second of every day. And I'm especially grateful for my faith, for my two precious kids, Josef and Karina . . . my friends and my health and survival, all by your grace. Thank you, dear God, the Father, and thank you, Jesus Christ, His Son and my Savior.

I ask you, dear God and Jesus Christ, to please stay with me and continue to show me the way. And help me to be the best I can be: first, for you, my Lord and Jesus Christ; for my precious kids and future grandkids; and for my friends . . . my dog, Rommel, and horse, Pegasus.

Steven glanced at Rommel and noticed his head bowed and eyes closed, seemingly praying, too. And Steven said the Lord's Prayer out loud:

Our Father, who art in Heaven, hallowed be thy name . . . thy kingdom come . . . thy will be done, on earth, as it is in heaven. Give us this day our daily bread and forgive us our debts as we forgive our debtors. And lead us not into temptation but deliver us from evil, for thine is the kingdom and the power and the glory, forever and ever, in Jesus Christ, your Son's name, Amen.

Steven opened his eyes and rose from his knees slowly, grasping the railing with his hands. He yawned, deeply breathing in the cool, dry desert air, and looked into God's brilliant and eternal expanse. Rommel stood beside him, staring at this master and best friend adoringly.

Steven looked down at Rommel, fully visible in the brilliant light show before them, and smiled again. From his dog, Steven looked back out on God's giant screen and focused on the jewels of the entire universe before him and downtown El Paso and Juarez sparkling below.

Steven looked at the giant, lighted American flag totally illuminating the Wells Fargo bank tower in the red, white, and blue lights of the stars and stripes. It stood above and in the midst of the downtown like a majestic beacon and shimmered as brightly as the Christmas tree that had lit the downtown until Christmas Day, a few days ago.

Right below, Interstate I-10 was almost completely deserted in the early morning hours. Just a few tiny-looking vehicles were visible, their headlights like fireflies moving in the far distance.

Steven and Rommel both stood in awe looking at God's magnificent screen.

Suddenly, with a very loud crackle and an electrical explosion, a cascading blackout extinguished all the lights downtown, the bright and brilliant American flag going completely dark. Then the blackout rolled out slowly into the far distance, both to Steven's right and left, all lights going out. The bright, sparkling quadrants of light went dark, one by one, until there was nothing.

And in that instant, the Lord turned out the lights of the world. The immense screen before them went completely dark. Only absolute darkness, silence, and oppressive gloom were left.

And El Paso died.

As Steven and Rommel stood in complete, pitch-black darkness, which enveloped both like a funeral shroud, Steven raised his arm to his face, clicked the luminous dial of his Timex calendar wrist watch, and read the brightly lit face: three o'clock in the morning, Friday, January 1, 2016, Anno Domini.

And then there was nothing.

CHAPTER 3

Steven Vandorol and his dog, Rommel, stood side by side in complete, absolute darkness.

Steven now understood what it would be like to be blind. He couldn't see a thing, but after his eyes adjusted, he could make out Rommel's outline, as well as that of a few buildings. No stars were in the sky. Where the earth met the sky was a total mystery.

"No stars in the entire sky!" Steven exclaimed to his dog. "It must be overcast . . . and it smells like it might rain." And just at that moment, a dazzling blue-white lightning bolt flashed and streaked down into Juarez and the distant horizon, turning the black gloom into blinding daylight, like a giant strobe flash, startling both Steven and Rommel. Both flinched involuntarily. Steven shivered and patted Rommel to calm him. The dog barked, a moaning howl that broke the deadly silence. And then all was back to dark gloom again.

Then another bolt, a deafening explosion, like bacon sizzling in a giant pan, struck downtown El Paso, lighting the downtown momentarily into sparkling daylight. Then, like a freight train, rolling thunder followed in waves, booming and deafening at first, then softly echoing into the distance, then back to nothing again.

Steven squatted down and held his dog close, feeling his warmth, yet the dog was shivering. Steven said a silent prayer as he held his dog for what seemed like an eternity.

Steven stood and walked inside, careful not to run into furniture. He picked up the LED flashlight that he kept on a small table by the screen door, turned it on, and walked back outside to his dog. He passed the light beam all around and on Rommel, who stared up at him with huge, black-pearl eyes that shined quizzically, looking like a big question mark.

"It's okay, boy," Steven said and petted his huge head, calming him even further. "Everything will be alright." He shined the beam all around the outside, left and right, to the back of the house and down into the gloom of

15

the mountainside. He saw nothing but the usual rocky scrub on an almost sheer decline.

"Let's go inside, boy. I think a big rain is coming! I can smell it in the air." Rommel willingly followed his master.

Just as both got inside, another huge lightning bolt lit the plate glass window, turning the living room into daylight for just an instant. Steven counted the seconds, waiting for the blast of thunder that eventually echoed outside like a tank gun firing.

"That one was just a few miles away, Rommel," Steven said. "Probably struck downtown again." His peaceful voice and manner continued to calm the dog.

Steven, with the flashlight beam shining ahead and Rommel alongside him, walked all around his oasis, checking the windows and making sure none were leaking. "I'm sure glad Eddie and his guys got our home all repaired after the home invasion blast while we were in Great Bend rafting." Steven paused, then said, "Once again, Little Buddy, the good Lord works in mysterious ways." They walked back into the living room, and both stood looking out the picture window, seeing only darkness, apart from a few car headlights, and oppressive gloom.

"It won't be long until sunrise, my friend." Rommel woofed, understanding written all over his intelligent face. He woofed a second time.

Then the sky fell down. The rain was a deluge of water on the plate glass, with huge raindrops slamming against the glass as if a fire hose were on it. Deafening sounds rose as rain hit the pane like machine gun bursts. It felt like their oasis was under attack, with the outside and inside lit to daylight as lightning bolts exploded over downtown El Paso—all followed by booming explosions of thunder.

It seems as if an angry Lord is voicing His displeasure with a wayward world and the evil in it, Steven thought.

As of yet, Steven's lights had not come back on, so he and Rommel huddled together in pitch-black darkness. Steven again raised his arm to his face, clicked the luminous dial of his wrist watch, and read the time: a quarter to four.

Steven thought to retrieve his cell phone from its charger in the kitchen, but when he tried it—nothing. "No electricity and cell towers are out as well!" he said out loud. "Might as well be patient, Rommel. I guess we just have to wait."

Steven got candles from the kitchen cabinet and lit them with a small lighter he took from a drawer. He picked up two, set them on two end tables, and went back into the kitchen to pour himself another Courvoisier. Back in the living room, he sat down in his favorite chair, and yawned. Rommel, now draping himself on the couch, watched his master intently.

Outside, it was still raining buckets. Steven took a sip and looked at his watch again. "Now a quarter past four; the lights have been out for almost an hour!"

Steven woke with a start and looked at his watch, almost five-thirty now. He looked over at Rommel to find his dog sleeping peacefully. Sensing his master was awake, he perked up and looked at Steven in anticipation. The two candles had burned down, wax gathering on the holders.

The rain had stopped, and the plate glass was a black void reflecting only the burning candles inside.

Steven got up, walked to the glass door, opened it to step outside, and immediately felt the oppressive humidity. He could smell the purity of wet concrete and fresh air. Rommel followed him out. Steven slowly walked to the railing with Rommel right behind.

As Steven looked out in the distance, a twinkling of lights was returning, as if the Lord were turning the lights of the stars in the sky back on. From the farthest distance, slowly at first, one sparkling quadrant of light at a time started twinkling, rolling forward right back into downtown El Paso, lighting even the American flag on the Wells Fargo bank tower once again.

The panorama of sparkling lights had gloriously returned. God's IMAX theater screen was back on.

Right below, even I-10 was completely lit again. Many cars, ambulances, fire engines, and other vehicles were visible in the middle of the night, racing all over, their lights flashing and pulsating.

Steven and Rommel quietly looked out over the lights and listened to the noise below. Steven checked his watch: 6:59 a.m. on Friday, January 1, 2016. New Year's Day in El Paso, Texas.

Suddenly, in a bright flash like a miracle of the Lord, the dark sky broke and a sliver of sunrise, a beautiful El Paso sunrise, shone right before their eyes.

They watched the sunrise for a few minutes, enjoying the cool air and the lights turning off, welcoming the El Paso sunrise again.

Steven again checked his watch: 7:06 a.m. El Paso, Texas, and his home on Golden Hill Terrace was bathed by the most brilliant sunshine ever.

Steven felt the storm had washed the world once again, renewing it with God's eternal promise and grace. He breathed the fresh morning air for several more minutes and then, followed by his dog, went to the kitchen and checked his cell phone. The face lit up. It was back in service.

"Well, that's that, Rommel!" Rommel nonchalantly strolled to the couch, hopped up, settled in after turning once, then closed his eyes to sleep.

Steven grinned at his dog and yawned. With his cell phone back on the charger, he walked to the bedroom and flicked on the light. He paused to stare wistfully at his favorite picture—a very sharp, high-definition color photograph of two dolphins leaping in synchrony in the wake just ahead of a massive tramp steamer slicing through the ocean.

He then undressed in a flash, settled under the covers, and had a nice conversation with the Lord before falling fast asleep.

CHAPTER 4

Steven Vandorol, in El Paso now for almost five years, parked his Ford Taurus in a reserved space of the courthouse parking garage on San Antonio Street in downtown El Paso early on Monday morning.

Built in 1991 on the site of the demolished courthouse originally built in 1917, the new structure was made of steel and concrete with an Alamo-shaped granite entrance and sky-blue reflective glass that mirrored the Franklin Mountains, the divider of affluent west and military east El Paso.

Steven got out and crossed the skywalk into the courthouse.

"Morning, Judge," the courthouse security officer said as Steven approached the security gate, X-ray monitor, and conveyor.

"Good morning, Manny." Steven nodded to the second officer behind the X-ray monitor. "And to you as well, Fernando."

Without being prompted, Steven unclipped his holstered Glock 22 from his belt and handed it to Manny. He then reached into his back pocket and pulled out a pearl-handled switchblade and handed it to Manny as well.

A ten-inch German tungsten carbide steel throwing knife was concealed in the thin leather sheath of his right sea turtle Tony Lama boot. And it stayed right where it was concealed as it always cleared the X-ray metal detector.

Manny asked, "Well, Judge, any threats against your life this week?"

"Not this week, Manny," Steven answered, smiling and handing him the weapons. "But it's just Monday. "

"I heard that, Judge."

Manny took the weapons as Steven walked through. On the other side of the machine, Steven clipped the pistol back and pocketed his switchblade. "You guys have a great day," he said as he walked to the third-floor elevator.

Steven punched the up button on the full-length mirrored panel at the elevators and waited. He was wearing jeans and cowboy boots shined to mirror-high gloss. He really liked his maroon sea turtle boots. They were the only luxury he had permitted himself since arriving in El Paso from

Washington, DC. He was also wearing a blue blazer; a snow white, starched, 100 percent cotton short-sleeved shirt for the El Paso heat; and blood-red tie—all standard wear for male El Paso lawyers at the courthouse. Since he wasn't going to court but to see his boss, District Attorney Ernesto Martinez, his tie was loosened and collar unbuttoned.

Steven continued waiting on the elevator. Staring at his reflection in the mirror, he admired his physique. *I feel great,* he thought, *and look okay, too.* He winked at himself in the mirror and gave a wry smile.

He then straightened his shoulders and noticed the serenity and calm apparent in his face. After recovery from the previous evil of Washington, he had earned a new degree of freedom. *Free at last from most of my evil ways,* Steven thought and smiled again. "Still a work in progress," he said out loud to no one in particular.

Steven Vandorol survived Washington, DC, with divine guidance and designated angels that the good Lord in His mysterious ways provided. He managed to beat two overpowering addictions and was working to see and know himself as he was, not as others wanted him to be. After a lifetime of chaos, violence, anguish, and pain, he was finally at peace with himself.

Since I'm not dead, I guess I'm stronger. He thought of German philosopher Friedrich Nietzsche's mantra: *That which does not kill me makes me stronger.* He smiled ruefully as the elevator opened to his usually smiling best friend, El Paso Police Department chief, Captain Edward "Eddie" Egen.

"Hi, Judge," Eddie said, stepping out of the elevator. "Can I talk to you for a second?" The elevator was crowded. His best friend seemed very serious today.

"Sure, Eddie . . . what's up?"

Eddie was huge: six foot five and two hundred and sixty pounds; bulging, muscled arms and legs; thick strong neck. He was an ex-army military police major who, after sixteen years in the army, came to Fort Bliss for his last military assignment. He fell in love with Texas in general, El Paso in particular, and married Andi, his fifth wife. At that time, army downsizing had been the order of the day, and when the 3rd Cavalry downsized to ten thousand men, Eddie retired, just in time to apply for the then-open City of El Paso Police Department chief position.

Eddie was a handsome man with gray hair; sharp, intense, and sometimes violent blue eyes; and a perpetual sly smile. He reminded Steven of a middle-aged John Wayne in one of his favorite John Wayne movies, *Brannigan*.

Not long ago, Eddie had been a player and a womanizer. Glib and a jokester, he had a joke he could tell at every occasion and could talk a woman into bed at the drop of a hat. Steven had seen him do just that. Steven accepted his best friend, the big, funny Irishman, for what he was: a many layered individual with emotional issues but a good, compassionate heart. Their commonality rested in chaos, violence, aggression, intensity, and personal survival. And there was nothing that either would not do for the other.

Chief Egen was probably the best PD chief El Paso ever had. It was a department established in 1884 in a very violent border town that was part of the untamed West.

Then 9/11 changed everything. Fort Bliss expanded and became one of the centers of the War on Terror. The United States was now fighting two wars: the War on Terror, for which Fort Bliss became one of the centers, and the previous War on Drugs, with the El Paso Police Department and its over one thousand uniformed police officers protecting the underbelly gateway of drugs into the US.

Steven and Eddie met through Eddie's wife, Andi, who ran a travel agency, Adventure World Travel. Steven would often get airline tickets through her for his weekend trips to Tulsa to visit his kids, now teenagers: son Josef and daughter Karina. Eddie was the silent partner of the agency, and when a dispute arose with the previous owner, Eddie became one of Steven's first El Paso clients.

Steven and Eddie became fast friends that first year Steven was in El Paso. Not only did Steven successfully defend the suit by the previous owner of the travel agency, but he countersued and won a half-a-million-dollar judgment for punitive damages for the Egens, which judgment Steven promptly collected by levying on a herd of fine quality quarter horses. Eddie, a fine horseman himself, agreed to settle the lawsuit by taking the entire herd, some fifty horses, valued at ten thousand dollars for each horse, and releasing the whole judgment.

Steven was a frequent weekend visitor to the Egen ranch near Canutillo, New Mexico. Steven loved horses since his childhood back in Brazil on a Brazilian mega ranch, called a *fazenda*, so he purchased a beautiful snow-white Arabian from Ed and promptly named it Pegasus after his first horse he had as a child on that fazenda. And a collected attorney fee of two hundred thousand dollars kickstarted his solo law practice.

Eddie touched Steven's shoulder and pulled him over to the fourth floor's expansive plate glass window, overlooking downtown El Paso, sparkling and shining in the early mid-morning sun. Eddie was holding a copy of the *El Paso Herald-Chronicle* newspaper.

Eddie said, "The elevator was too crowded with ROW which both of us barely tolerate." He was smiling now.

Steven smiled at his best friend and asked, "You goin' to see Ernie?"

"Yeah, he wants an update on the New Year's Eve massive blackout that's been all over the news since it happened."

"Good! I want to hear all about it myself. It was scary there for a while. It sure scarred poor Rommel."

"I bet," Eddie said. "That's just like making love in a hurricane!"

"How so?"

"Well, you are having a really good time, but a whole lot of scary things are goin' on around ya!"

Steven chucked and just shook his head.

"Are you heading up to see Ernie, too?"

"Yep, I guess he wants to talk about the *Hernandez Herald-Chronicle* interview. Did you read it?" Steven glanced at the newspaper under his arm. "He also wants an update on the indictment."

CHAPTER 5

Steven and Eddie took another crowded elevator to the fifth floor where the entire floor was occupied by the offices of the 65th district attorney, Ernesto Luis Martinez, and his assistants, a total of thirty-five lawyers and more than fifty paralegals and investigators.

The reception desk was flanked by two massive wooden doors to either side—both with bullet-proof peepholes, the obvious second line of security defense to the inner offices.

The pretty young receptionist asked, "Chief Egen, how are you today?"

"Fine, darlin'. How you been?" Eddie was smiling brightly. His previous lustful interest for her was gone since his commitment to his wife Andi had been renewed. "Ernie is expecting us."

"I'll let him know you're here. Oh, hi, Mr. Vandorol . . . I'll let him know that you are both here." She buzzed Ernie's office. "Chief Egen and Mr. Vandorol are here."

This time Steven reached the door first, opened it, and held it for Eddie.

They entered a hallway at least twenty-five yards long with plush, dark-brown carpet, honey-brown oak paneling, wainscoting, and crown molding down the entire length, large wooden doors on either side, ten feet apart, twenty doors total. The door at the end of the hall had the nameplate, Ernesto Luis Martinez, 65th District Attorney.

Down the carpeted hallway on both walls hung the original six flags over Texas framed behind glass, and between the doors on each side were offices for the DA and his almost fifty assistants, headed by the criminal and civil first assistants on either side.

As they approached, the door at the end was opened by Ernesto Luis Martinez himself, who smiled broadly.

The DA was short and stocky with dark olive skin. His black hair, combed straight back, was graying at his temples. He had large brown eyes, ample eyebrows, and was clean shaven. A handsome man, he was probably in his mid-fifties and was impeccably dressed, as always, in a navy-blue tailor-made suit, white linen shirt with French cuffs, and gold nugget cuff links. He also had on a Bijan silk powder blue tie, with matching pocket square, and polished alligator cowboy boots.

"Good morning, Chief." Ernie smiled at Eddie. "Thanks for coming on such short notice." He turned to Steven. "Nice boots, Steven."

"El Paso's best: Tony Lama."

"Alligator?"

"Sea turtle."

"Very cool . . . and great shine as well. Very, very nice!" Ernie said as he closed the door and walked to his glass-covered mahogany desk. "You guys want anything? Coffee?" Ernie cleared a speck from the corner of his right eye with a manicured, slender finger.

"I never turn down good coffee, thanks," Steven replied, sitting down in a red leather upholstered armchair in front of the desk.

"Me, too," Eddie said. "And doughnuts, too, if you got 'em." He took a seat beside Steven.

Ernie smiled. "Cops gotta have doughnuts. Right, Chief?" He picked up his phone. "Marcy, can we get some coffee . . . and doughnuts if we still got 'em from the morning rush? Thanks."

Ernie sat down behind his desk piled with neat stacks of files, some eight stacks of ten to twenty files each, and a red leather desk pad holding only the *El Paso Herald-Chronicle* and a sterling silver pen and pencil desk set engraved with his name.

Behind his desk was a mahogany credenza also with a glass top, and two ornate golden flag stands topped with golden eagles were flanking it: the state flag of the Lone Star State on the right, the flag of the United States of America on the left.

"Hey, Ernie, did you hear about Hillary Clinton addressing a large gathering of Native Americans at their Indian First Nations Summit in Austin?" Eddie Egen was smiling broadly. Steven had heard the joke before but knew Eddie wouldn't miss the opportunity to tell it again. He had quite the reputation for being a real wag.

24

Ernie smiled broadly at his chief of police. "Tell me."

"Hillary spoke for almost an hour about her plans to implement totally free government grants for college education, free Medicare for all, blah, blah, blah. And although she was vague about details for the funding of her plans, she spoke eloquently about what she would do if she were to win the White House this fall in the 2016 November election.

"At the conclusion of her speech, the chiefs presented her with a beautiful plaque inscribed, 'Walking Eagle.' "A news reporter later asked the chiefs how they came to select the new name for the Democratic presidential candidate. They explained that 'Walking Eagle' is the name given to a bird that is so full of crap, it can no longer fly."

They all laughed hardily. Eddie had great timing and a talent for joke telling, for sure.

With a knock on the door, Marcy walked in carrying a tray with two mugs and a plate of doughnuts. She set it down on the table between Steven and Eddie and walked out.

"Eddie, you should do stand-up comedy," Steven said, smiling and shaking his head.

Ernie added, "Good one, Ed! Thanks again for coming."

"Sure thing, Boss!"

Ernie turned serious, his mouth now a straight, sharp line. "The New Year's Eve blackout has been all over the news media since it happened. What's going on in El Paso, Chief?"

"Spin, fake news, and hysteria!" Eddie answered, handing Steven the *El Paso Herald-Chronicle* from Sunday, January 3, 2016. Steven already knew it was flooded with news of the blackout and the chaos of West Texas-northern Mexico in its aftermath.

Steven took the newspaper and started reading, as Ernie did the same…

El Paso Herald-Chronicle

$ 2.00 SUNDAY EDITION $ 2.00
Volume 113, Issue 282 Sunday, January 3, 2016

MASSIVE TOTAL BORDER BLACKOUT FIRST IN EL PASO HISTORY ENTIRE EL PASO AND JUAREZ BORDER SUFFERED COMPLETE BLACKOUT—FIRST IN TEXAS HISTORY; EL PASO POWER AND ELECTRIC BLAMES POWER GRID COMPUTER SYSTEM FAILURE

BY ARMANDO VILLALOBOS

EL PASO HERALD–CHRONICLE BUREAU CHIEF

A massive blackout struck the entire El Paso-Juarez Border-plex at exactly 3:00 a.m. on New Year's Day, rendering all of southern El Paso County and northern Chihuahua into complete darkness, likely starting with downtown El Paso and rolling north and south, 250 square miles of southern Texas and northern Mexico, all in all.

The total blackout was followed by an unseasonably heavy rainstorm, with wind gusts of up to 60 miles an hour, that dropped over five inches of rain in an hour with lightning and thunder striking downtown El Paso and Juarez Border-plex several hundred times during the storm. This caused an estimated damage of five million dollars of destroyed cell towers and electrical power lines, according to an El Paso Power and Electric spokesman.

"Our investigation is far from complete, but our engineers suspect a massive computer systems' failure that shut down all four substations," spokesman James Conrad said this morning. "The investigation will continue for the next several weeks and, when completed, will be made public as El Paso Power believes in complete disclosure, transparency, and honesty regarding threats to our power grid infrastructure," he said.

When asked about the possibility of cyber terrorism, Conrad said the Power Grid Computer Control System was designed, implemented, and monitored since 1990 and has had no incursion threats in almost ten years. The last recorded intrusion was blocked completely by the system's security controls, as was reported at that time.

El Paso Police Chief Edward "Eddie" Egen confirmed widespread looting, vandalism, and property damage and confirmed four deaths and hundreds of injuries during the 24 hours following the blackout which ended at 5:30 a.m. when the electrical grids were fully restarted in the downtown El Paso-Ciudad Juarez metroplex.

Also, a spokesperson for AT&T said that at least a dozen cell towers were damaged by the storm and all cell phone service interrupted by the blackout for almost six hours, but was restored by sunrise.

In a related story, on an anonymous tip, Jason Warren, El Paso Power and Electric chief engineer and executive vice president and member of the Board of Directors, and his wife, Jillian, surgical nurse at Providence Hospital, and their eight-year-old daughter, Michelle, were found dead in their home. The three were apparently victims of a home invasion/robbery by Juarez/south El Paso street gangs. EPPD investigators and the coroner said they had been dead since the afternoon of New Year's Eve.

When asked if the deaths were related to the blackout, El Paso Power and Electric spokesman Conrad said, "Absolutely not. While Mr. Warren supervised the entire power grid and computer security system, we feel the deaths are not related.

"We are saddened by the deaths of the Warren family. Mr. Warren had been with our company since 1970, was a graduate of Texas A&M, with a post graduate doctorate in computer science from UTEP, and was a nationally known expert in power grids. He will be sorely missed, and our hearts go out to all his family, co-workers, and friends.

"The blackout ended at approximately 5:30 a.m. on New Year's morning in the metroplex, and all power will be restored completely on the border by this coming weekend." Repairs to power lines and towers will continue in outlying areas with power lines to be restored in the next few weeks.

In related news, the Sun Bowl football game between the Stanford Cardinals and the Oklahoma Sooners was played as scheduled as all power had been fully restored for the game kickoff on New Year's Day at two thirty in Sun Bowl Stadium. Oklahoma beat Stanford 46-10. (See Sunday Gameday, Section D)

Steven folded the newspaper and put it on Ernie's desk. "Well, at least Oklahoma kicked the crap out of Stanford's butt!"

Ernie and Eddie both chuckled.

"It *was* a good game," Eddie said. "And a great evening with you and Rommel and Ray and Jessie at the ranch watching all the New Year's Day bowl games!"

"And the Mexican buffet Andi cooked wasn't too shabby either." Steven raised his coffee cup and toasted Eddie. "Eddie, what's the deal on the Jason Warren murders? Did you realize that Jillian Warren was the nurse who attended to you at Providence Hospital when you were almost killed on the highway returning from Pecos? Remember, that's where our special prosecution witnesses were hidden."

"You're absolutely right! You met her that day when I was in the emergency ward . . . just a little drugged up."

Steven interrupted, "But not enough to miss joking and flirting with her, right?"

"That was the old Eddie Egen, the flirt!"

"Got ya, Eddie, not only were you saved that day by the grace of our Lord when He entered your heart and soul, but He transformed you radically as well."

"And you helped so much, my friend. I can't thank you enough!"

"You already have. I'm proud of you."

"Amen," Ernie said. "You're the best police chief El Paso's had in its long, Wild-West history!" Ernie paused. "Was it a robbery murder?"

Eddie looked directly at Ernie, swallowed, and said, "No, it was *not* a robbery murder." He swallowed again. "It was a very professional assassination!"

CHAPTER 6

Steven was surprised. He looked between the two men and then back at his friend Eddie, who was very solemn as he said, "It all happened at approximately midday New Year's Eve. Jason and Jillian Warren were found on January second by officers dispatched there when the son, Jacob Warren, found them all dead.

"For the son's protection, we said it was an anonymous tip! Forensics put the evidence together and figured it happened something like this: Jillian was apparently arriving home, having picked up the eight-year-old daughter from day care, and was shot twice in the face."

Usually stoic, Eddie was getting visibly emotional. "Then the little eight-year-old came in from the garage to the kitchen and was shot in the mouth, probably as she screamed. The coroner says she died instantly, just like her mother."

"Forensics figured a period of one to two hours passed before Jason Warren arrived from work, drove into the garage, walked into the kitchen, and was shot in the face. He also died instantly, but two more shots were delivered right in the heart."

Ernie interrupted, "A killer who enjoys it?"

"Yes, and very thorough!" Eddie looked at Steven and continued, "All shots were 9mm parabellums from a Barretta MP9. It was just a horror show. Blood everywhere! The bodies hadn't started to decompose in the three days' heat as the air conditioning was apparently turned down after the killing. The estimated time of death for all three was between noon and four o'clock on New Year's Eve. No witnesses whatsoever. It happened during the hottest part of the day when streets were likely deserted. Neighbors heard nothing, saw nothing. There was no apparent reason that it was a robbery."

"What about the boy?" Steven asked.

"Entry was through the back gate; the back-porch screen door was open, unlocked. It was an easy deal. Well scouted. No prints. House completely undisturbed. It was a well-executed, professional assassination."

"But what about the boy?" Steven asked again.

"We've got him in protective custody. He's just devasted. He's twenty and a sophomore at UTEP majoring in computer science. Their neighbors described them as a very happy family. Both Jason and Jillian had jobs they enjoyed; both made good salaries. They seemed devoted to their kids and had a great life. Jason just got his Christmas bonus from El Paso Power and Electric of fifty *G*s. The only saving grace is . . . none suffered."

Steven looked at his best friend. "Do you think the killing had anything to do with the special prosecution, Eddie?"

"I don't know. We're still investigating everything at El Paso Power."

"So, the son is in protective custody?"

"Yes, we didn't want a fourth Warren assassinated. He's almost catatonic . . . listless . . . not talking at all. The state psychiatrist has been talking to him."

"Eddie, if there's anything I can do, let me know, okay?" Steven really felt for the young guy who had just lost his parents and little sister and was now all alone.

Ernie focused the meeting: "I guess we'll see. By the way, how is the amended indictment going, Steven?"

"As I told Judge Carbon—"

Ernie interrupted, grinning from ear-to-ear, "Yeah, I heard you had a New Year's Eve date with her! Well, did you kiss her good night?" He winked at Eddie.

"Ernie, she's become a really good friend—but not that good!"

Ernie laughed out loud. "I've got it! I wouldn't mind a date with the judge myself. Can you put in a good word for me?"

"Boss, you're on your own there!" Steven laughed.

"Well, I'm gonna work on just that! Seriously, though, how is the special prosecution and amended indictment going?"

"Well, as I told the judge, when I get the help in my law office so I don't lose my practice, I can work on it full time. Beth Barker, North Anderson, and I pretty much reviewed all the evidence and interviewed all the well-secured witnesses and documentary evidence with Eddie and his investigative team. I will be ready to hit the ground running on the amended and superseded indictment full time, probably next month."

Ernie interrupted, "You told me you're expecting a friend and colleague to join you soon. Where's she from?"

"From Washington, DC. She had just made partner in the law firm where I was of counsel at Henderson and Lane on K Street."

"Yeah, I remember. What's her name again?"

"Vanessa Moore." Steven paused, thinking back to the agony of his time in DC when he was betrayed by the two people he trusted most. "She was a real help and was there for me when I was going through emotional hell during the blow up of Project Triple X, a corruption of the Clinton administration by North Korea."

"I do remember you telling us all about it," Ernie said."So, when is she coming to join you?"

"She said the first week in January," Steven answered with a shy smile. "But I haven't heard from her yet. I expect to anytime now."

"Well, that's great, Steven. I'm glad you're getting some help in your office so I can have you full time! We're all ready to go after all those high-profile criminals!" Ernie paused a beat and, as an afterthought, added, "Did you read the article about your interview with Raul Hernandez last November in the *El Paso Herald-Chronicle*?" Ernie held the paper in his hand. The article was a reprint of an interview with Steven about his novel, *Sunbelt*, which he wrote and published while in DC.

Steven smirked, shaking his head slightly. "Yeah, I read it . . . again. It was embarrassing last November when the media made a big deal about it, when I became your special prosecutor, and it's still embarrassing now." Steven blushed. "Running it again now, I guess, is the *Herald* joining the main-stream media in diverting attention from yet another government failure and the blackout, and putting the focus back on the indictment and that particular government corruption."

"No, that's great, Steven! Not only are you now a conservative media star nationwide—and especially in Texas—but you're also a rallying cry for conservatives all over America. So, I'm not just proud of you as my special prosecutor, I'm extremely proud of *you*." Ernie handed the *Herald-Chronicle* to Steven.

"Dilly-dilly!" Eddie interjected, raising his coffee cup to his best friend. "As Bobby Vee says in 'Lavender Blue'!"

"Dilly-dilly," Steven answered.

Ernie just smiled.

CHAPTER 7

Steven Vandorol did a double take. Vanessa Moore, his good friend and former colleague from Washington, DC, sat in a chair, legs crossed, smiling brightly. She was a shining star with a dazzling smile that radiated in the austere and simple reception room of Steven's law office.

Vanessa looked back at him through hypnotically hazel eyes. She was more beautiful now than Steven remembered, her small, strong hands folded together, showing well-manicured nails tinted pink. And at that moment in time, Steven fell in love with her all over again.

Steven's smile broadened as he stared, speechless, at the gorgeous Vanessa. She was wearing a simple white blouse with a deep blue skirt. Open toe heels revealed light pink polished toes. A jacket was lying on the back of the chair. As she rose, her beautiful smile broadened. "Surprise, Steven Vandorol!"

Still stunned, Steven set his burger sack and drink on a chair and rushed over to her. She held out her arms, and the two old friends hugged each other. Steven bent down to five-foot-tall Vanessa and said, "I can't believe my eyes. Is it really you?" They kept hugging as her eyes teared up and glistened in the bright light of the reception room.

"Five years older and a lifetime wiser," Vanessa answered, squeezing Steven more tightly. She was now crying.

"Wow!" Steven managed, holding Vanessa. "Has it been five years, really?" Steven pulled Vanessa back. "Let me look at you." He grasped her face tenderly with both hands, and with his thumbs, he gently wiped her tears away. "Hey, no crying. This is the happiest moment of my five years here in El Paso. You are absolutely stunning, Vanessa. More beautiful than I ever imagined or remembered. Wow!" Steven was grinning like a silly teenager.

Vanessa went back into the hug. "Mine are tears of joy . . . and relief." She paused, "It's not Vanessa Moore anymore."

"What? That's right, when we talked, you told me you got divorced! When was that?"

"I divorced Dudley two years ago . . . and took back my maiden name . . . and my life. So, it's Carson now." Vanessa smiled the most radiant smile Steven had ever seen in his life. He was having a hard time letting her go.

"Well, come into my office and let me introduce you." Steven put his arm around her slim waist. "Christina, would you buzz us in?" The door buzzed almost immediately. "Thanks."

Steven opened the door and stepped into the hallway facing Christina. "Chris, this is my friend from Washington, DC, Vanessa . . . uh . . . Carson."

"Nice to meet you, Ms. Carson." Christina smiled but looked at Vanessa intently, her dark eyes flashing, a gaze Steven noticed.

Vanessa smiled back at her warmly. "Good to meet you, Christina."

Steven turned the other way, with Vanessa still on his arm. "And this is my good friend and investigator, Ray Ortega." He too smiled broadly but was also staring noticeably.

Ray stood up by his desk and came around. "So nice to meet you, Vanessa."

Vanessa extended her hand, which Ray took. "Likewise, Ray. Are you Christina's father?"

"That I am." Ray's smile widened. "Is it that obvious?"

"It sure is," Vanessa answered, smiling warmly.

"Excuse us, Ray. We've got lots of catching-up to do." Steven, arm held against her back still, walked down the hall and stopped by the office on the right. Marce, the legal assistant Steven had just hired in January, looked up and rose from her chair.

"Marce, this is Vanessa Carson. Vanessa, this is Marce; she's our legal assistant."

"Good to meet you, Ms. Carson, and welcome to El Paso." Marce smiled warmly.

"Thank you. Good to meet you, and please call me Vanessa."

Steven led Vanessa back to his office and pointed to the wingback chair. Vanessa was about to sit down when Steven closed the door and went to hug her again. She turned and hugged back, and the two held each other tightly, both smiling, for what to Steven felt like an eternity.

"I could hold you all afternoon," Steven said, disengaging. "Tell me everything." He sat in the wingback chair opposite hers.

It all came out in a rush.

"I was completely devastated by your disappearance from DC and the complete silence at Henderson Lane. Dudley dismissed my questions, saying, 'Steven was treasonous.' It wasn't until the FBI served search warrants on Henderson Lane and arrests were made that I knew Project Triple X had died a very ugly and agonizing death. *The Washington Post* published a brief article stating that Project Triple X had been withdrawn; that your then best friend, Martin King, committed suicide; that attorney and former of-counsel to the firm, Steven Vandorol, had left DC; and that his whereabouts were unknown."

"My marriage to Dudley was on the ropes, which it had been for a while, as you knew from our conversations back then. I withdrew from the firm, enforced the buy-out provisions of the law firm partnership agreement, and filed for divorce. Dudley, being the little narcissist Napoleon he always was, fought me, tooth and nail." She paused and swallowed, her hazel eyes tearing up.

Steven said nothing.

"I prevailed in that lawsuit. Henderson Lane paid me off, and the divorce was granted favorably to me, Dudley being the 'womanizing scumbag' that he was. End of story!"

"I realized my responsibility in both the marriage and divorce. I sought counseling and spent eight months in therapy, working through childhood issues. I was raised by a tyrannical, alcoholic, and abusive father, an enabling mother, and controlling older siblings. Add to this the suffocating religious dogma that had enslaved me, making me feel everything was my fault and nothing I could do was right, with God always punishing me for my many errors, sins, and mistakes."

Steven still said nothing.

"I had an addiction, a religious dogma addiction. And my childhood trauma enslaved me and was robbing me of my freedoms." Vanessa paused and her beautiful eyes looked out the window. She was pensive for several moments.

There is something she's not saying, something deep inside, Steven thought, but still said nothing.

"I had an angel for a therapist. She was a Christian counselor." Vanessa paused. She was tearing up again. "She quoted from the Bible, John 14:6, which says that Thomas asked Jesus Christ, 'Lord, we don't know where you are going, so how can we know the way?' and Jesus Christ answered, 'I am the way and the truth and the life. No one comes to the Father except through me.'" Tears eased down her cheeks. She paused and dabbed with a Kleenex.

Still Steven said nothing.

Vanessa looked back into Steven's eyes. "And I had an aversion to the sexual . . . an abhorrence . . . because of past horror. I'll tell you about it sometime." Tears were flowing down her beautiful face.

Steven still said nothing. He gave her space and continued to listen. He guessed that there was much, much more to that particular anguish. As the good friends they were, he would allow her to share it in her own time.

Vanessa sniffed, once, twice, blew her nose, wiped her eyes, and said, "It was divine guidance, Steven. It was grace from the Lord, that moment I understood and found freedom: freedom from my past, freedom from my father and enabling mother, and especially freedom from the religious enslavement and propaganda that some priest needed to consent to my salvation and grant me entrance to paradise."

Steven nodded slightly.

Vanessa grew angry. "It was all lies to me! At that moment, I realized that the good Lord and Jesus Christ were in my heart, and that I didn't have to look anywhere else, especially not to some priest. I had nothing to confess. I saw myself, my utter sinfulness and need for a savior, Jesus Christ. I'm a good person. The Holy Spirit came into my heart and soul."

Steven blurted out, "I loved you from the first moment I met you, Vanessa. Dudley had picked me up at the airport and brought me to your home in Chevy Chase to stay prior to starting with the law firm. And I fell in love with you all over again just a few minutes ago when I saw your sunshine smile."

"Oh, Steven, I loved you too, from that first time I met you at our house, at the reception held in your honor when the buffoon Dudley introduced you to Henderson Lane partners . . . just a big show! Your then best friend, Martin King, orchestrated to enslave you at a time when you were really vulnerable."

"And he succeeded, just to then betray me!" Steven said. He could hardly contain his feelings. He wanted to rush to her, hold her, kiss her, but he didn't. "You left the church?" *She had an addiction just like me, but of a different kind, both equally enslaving,* Steven thought.

"It left me, taking all their blah, blah, blah . . . the pomp and rituals with it."

Steven smiled. "Tell me how you really feel!"

Vanessa laughed. "I made a decision. I was done with my past. After months of therapy, I realized I had a choice regarding my future; I had personal decisions to make." She wiped her eyes again. "My counselor explained the 'Therapeutic Cycle,' meaning that any issue of evil you want to change in your soul, first you have to become aware that it's harmful and self-defeating; then you have to understand why you do it; then you make a decision to change; and then comes the hardest part: practicing that decision to reach a higher level of human growth. My therapist, Susan, said the Therapeutic Cycle was best said in Hebrews 12:11: 'No chastening seems joyful for the present, but painful; nevertheless, afterward it yields the peaceable fruit of righteousness.'"

Vanessa was much calmer as she poured out this part of her story. Steven was nodding and felt he understood Vanessa very well. Doc Bill, Steven's own Christian counselor, had said the very same things to Steven and had discussed the Therapeutic Cycle with him many times.

"I've always hated DC, but I finally understood it was a toxic environment, like a nuclear waste site. So, my next decision was that I was done with the corruption, slime, and outright evil of DC." She paused with a wry smile, like she had a little secret. "I remembered your friend Courtney Wellington was in DC. You introduced me when he came to the office."

"Right."

"That was big-time grace, all in itself! The good Lord led me to Courtney." Her dazzling smile was back. "So, I called him and asked, 'Where is Steven Vandorol?' He told me, so voilà,' here I am!"

"So, that's why Courtney was so guarded about you when we talked back in September of last year. It wasn't until we talked again at Christmastime that he said you'd gotten a divorce, left the law firm, and were probably looking for work. That's when he told me to call you."

Steven felt himself getting warm all over. "But when we talked later, before New Year's, and you said you would come to El Paso the first week in January, I had no idea you were already planning to find me! But here it is, February, so I'm really pleased and excited, but still surprised. What happened?"

"Well, my friend, a girl has to pretend to be a little hard to get!" She shone a dazzling sunshine smile at Steven again.

This time Steven couldn't resist. He rose and stepped toward her, half thinking she would disappear when he reached out for her.

She rose, wrapped her arms around him, and kissed him. Surprised, Steven felt himself losing his sense of time and place and gaining something far greater. Something asleep in him was now stirring: passion for a woman. He pressed against her, kissed her back.

"Well, what was that all about? Not that I'm complaining," Steven said.

"The other big decision I made when I was still in DC was: I'm going after what *I* want, and Steven, I want you. I think it was love at first sight, but I surprised my feelings, seeing how I was married then. But now . . . I love you! There, it's out!"

Steven pulled back and, still holding her in his arms, said, "I love you too, Vanessa. I have since we first met!"

The two kissed again, deeply, and Steven tasted the sweetness of her mouth and felt her tongue. Their lips finally parted reluctantly.

"So, when did you get to El Paso?" Steven asked, still holding her.

"I've been in El Paso since Thursday, October fifteenth of last year!"

Steven was stunned. He sat in the chair. Vanessa followed, sitting on his lap. Arm around his neck, she said softly, "I didn't want to burden you or assume upon our past friendship. I wanted to come to you independently and without hesitation or need." She kissed him again.

As their lips parted, he said, "Thank you, Vanessa."

"You are most welcome, Steven."

"Tell me everything."

"I got in on Thursday and stayed at the Hilton, rested, and made some plans. On Monday, I went to the Ford dealership, bought a used Kia Soul, a cute little thing . . . I negotiated a great deal."

"I bet. I've seen you negotiate."

"Then, I went to the Chamber of Commerce to get my El Paso bearings, looked up your address and that of your office and the courthouses, state and federal. Once I located it all on a map, I decided that I wanted to live on the west side of El Paso."

"Let me guess." Steven put his index finger to his lips and looked up. "A high-rise apartment on Stanton Street?"

"Wow, how did you know?"

"You're a city woman, and the Stanton House is seventeen stories with balconies and a great view, day and night."

"Did you live there?" Vanessa asked.

"Sure did, when I first came to town." Steven kissed her on the cheek. "You've got to see my view now at my home on Scenic Drive."

"The view of downtown is what sold me. Plus, it has secure underground parking. It's really nice and secure."

"What apartment?" Steven asked.

"1604," she answered. "Yours?"

"1704, right above yours . . . top floor. I'm now at 4506 Golden Hill Terrace by Scenic Drive."

"I know. I've driven by there several times . . . and went up to Scenic Point. I even rode the Wyler Aerial Tramway up the top to Ranger Peak and looked at your house."

"My view is almost as good." He was holding her tightly. "I really love it up there on Ranger Peak; it's more than 5,600 feet up."

"Wow, over a mile high!" Vanessa's beautiful hazel eyes were wide.

"Yes! We'll have to go up to Ranger Peak together . . . but please continue."

"Well, I rented furniture, a washing machine, everything I would need. By then it was pretty late, so I went back to the Hilton pretty exhausted. Steven, I want to tell you, it's probably the best night's sleep I've had in years." Her eyes were sparkling. The entire time, they were exchanging kisses. She finally said, "Stop! No more kissing until I finish telling you, okay?"

Steven nodded.

"The next day, I went to the Bar Association and signed up for the exam—Professional Responsibility portion only since I'm licensed in Virginia, Maryland, and DC."

Steven nodded.

"By the way, I took the exam the Monday before Thanksgiving and passed." Vanessa frowned, and a dark shadow passed over her beautiful face like dark storm clouds.

Steven noticed again but said nothing.

Vanessa paused and swallowed as the dark cloud passed.

"So, you're licensed in Texas?" Steven asked, already thinking ahead.

"Yes, sir. So, after the Bar Association, I found out you'd been appointed special prosecutor in the Alvarado case . . . I never did like that jerk when he was your client in DC, but I digress. I went downtown to check the courthouses, and I walked around for a while and went to a Mexican restaurant—loved the huevos rancheros."

"Great food here!" Steven interjected.

"I went to see Don Stewart. You remember Don?"

Steven nodded. "We had him as local counsel on the Sunland Park Mall deal you and I handled for the Alvarados back in DC, remember? Don is a really good guy, good lawyer . . . still a good friend."

Steven shuddered slightly thinking back to the Alvarados—father, Alberto, and son, Ricardo—his clients in DC when he was practicing law there. Just recently, around Christmas, Steven met Ricardo Alvarado alone in Cloudcroft, and Ricardo tried to buy Steven off as special prosecutor for twenty million US dollars. Steven completely refused the rumored Mexican drug kingpin of the Juarez Sinaloa Cartel.

"Yes, I remember." Vanessa smiled. "Don and I had a nice chat . . . and I went of counsel. He let me have a vacant office next to Jim Maxwell . . . and let me have some cases. Imagine my surprise when you called me to come to El Paso, and I was already here. I almost screamed with joy. I just couldn't believe it!"

"Well, my dear, the good Lord works in mysterious ways. So, why now? Why didn't you come see me in the first week of January?" Steven asked.

"I had some emotional stuff to work through, and I had to do it myself. I wanted to clear my psyche and come to you unencumbered."

"Well, did you work through it?"

"I think so, but do we humans ever really know? I'll tell you all about it someday."

"Let's change the subject, love! So, what's your obligation to Don?" Steven was still thinking.

"None really. They gave me a couple of real estate deals to work on in December, but that's it. I'm almost finished with them. I guess there'll be others."

"Do you want to stay there?" Steven was now smiling.

"Not really, Steven. What do you have in mind?" she asked coyly.

"Do you want to be law partners? I need help. I need and want you."

"Yes! Yes! When do I start?"

"Well, that was easy. How about right now?"

They sealed the deal with a passionate kiss.

After they broke from the kiss, Steven whispered, "What about us?"

"Shall we just leave that in the good Lord's hands?"

"Done," Steven said. "Any plans for this evening?"

"Dinner with the man I love."

He was beaming. "Great! By the way, do you have a dog, or do you even like dogs?"

"Oh, I love all animals, and, yes, I have a silly little female part-Yorkie mutt named Harley . . . and a contrary cat named Caspurr."

Steven laughed out loud.

CHAPTER 8

Vanessa was to arrive at six. Steven walked into the bathroom and looked at himself in the mirror. His physique was that of a much younger man. He thought himself passably handsome, but had never known what to use his looks for.

Now, for the first time, he wanted to be attractive to a woman. But not just any woman, Vanessa. He was wearing a new white shirt—when any old shirt would have been fine—a navy blazer, and starched jeans.

The 9mm Glock was holstered in the small of his back, an eight-inch stiletto switchblade in his back pocket, and his high-gloss maroon sea turtle boots, with his throwing knife in his right boot, finished the outfit. The rest of the world—or ROW as Steven laughingly called the masses of humanity in a downward spiral of rot and mediocrity—and the special prosecution—now required increased vigilance and security.

Steven had his hair trimmed, and his sideburns were razor sharp. He had shaved again very close when he usually would have only done so the next day. He reached into his pocket for a breath strip and swallowed. He felt a nervousness not felt in a very long time, like a teenager on his first date.

He walked to the large glass window in his living room facing downtown El Paso-Juarez. The sun was setting. The cloudless sky was made brilliant by the sinking sun and was a spectacular rainbow of brilliant colors: crimson, orange, violet, yellow, silver, and gold—God's ultimate artist's palette of colors. Outside it was a cool and dry February evening.

Steven was anxious and nervous but still so very happy. He remembered what his daughter Karina had said: "Happiness is like a butterfly; you can chase it and chase it and never catch it. But as soon as you sit down to rest, it lights on your shoulder." The butterfly had landed. Vanessa had come to El Paso just for him—not for what he could do for her or what he could give her. It was just because she was a friend and they were connected spiritually by love. Steven felt a happiness he hadn't felt since childhood with his brother on the fazenda.

He checked his watch—almost six o'clock. Vanessa would be there any minute. He knew her to be punctual as she was as conscientious as Steven, just a small part of the commonality they shared.

He was half excited, half worried, and also wondered whether Vanessa was real or something he had dreamed up. He had allowed himself to share more of his thoughts and feelings with her than with any other woman ever. Was that because she was his soul mate or because he wished he were the kind of man who could have a soul mate? Did he have the potential to be fully human or would his prior addiction, now in remission, defeat this relationship as well, as it had many times in the past? He would leave that for the good Lord. He whispered a prayer for Vanessa, his children, his friends, Rommel, and Pegasus.

A knock at the door woke Steven from his reverie. He froze. But the fear was irrational; it could be no one else but the love of his life, Vanessa. The fear was related to the previous attempts on his life and the attack on Rommel.

During their long conversation earlier that afternoon and in the spirit of full disclosure as to the actual physical danger of becoming his law partner, Steven had told her everything. Shared it all. From when the sinister surveillance started last year, to the attempt on his life and near destruction of his home, while he had been on the rafting trip with his children before Thanksgiving, and the explosive placed in his office around Christmas, the attempt on Ed's life, and the shots fired at Rommel from Scenic Point. Steven was especially vigilant and well-armed as a result of recent events and also had the street smarts gleaned from a life in an evil world.

Vanessa's answer after listening calmly had been, "As partners, we have to share the good, bad, and ugly, all of it, all the time." At that very moment in time, Steven was a completely free human being beginning an upward progression with another free and good-hearted soul, with the good Lord in both of their hearts. Steven breathed deeply with that thought and prayer and headed to the door.

As an act of faith, he didn't even look through the peephole before opening the door. *After all, Vanessa has already taken the leap of faith to come to El Paso,* he thought.

Vanessa Carson stood outside in a simple black dress, short-waisted jacket, and high heels. She was stunning. His heart was racing—a new feeling but a feeling he really liked. Once again, for the third time this day, he saw her dazzling smile, reflecting their happiness together.

Steven held out his hands and Vanessa took both. He backed into the entryway and let the door swing shut. They were in each other's arms, holding each other as tightly as possible.

"You look spectacular, my precious angel," Steven said, drawing back to look at her at arm's length.

"And you look wonderful, my Steven," she replied. "My handsome law partner!"

Steven was in a dream, a tender, loving, and passionate dream. He could feel the warmth flowing between them as they kissed to a new life of happiness to last a lifetime. The two drew apart, both smiling.

Vanessa spoke first. "This is my dream come true, Steven, my love!"

"You just read my mind, Vanessa, *my* love." He led her to the living room.

"Let me introduce you to Rommel." The Great Dane was regally laying on all fours like a living sphinx before an Egyptian tomb.

Rommel's ears pricked up, black eyes shining, when he saw Vanessa. The huge Great Dane rose up and slowly eased toward her, half crawling, sheepishly almost, as if not to startle the beautiful woman.

"This is amazing," Steven said, still holding Vanessa, who was smiling brightly at his dog.

As Rommel eased directly toward her, Vanessa went down on her knees at eye level with the magnificent dog, put out her arms, and hugged his huge neck. Rommel moaned from deep in his throat, almost purring like a beautiful black panther.

"Wow," was all Steven could say. It was an amazing reaction for Rommel.

Vanessa, still holding the dog, smiled again. "It's not me. He just smells my little girl dog, Harley."

They both laughed. It seemed like Rommel did as well, his huge head nodding up and down.

Steven laughed out loud. "Vanessa, my love, you truly have all the weapons of angels," he said, alluding to Arlene Wellington's saying that if one has truth, beauty, goodness, and love, along with a good sense of humor, you can face anything, for those are the weapons of angels.

She rose, and Rommel came to her waist. Still petting Rommel, she said, "Show me your home."

Steven put his arm to her back and led her down the hallway, Rommel obediently walking beside her. "Can I get you a glass of wine while you look, my sweet angel?"

"Sure. Everything goes better with wine!"

Steven went back to the kitchen, poured two glasses, and returned to Vanessa. She was looking into his bedroom. Rommel, standing beside her, was almost as tall as she was.

"Chianti okay?"

"Perfect." Taking the glass, she raised it and said, "To us and our love."

"To you—us . . . I love you, Vanessa."

She answered, "I love you too, Steven." They clinked glasses and sipped their wine as Rommel woofed out loud, wanting to be a part of the fun.

Vanessa noticed the print above Steven's bed. "Wow! What a really wonderful photograph! It's just exquisite. Where did you get it?"

"When I first arrived in El Paso, I found it in a local photo gallery. The two dolphins swimming in sync before the massive tramp steamer's forward wake represents perfect emotional intimacy between soul mates handling the rest of the world—ROW, as I like to call it."

"Wow, you are quite the philosopher! You're going to have to explain that most intriguing metaphor."

"I'm *no* real philosopher—just a SAG philosopher."

"SAG? I've never heard that term before."

"SAG: silly a** guesser!"

She started laughing.

"But I'll be glad to explain the metaphor, my angel. Maybe at dinner, okay?"

"Sure, my handsome law partner," she responded before changing the subject. "I guess you feel pretty secure here?"

Steven had told her in detail about the hit contract and assassination attempts on his life, and about his various conversations with the district attorney, Ernie Martinez. He also told her of the subsequent conversations with his friend, Courtney, about Courtney working for the CIA, and being Steven's contact in DC, who had heard through his work that the Alvarados had issued the contract marking Steven and the whole prosecution team for assassination.

"Aren't you a bit exposed, living up on this mountain? A bit isolated?" Vanessa asked while looking into Steven's study.

He took Vanessa's hand and led her back into the living room. "Vanessa, my angel, in the spirit of full disclosure, I'll tell you my life story . . . but briefly because I'm getting hungry. Okay?"

With his arm around her and Rommel still following, they ambled back into the living room and took in the vast panorama of El Paso-Juarez. The view was absolutely spectacular as the sun was setting, washing the horizon in a spectacular spectrum of stunning colors and hues.

Looking out, Vanessa remarked, "Wow, you're right about the magnificent view!"

The two partners sat down, and with the amazing view before them and a Great Dane at their feet, Steven told his story of living in Germany, then Brazil, New York City and south Bronx, Japan, Oklahoma, West Point, the Sunbelt agony—where he almost took his own life—and DC, ending with El Paso.

Steven shared all in his mind, heart, and soul with Vanessa, something he had never done with anyone else before, especially a woman. Steven shared it all: the lifetime of violence, street smarts, and vigilance, all he learned in a corrupt and evil world. Vanessa listened intently and in silence. He felt this was the first time someone really cared.

When Steven was done, he asked, "Do you have any questions?"

"Not really, we're both products of all that's gone before, but I do love your boots, Mr. Vandorol!"

"Well, thank you. They're my favorite. Custom-made sea turtle Tony Lama, El Paso's own."

———

"You were certainly a big hit with Rommel, my sweet angel," Steven said as they sat next to each other at Cafe Central. Steven looked at his menu as they listened to the background music—Gipsy Kings, "Bamboleo"—in the candlelit restaurant.

Vanessa had insisted on driving, ostensibly for more familiarity with El Paso, yet he sensed that a different car would be better for their mutual security. Steven had agreed. They parked in the courthouse parking garage in the DA's marked parking spot and walked a block and a half to Cafe Central, one of the oldest restaurants in the El Paso del Norte region, open since 1918. Inside, they were seated by Tony at Steven's regular private table in the opulent dining room.

The two were looking at engraved menus featuring dishes that were a combination of decades-old traditions and bold, innovative flavors incorporating a Southwestern twist.

Steven was positively shining, as was Vanessa. He was the happiest he'd ever been in his entire life. And Steven was proud to be seen with the woman he loved. When they had entered the restaurant, he had noticed all the rubbernecks of the El Paso legal community buzzing about this spectacular woman with him. Yes, Steven was a proud and happy man.

"Rommel is just a magnificent animal," Vanessa said while looking around the restaurant. "And this is a really great place. What do you recommend?" she asked, hooking her ankle around his leg.

Steven smiled as he felt her warmth. "You must have the green chile soup. It's the best, and I love the tenderloin, medium rare. What do you feel like, sweet angel? American, Southwestern? Mexican or Tex-Mex?"

"I'm starving. How about Tex-Mex. What's good?" She was positively enchanting, hazel eyes shining like jewels in the candle-light.

"I love you, Vanessa, and thank you again . . . for everything." Steven looked directly into her beautiful eyes. "Thank you, Lord, for bringing her here." Steven's eyes were tearing up. He took a deep breath, wiped away a tear. "The steak and green chile enchiladas are really very good."

Vanessa had been looking directly into Steven's eyes and dabbed her own. "Thank you, Steven, thank you for who you are and for loving me. I'll love you forever and always."

Steven leaned over to Vanessa and whispered, "I'm going to kiss you, my angel!"

Taken aback but still smiling brightly, Vanessa asked, "Here?"

And Steven Vandorol and Vanessa Carson, new law partners, kissed at the Cafe Central in El Paso, Republic of Texas, United States of America.

Tony discreetly appeared by their table. "Are you ready to order, Mr. Vandorol?"

"I think so, Tony. What would you like, sweet angel?"

Vanessa gave Tony a totally disarming smile and said, "I'll have the green chile soup . . . and the steak, medium rare, and green chile enchiladas, please—both of which Steven recommended, Tony."

"Excellent choice. And would you like a salad?"

"Yes, Steven and I will share the Caesar salad. That okay, Steven?"
Steven nodded.

"And we'll look at your dessert menu later. Thank you, Tony."

"You're most welcome." Tony turned to Steven. "And you, Mr. Vandorol?"

"I'll have the green chile soup as well and the prime filet, medium rare. I'm starving."

"Very good, Señor Vandorol. I la señorita es encantador! ¿Redondo de chianti?"

"Si, muchas gracias, Antonio. Para el vino y para el cumplido," Steven replied.

Tony smiled, nodded, and walked toward the kitchen.

Vanessa was looking at Steven, smiling. "What was that little exchange about?"

"Tony asked if we wanted more wine, and he also said that you are most enchanting." Steven kissed her again. "I agree, Vanessa Carson, and I love you!"

"I love you, too, and I want to shout it from Scenic Point."

"I'll have to teach you to say that in Spanish!" Steven was smiling at the woman he now prayed would be the love for the rest of his life. "It really is a beautiful, romantic language."

"That's good, Steven, and I can teach you to sign." She made a gesture with her right hand: thumb, index, and little finger up, the two other fingers down. "This means, 'I love you'!"

"Wow, I didn't know you knew sign language." Steven made the same gesture back to her. "Tell me about signing, sweetheart. It's very interesting to me."

"Remember when we were in DC, on K Street?"

Steven nodded and held up the sign for "I love you" again, albeit a little out of form.

She signed back and continued, "A really sweet deaf girl worked in the mail room. She had a good heart and was such a hard worker . . . but no one talked to her or ever noticed her."

Steven listened.

"Well, one day, when she brought my mail to my desk, I was eating a bacon cream cheese bagel. You know . . . those you liked to get, remember?"

Steven nodded and remembered those wonderful times he and Vanessa had occasionally met at the little coffee shop in their building for coffee and bagels. It had been their oasis amidst the ilk, corruption, sleaze, evil, and chaos of DC.

"Her name was Lucy—"

"Yes! I remember her, a sweet young girl with blonde hair. I'm afraid I was among those who ignored her. And I'm sorry for that."

"Well, you had a lot on your plate then, Mr. Vandorol. So, anyway, I asked if she would teach me to sign, so we could talk. She read my lips, I think, and every day on her break we'd meet for coffee, and she would teach me. We became friends! Before I left DC, she met the love of *her* life; they married and have a little girl now."

"Gosh, what a great story! Would you teach me how to sign, my love?"

"Okay, I will. But only if you teach me to speak Spanish, Señor Vandorol!"

With a fist bump, they made it a deal. He leaned over and kissed her full on the lips again in the restaurant, not caring if anyone was watching.

Tony was showing a couple to their table nearby. It was Chief Judge Kathy Carbon and Steven's boss in the special prosecution, District Attorney Ernie Martinez.

Steven stood and both the judge and Ernie noticed and detoured over to their table. "Steven, how are you?" Ernie asked, sticking out his hand to Steven but looking directly at Vanessa.

"Ernie." Steven shook hands with Ernie and acknowledged the chief judge. "How are you this fine evening, Judge?" Steven asked, smiling broadly at both.

Kathy was also looking directly at Vanessa.

"Judge, Ernie, I would like you both to meet my new partner, Vanessa Carson, previously from Washington, DC. I told you both that she was coming to El Paso."

Vanessa rose and extended her hand. "Very nice to meet you, Judge . . . and you as well, Mr. Martinez."

"Ernie, please. May I call you Vanessa?" he asked.

Steven watched Ernie looking directly into Vanessa's beautiful eyes and thought, *Her eyes have captivated for the third time today: me first, then Rommel, and now the DA.*

Vanessa nodded.

Steven jumped in. "Can you join us . . . for a drink at least? I was going to take Vanessa by the courthouse to meet you both tomorrow."

Judge Carbon smiled. "Sure . . . but just for one drink. It's not often that I get to have dinner with the district attorney."

Ernie pulled a chair out for the judge and then sat down himself. "Well, this is a real surprise."

"For me, too. She's been in town since mid-October . . . checking out the lay of the land," Steven said, motioning for Tony.

Tony appeared again. "Mr. Vandorol?"

"The judge and Mr. Martinez will have a drink with us . . . before dinner."

Tony looked at the judge. "Your Honor?"

Judge Carbon replied, "Vodka martini, up with two olives."

Tony looked at Ernie. "Señor Martinez?"

"Tequila, one shot!"

Tony was gone.

Ernie laughed. "Tony plays the invisible man well, doesn't he?"

Judge Carbon laughed also. "That he does." Looking at Vanessa, she continued, "Did you know Steven in Washington, DC?" She had noticed Steven's beaming expression and knew this must be a special friend.

"Yes, we practiced law together at Henderson Lane for a brief time . . . five years ago!" Vanessa said, smiling at the judge.

"So, what made you come to El Paso?"

Vanessa Carson proudly answered, "Steven Vandorol."

CHAPTER 9

"Steven, my love," Vanessa said, "you conveniently left out 'law' from 'law partner' when you introduced me."

Steven could tell the chief judge and district attorney had both been mesmerized by Vanessa. Ernie was excited that Steven had found experienced legal talent and said so to all, saying that Steven could now devote full time to the special prosecution of the Alvarados and others. However, Steven noticed the DA coughed nervously after he expressed that. After a round of drinks, they had adjourned to their own table on the other side of the restaurant and were now deeply engrossed in conversation.

"I also want to shout it from the mountaintop, from Ranger Peak. Everybody in town will know soon enough that ours is a forever and always love."

Steven's eyes were drawn to another couple walking into the restaurant. They were met by Tony, who led them to a table. It was Beth Barker and her husband, a younger Francisco Montes. Before Steven looked away, Beth saw Steven—and Vanessa—and grabbed her husband by the arm, dragging him toward their table.

Under his breath, Steven whispered, "Get ready for the Cat Woman." Steven stood as the couple approached. "Hello, Beth . . . and Francisco."

Beth and Francisco were looking directly at Vanessa, yet Beth said to Steven, "How nice, Steven Vandorol. How are you?" Steven noticed a slight top spin in her voice.

"Beth Barker, I would like for you and Francisco to meet Vanessa Carson, my new partner. Beth is on our special prosecution team."

Beth looked very beautiful this evening. She was not only a tall, statuesque woman with what some might call a handsome face, but she was also a fireball in the courtroom. She had short red hair showing strands of gray and bright blue eyes. Her only real flaw, if you could say that, was a small scar on the side of her straight aquiline nose. She wore a tight, red silk dress that left little to the imagination. Blood red Jimmy Choo high heels, which made her almost a foot taller than her dark-skinned and several years younger husband. He was well dressed also and had his long, jet-black hair pulled into a ponytail.

Vanessa, looking at Beth, said, "Nice to meet you, Beth . . . and Francisco." Vanessa extended her hand for Francisco, who had offered his. Francisco kept her hand longer than necessary, but Vanessa finally pulled away.

Beth asked sweetly but with a sneer, "So, when did Steven hire you, Vanessa?"

"Steven didn't hire me; we're partners."

"Well, that was quick. Have you known each other long?" Beth was frowning.

"We practiced together in DC, and I'm thrilled she is here now. Have a nice dinner this evening." Steven sat down, dismissing them both.

Tony, who had been standing by, was perceptive. "Ms. Barker . . . Mr. Montes . . . your table is ready." Tony led them away.

Beth turned back. "It was very nice to meet you, Vanessa. I'm sure we'll see much of each other." She turned and walked on behind Francisco, leaving Vanessa nodding and still smiling sweetly.

"Not if I can help it," Vanessa whispered under her breath, leaning toward Steven. She kissed him, and he kissed her back.

"Well, that was awkward," Steven said, whispering as well.

"The good, the bad, and the ugly. So, which one is she?"

Tony and another waiter served their green chile soup and both walked away.

"The bad . . . to answer your question," Steven said, tasting his soup. "She proposed that we have an affair."

"What? She's got the hots for you? I can tell." She picked up her spoon and tasted the soup. "This is marvelous." She took another spoonful. "What did you say?"

After another spoonful of soup, he responded, "I said thanks, but no thanks."

"What did she do?"

"She was put-out by the rejection, I think. She was a bit testy tonight. Couldn't you tell from her voice?"

"I sure could. Will it affect the special prosecution?"

"I don't think so. At least I hope not. She's a ruthless prosecutor and a good lawyer, but I don't trust her. I have this weird gut feeling about her. She's extremely aggressive, takes no prisoners and opponents are immediately executed . . . verbally. I've seen her in action. She can be manipulative, ruthless, and sometimes downright vicious." Steven finished his soup. "That was delicious."

"I noticed the small scar on her nose," Vanessa said. "Did you see it?"

"I sure didn't, maybe she got it dueling!" Steven was smiling.

Vanessa laughed and finished her soup as well. "That *was* excellent."

Tony approached with plates.

Steven and Vanessa were sitting so close that they were almost joined at the hip. Steven could feel her warmth as her left leg was again hooked over his right. He felt her passion and pride and pulled her even closer, his right arm around her delicate shoulders as Tony set down plates before them.

Both looked up and in unison. "Thank you, Tony!"

The waiter smiled and left.

"It would be so easy to take you home tonight, my love." Steven's passion was rising in his mind and heart. "You are so astonishingly beautiful, inside and out."

"But?" She smiled and squeezed his leg with hers.

"But . . . I'm turning *that* over to the good Lord, as you said, as well." Steven pulled her even closer and kissed her again. She kissed him back, lingering.

She knew exactly what Steven meant about their love. "I agree completely, Steven, our love means everything, and I understand what you have been through these last few years. I'm so proud of you for working through the struggle you've had." She touched Steven's face. "Your struggle and survival with relationships, with women, and with the evil in DC were my example to cure the evil in my own heart. Thank you, Steven."

"You're welcome, my sweet angel." Steven held her closer yet. "Our love means all the world to me as well. You have made me the happiest man on earth. Thank you for your love."

"My pleasure. We're doing the right thing, baking a cake." She paused and smiled sweetly before continuing.

Steven's eyes widened. "Baking a cake?"

"When I talked to Courtney about your struggles and about relationships, he told me how much you liked his 'baking a cake' analogy about a good relationship between a man and a woman."

"Yes, and from my conversation with him, I finally learned what real love was and what a real relationship between a man and a woman should be. I then developed my own One, Two, Three, Four Theory about human relationships."

"I really liked the baking a cake analogy, especially what the cherry on top represented," Vanessa said, hazel eyes flashing, "but I'm gonna love your theory . . . I'm certain." She took a bite of steak.

"Brief or at length? I don't want to bore you with too much blah, blah, blah, my love."

"At length, of course."

"Okay, point *one* is the self with the good Lord in your heart." Steven teared up as he always did when he thought about and mentioned his Lord and Savior, Jesus Christ.

Vanessa noticed. "You need to help me in strengthening my faith, will you?"

"I certainly will. *Two* is the two most important things in life: survival and the quest for emotional intimacy in various human relationships. The top-of-the-line relationship, as the good Lord intended, is between a man and a woman: Adam and Eve in the beginning, and you and me right now." Her shoe had come off, and Vanessa was rubbing her bare feet under the table against his left calf.

"So, is that what you meant about the intimacy of the two dolphins in that photo above your bed?" Vanessa asked.

"That's right!" The touch of her soft, bare feet, so natural and unsolicited, warmed his heart. "Thank you, my love."

"For what?"

"For just being you . . . and not trying to be anyone else."

"You're welcome. Please go on."

So, Steven told Vanessa all about his theory, the One, Two, Three, Four Theory of Intimate Human Relationships, 4LIFE, as he called it.

Vanessa exclaimed, "Wow, Steven, I love the theory as it covers all intimate relationships between two humans. It's like the *three* important things in life on our planet: the self, how the self-connects with others, and the ingredients of that connection!"

"Now, it's my turn to say wow!" Steven said. "In one simple sentence, you summarized my entire theory, which 'took me lots of blah, blah, blah . . . for almost ten minutes, to explain."

Vanessa laughed. "That's why we lawyers charge by the word!"

They both laughed out loud. "You know something, my Vanessa? We're not only philosophical equals but intellectual equals as well."

Vanessa kissed Steven's hand. "Any of those intimacy issues my problems?" She raised her eyebrows in anticipation.

"My sweet angel, now that I've seen myself, I don't analyze, criticize, control, or make judgments of my friends . . . I can only control myself . . . and I'm not going to do that to the love of my life."

"But I'm asking you for your opinion," she interrupted. "Your opinion of me is important in our honestly sharing everything."

"Okay, then . . . I think it's self-tenderness," Steven answered. "You are so hard on yourself and you worry too much. And it'll be my job to keep you from getting beaten to death with your own goodness, as Ayn Rand suggests in *Atlas Shrugged*—my favorite novel."

"My favorite novel as well!" She paused a beat, then, "Thank you. You are the angel the good Lord put in my life to help me do just that . . . and to see myself as I truly am . . . I am carrying around a lot of guilt . . . about everything." That dark cloud Steven had seen earlier in the day when they were talking in his' office was again passing before her beautiful eyes.

After finishing their delicious dinner, they sat sipping their wine when a sad look came across Vanessa's face.

"What's wrong, honey? All of a sudden you seem sad," Steven asked.

"Oh, I'm sorry. There was a man sitting behind you that made me remember something I'd rather forget."

Steven took her hand and said, "I'm here to listen, not judge or analyze, so if you ever need to 'let it out,' I'm here for you." He gave her hand a squeeze and smiled. "I can see some horror touched you, my love, and I'll be there for you. . . all in your own time and choice, okay?"

"Thank you. In our upward progression, we can each close the circle. I agree, my love. Here's to the upward progression of our love . . . to become one before the good Lord in paradise."

"You have restored my faith in womankind, Vanessa Carson!" Steven raised his glass.

"How is that, Steven Vandorol?" Vanessa said, cuddling even closer. They now appeared to be one body, with two heads, both smiling happily.

"You took the ultimate leap of faith when you called Courtney to find me and came to El Paso as your free choice, without letting me know. As you said, 'I wanted to come to you, independently and without hesitation or need.' That's why you restored my faith in womankind."

Tony almost magically appeared again. "Care for dessert, señorita?"

This time Vanessa answered immediately, "Si. Gracias . . . Do you have a layer ice cream cake?"

"Yes, ma'am, we sure do. It's a four-layer ice cream cake: chocolate, strawberry, vanilla, and raspberry topped with whipped cream."

"That sounds wonderful. Please bring one and two forks. We're sharing."

"Very good, Miss." Tony turned to walk away.

"Oh, Tony?" Vanessa called after him.

Tony turned back. "Yes, Miss?"

Vanessa smiled her sunshine toward Steven and said to Tony, "Please put a cherry on top for us!"

CHAPTER 10

"So, you call yourselves professionals?" The gravelly, almost hoarse voice—obviously using a voice mixer—came through on the untraceable burner cell phone. "Your team botched every attempt. You couldn't even kill a stupid animal." The sarcasm was palpable as the hollow voice continued, dripping with cynicism. "Well, Colonel Lemev? What have you to say for yourself and that team of incompetent, so-called professional assassins?"

Colonel Stanislav Lemev was one of the leaders of the assassination team and a contract killer himself, contracted for millions of US dollars by "Gravelly Voice," as the assassination team now called him. The very familiar voice was encrypted and modified, coming from somewhere in America, somewhere in Washington, DC, they all guessed.

Colonel Stanislav Lemev, Communist Chinese Colonel Qiao Liang, consummate ninja assassin, and Chinese General Wang Xiangsui, all three, sat at the same table as before in the darkened safe house that was now the strike team's headquarters in Sunland Park, a suburb of El Paso, along with the rest of the assassins scattered about.

All in the room remained totally silent.

Fat General Xiangsui was fanning himself with a folded newspaper while Colonel Liang, as always, held a delicate, fine china saucer and daintily sipped hot tea from an even more delicate gold-inlaid china cup.

The Chinese communists, the Russian Spetsnaz, and Muslim radical terrorist killers all remained silent as Colonel Lemev received a tongue-lashing from Gravelly Voice.

General Wang Xiangsui and Colonel Qiao Liang had broad smiles on their faces—very unusual for the dour and stoic Communist Chinese. They were gloating and seemed elated with Colonel Lemev's utter discomfort. Both just tolerated the moronic, muscle-bound Russian, whom both knew to be Vladimir Putin's personal "fixer" thug.

The two Chinese men were still completely unknown to Gravelly Voice, Ward Powell knew for certain. He was sitting on a couch beside Uri Gagarin, his look-alike "almost" brother, and he smiled to himself as he looked around the room at all the players.

What a bunch of creeps, Powell thought. *I'm gonna really enjoy killing all of them. Even Colonel Lemev, our wonderful leader, who's well placed with Vladimir himself. He's just a hypocrite, salivates like a puppy dog when I talk about my sexual escapades, but threatens to kill me when I say something crude and sexual, especially about mothers or his beloved Mother Russia. I'm still going to turn him into my "slave buddy," especially since I found out from Liang what he did in the cabin near the US-Canadian border, near Melita, Canada, and one hundred miles from Carrington, North Dakota.* Powell's thoughts mimicked and parroted the location names, as he had memorized, and then destroyed, his written instructions for last year bringing the reinforcements from ghost headquarters, near Anchorage, Alaska, to where Russian and Chinese communists continued to infiltrate North America by the thousands directly from mainland Siberia across the Bering Strait.

Major General Wang Xiangsui was a large, very fat man, both by Chinese and American standards, fitting in well with an obese American nation. Almost five and a half feet tall and about three hundred pounds, he resembled Jabba the Hutt. He was dressed in an oversized tan linen suit—tailored to perfectly hide his obesity—a custom-made, white, 100 percent cotton shirt, monogrammed in Chinese kanji, French cuffs with gold American flag links, and a pink Christian Lacroix silk paisley tie. His shoes were Gucci, very expensive—not just cheap Chinese knockoffs. He was sweating profusely, and the perpetual scowl on his fat face made him look like he had indigestion from swallowing a large lizard.

The book *Unrestricted Warfare: China's Master Plan to Destroy America,* co-authored by then-colonels Wang Xiangsui and Qiao Liang, vaulted both men to Communist China's top military leadership. General Xiangsui rose much faster to a generalship in communist leadership than his colleague, as he was a master manipulator and corruptor, not unlike his idol and mentor, Mao Tse Tung, the killer of seventy million Chinese during and after World

War II. And though his co-author did most of the writing, General Xiangsui had taken full credit.

General Xiangsui was the designated dictator of America, and in complete charge of the sword-point of all the ground forces massing on the Canadian and Mexican borders of the United States. All such forces were unknown to most of the assassination team and totally unknown to all their Washington, DC, contacts within the current administration, especially their apparent spokesman, Gravelly Voice, right then talking on the speaker.

Once his job was done, America would be subdued and neutralized as a power. The general would then foreclose on the United States' massive debt of trillions, and Communist China, as the lone remaining world power, and the general personally, as dictator, would, in effect, own all public American lands. *We Chinese will then truly be the Kings from the East as their nonsense Christian Bible foretells in the Book of Revelations,* the general thought.

General Xiangsui was first going to discipline the assassination team for their various failures and make way for further reinforcements that were waiting just outside Ciudad Juarez, a stone's throw from downtown El Paso.

General Xiangsui was not a believer in the old Chinese adage about the "enemy of my enemy being my friend." He would kill all enemies, regardless of any alliances, and had been in daily contact by cell phones (far more advanced than any in America) with Colonel Liang, his partner and co-author who *claimed* to be just an observer on the assassination team but was actually the leader of the advance guard already well hidden and dispersed in El Paso.

The general smiled to himself as he thought again about how he managed to insert his co-author into Vladimir Putin's closest thugs and gangsters. As a member of Putin's Russian Mafia inner circle, Colonel Liang could and would join the assassination team merely as an observer. *Liang will be the cobra in the henhouse as the ancient proverb says,* General Xiangsui thought as he looked around the room, surveying all the distasteful killers and assassins, especially the degenerate Muslims in their midst.

General Xiangsui was livid that the attempts on both Egen and Vandorol had failed. Steven Vandorol was still alive and continued to be a factor in this prosecution with national implications. General Xiangsui would make sure that Vandorol would be destroyed this time.

General Xiangsui hated Vandorol and knew exactly why. Not only had Steven thwarted the Kings of the East from the takeover of the United States government by blowing up the failed Project Triple X several years ago, but Vandorol also represented everything about America that communists and the American left hated most.

As for hating America, the general had first turned to a local El Pasoan for help carrying out his final plan, already authorized by the chairman himself, to neutralize American armed ground forces and pave the way for the invasion of America from the south, from Juarez, Mexico, and in the north from Canada, where the state of California was the first prize.

The general had already tested his final plan through his "Year of the Horse" surprise, which had caused a massive blackout of the entire southern border between Mexico and El Paso, Texas. Then he had the American traitor and his whole family summarily executed.

But the general made a mistake. He had ordered Ward Powell to eliminate the entire Warren family. He trusted him to get the job done, but Powell left the son as a most annoying loose end. *I'll have to get the job done right myself,* he thought as he continued to fan himself with the newspaper.

CHAPTER 11

Young Jacob Warren sat across from Steven Vandorol. He was looking down at this lap, very sad and obviously still in a deep depression, although he lost his family months ago. Jacob was brought to Steven's office on a Saturday morning by two armed and uniformed police officers in a white unmarked Dodge Charger with tinted windows. Steven was alone in the office with the young man as the officers sat outside in the waiting room drinking coffee.

Jacob was tall and had a slight nervous twitch that became more pronounced when he talked about the recent events, especially about losing his mother. A nice-looking boy, he reminded Steven of a younger Mark Wahlberg. Steven thought, *This kid just lost everything, especially the anchor of a father, and he still has all his own personal demons and growing up to handle.*

Steven, sitting opposite a very solemn Jacob, spoke first. "So, Captain Egen told me all about you and said you wanted to see me and chat."

Jacob raised his head and looked directly into Steven's eyes. "Yes, Mr. Vandorol, I researched all about you while I was in protective custody. Chief Egen said you were the best lawyer in El Paso and could be trusted."

Steven said nothing.

"I loved my dad and mom and still do . . . very much, but I'm really angry at them because they are dead and they let my little sister, Michelle, get killed, too!" Jason's eyes clouded. "My little sister was just a kid . . . and my mom hated her because she was Dad's favorite."

"And weren't you your mom's favorite?"

That got his attention. "Yes, and that was causing their divorce." Jacob put his head down again.

"They were getting a divorce before they were killed?"

And it all came out in a rush: "They were both having affairs. I know Dad had an out-of-town woman he was seeing regularly because he often took business trips." Jacob made air quotes with his fingers. "Business for his company, El Paso Power and Electric. Mom, who thought she was fat, lost all her confidence because Dad had turned away." Tears made paths down his face. Steven pushed a box of Kleenex across to Jacob. He took one, wiped his eyes, and continued. "Still, I think she was seeing this doctor, a gynecologist at Providence Hospital who kept an apartment at Stanton House."

Steven thought, *That's right where my Vanessa lives. I wonder on what floor?*

Jacob, wiping his eyes and getting a little angry, continued, "He lived in 821, on the eighth floor. I know because I followed him . . . I suspected the good doctor took lots of nurses up there, and my dad was a traitor."

Steven's eyes widened. "A traitor, your Dad? How's that?"

Now calmer, but still angry, Jacob was specific: "He betrayed our country to the Communist Chinese for money, a lot of money. And for what? So he could continue to have his little out-of-town "business" trips with his whore and maintain his toys, that stupid white Porsche and all his porno stuff."

Steven interrupted, "How did he betray America?"

"By selling out the electrical grid on the southern border of the US. Who do you think caused the New Year's Eve massive blackout, Mr. Vandorol?" Jacob's voice dripped with sarcasm.

"The company provided a news release to the media saying it was a grid computer malfunction," Steven said. "That wasn't it?"

"Mr. Vandorol, that was fake news to cover up the fact that my dad, who created the entire system for El Paso Power and Electric, sold the Communist Chinese the back-door code to the security system, which he alone knew, so the electrical grid computer system could be hacked as a test to create the blackout."

"So, the blackout was just a test?"

"Yes, just a test."

"For what?"

"I don't know," Jacob answered, shaking his head. "Something big, really big, where there'd be a massive blackout for the state of Texas's entire southern border with Mexico."

Steven asked, "Are the Russians involved?"

"I don't know that, but I know the Chinese definitely are!"

"How do you know?"

"Because Dad told me everything . . . and said that if something happened to him, I was to disappear for a while and then resurface to tell the police everything I knew."

"Well, did you?" Steven raised his eyebrows and waited.

"No, I didn't. I was afraid. Dad told me I should go to the police, but I thought a lawyer would know more. I feel like I can trust you. I can, can't I, Mr. Vandorol?" He locked eyes with Steven.

"That's a choice *you* have to make, Jacob. I could tell you yes, you can trust me. But trust is something that has to be earned. It's your choice, young man."

Jacob's eyes softened as Steven thought, *This is a sad young kid who just lost his parents and sister and is completely alone.* Steven resolved right then to try to make a difference in this young man's life. He reached out to Jacob. "Yes, you can trust me. And my partner, Vanessa, as well! Tell you what, why don't you have dinner with Vanessa and me, and you can tell us the whole story so we can help you."

"But I'm in protective custody, and two officers watch me all the time."

"I think I can arrange with Chief Egen for you to have a little freedom."

CHAPTER 12

Jacob Warren was smiling brightly today—a definite change.

Steven had, indeed, arranged with Chief Egen for Jacob to have a little freedom. Jacob was at Vanessa's apartment for dinner, and he couldn't keep his eyes off beautiful Vanessa.

Big Rommel and little Harley, invited by Steven and Vanessa for the occasion, lay together on the large oval rug, and an uninterested cat, Caspurr, was also in the audience.

Steven had shared with Vanessa his idea to help a lost kid with some guidance and to build a friendship and trust between them. "I think the kid needs some surrogate-parent role models right now," he had explained. Vanessa agreed enthusiastically, and she cooked a sumptuous Italian feast.

"This is wonderful, Ms. Carson," Jacob said to Vanessa. He was *not* just enthralled with the veal piccata. "Thank you for having me for dinner." Jacob looked directly at Steven. "And thank you, Mr. Vandorol, for arranging it. This is the first time since my sister . . . and parents were murdered that I feel safe."

Two uniformed police officers brought Jacob to the apartment: young officer Jesus Cruz, who remained with the police cruiser downstairs, and veteran officer Marty Schultze, who stood outside the apartment by the elevators. Steven knew both officers well.

Vanessa spoke first as she looked at Jacob. "First, you're most welcome!" She set her fork down. "Jacob, the 'Ms. Carson' stuff's gotta stop." She smiled brightly at him with her sunshine smile. "Please, *Vanessa* will be fine, okay?"

Steven, watching both, had to smile himself as the thought, *Jacob might just fall in love with my Vanessa tonight.* But he said, "Same goes with the 'Mr. Vandorol' stuff. Steven is fine; it makes me feel younger!" Steven looked at Vanessa and winked.

Jacob was enjoying himself, smiling brightly, with relief written all over his previously downcast face. "Thank you, Vanessa and Steven, thank you so much." His eyes teared up.

All three were silent.

Steven broke the silence. "Jacob, you're very welcome. You're welcome here at Vanessa's apartment, at our law office, and at my home, any time. All places are secure now completely, with round-the-clock surveillance."

Jacob smiled. "Yes, I've got two full-time babysitters, Officer Schultze and Officer Cruz; it's pretty neat riding around in a chauffeured unmarked police car."

Jacob was having a good time, enjoying the dinner with Steven and Vanessa. *Wow, she's gotta be the most beautiful woman I've ever seen in my life,* he thought.

Steven noticed the stars in his eyes but said, "Jacob, Vanessa can be trusted implicitly. She's a lawyer and understands confidentiality, as I do, and I trust and respect her. So, it's your choice, but anything you wanted to tell me tonight is safe, completely, with Vanessa as well."

Steven took a bite of piccata, swallowed, and gently laid his hand on Vanessa's. "If you want to tell just me, she'll understand that, too." Steven looked at Vanessa who was nodding in agreement.

Jacob responded, "I want her to hear it as well. My Dad was a louse, but I guess I was the only one that he could trust." He saddened again.

And Jacob told Steven and Vanessa everything as they said nothing, just listened.

Jacob told of his dad acting "weird" and "paranoid" and being more distant than usual, like he was hiding something. "He stopped talking to Mom completely, almost ignoring her, rather than talking only occasionally as before. He only talked to Michelle and was overly tender and loving to her. So, I followed him around and was watching him at Gold's Gym when a young Asian man—I think Chinese—used a device to bypass Dad's Porsche's security alarm. He opened the door, put a brown package on the passenger seat, locked the doors back, and left."

Jacob, a little breathless, continued, "I waited for Dad to come out of the gym. Finally, he got in the car and looked around, like someone might be watching. I think he opened the package. He then held up a bundle of money, counted it, and put in back. He seemed happier than I'd seen him in years."

Jacob took a deep breath, sighed, took a sip of his Coke, and stared out Vanessa's window. "Then I came home late one night, and Dad was out in the backyard talking on his phone. He had it on speaker because he thought he was alone, I guess. At the time, I assumed he must have gotten a new one because it wasn't his iPhone. I snuck out, hid close by, and heard him talking to someone who spoke very slowly and very distinctly. They were talking about the Year of the Horse surprise, and I heard something about a Chinese proverb. I thought it was a really weird conversation, for sure."

Steven and Vanessa still said nothing and continued to listen.

"So, I thought, *This is bull crap*, and I came out of hiding after he hung up. When I confronted him, Dad spilled his guts to me."

CHAPTER 13

After a delicious Italian dinner of veal piccata, Caesar salad, Ezekiel garlic bread, and fagioli con le cotiche, Vanessa served dessert: a lavish chocolate cake, which she made from scratch.

Jacob was in heaven. He couldn't stop saying "Wow!" and "Amazing!" to anything and everything Vanessa said or did: "Wow, Vanessa, this cake is just amazing! What did you call it in Italian?"

"Torta Barozzi, originally named 'black cake.' It was officially named after the famous local architect Jacopo Barozzi in the small village of Vignola, near Modena, at the end of the nineteenth century, where it was created by the talented pastry chef Eugenio Gollini. His namesake uncle, the owner of the Gollini bakery, which still exists in Vignola today, trademarked its name and decided to keep the recipe secret, turning the dish into a legend and helping it become the region's most famous culinary creation."

"Jeez, Vanessa," Jacob said as Steven watched in quiet amusement. "How do you know so much about that?"

"Vignola, Italy, is where my mother, Angelina, and my grandmother, Sophia, were born." A tear formed in her eye. Steven noticed.

"That's an amazing story," Jacob said, still looking at Vanessa with stars in his eyes.

Getting up from the table, Vanessa said, "Jacob, why don't you help me fix plates for Officers Shultze and Cruz. I'm sure they're pretty hungry by now with all the aroma."

Jacob was up in a flash and said, "Excuse me, Steven," as he followed her into the kitchen.

Steven nodded to Jacob and continued to smile as he heard the boy ask, "Can I take the food to them?"

* * * *

In Sunland Park in the meantime, Gravelly Voice was still talking: "Colonel Lemev, you and your team of contract killers have been paid

70

very, very well, and we . . . uh . . . *I* am extremely disappointed in your performance."

Colonel Lemev sipped more Stolichnaya vodka as he surveyed the room in quiet embarrassment, thinking, *Glad Powell tapped into some big Mexican money! I don't know how he did it, but I'm not taking any more der'mo from this gravelly voiced Muslim pretender.*

The general was also aware of the very uncomfortable and awkward silence. His entire assassination team, well situated, well concealed, and unknown to all, were perfectly invisible to regular life in El Paso, Texas.

As he sat in contemptuous and smug silence, General Xiangsui knew that Gravelly Voice—his superior intelligence had revealed—was none other than the former attorney general of the United States of America, a Muslim himself, who had resigned from the administration to head the Muslim Brotherhood's infiltration of American government, especially the State Department and Pentagon. *The stupid, arrogant Muslim*, General Xiangsui thought, *has absolutely no clue as to the whirlwind about to hit America.* He looked over at Ward Powell sitting by Uri, both completely silent, and was astonished; the smiling Ward Powell actually winked at him.

His co-author, Colonel Liang, was sitting next to Lemev, also in arrogant silence and smiling broadly and uncharacteristically; he was proud of his new-found sense of humor. He nudged the general with his elbow, and thought, *The American administration, especially the White House, just like the rest of America, is completely clueless about our invasion."*

Russian Spetsnaz commando Colonel Lemev squirmed and fidgeted in embarrassment, just like a teenager on a first date, as the whole assassination team watched and listened in very awkward silence.

Only Ward Powell was silently enjoying the festivities. He thought, *I bet the head Muslim in the White House, who's probably listening in, is enjoying it as well.* He again almost laughed out loud but stifled the laugh by feigning a cough. Only the general noticed.

The Russian colonel was a huge bear of a man. A full Spetsnaz, Russian Special Forces colonel, he could be identified by the tattoo on his right hand, a scorpion with claws open. The open claws signified him as an active combat veteran of the Russian fiasco in Afghanistan, the Russian Vietnam. He had a deep hatred for the United States, whose stinger missiles—shoulder-fired and CIA-supplied to Afghan freedom fighters—brought the Russian bear to its knees.

Lemev was at least two hundred and seventy pounds and well over six feet tall. He had a barrel chest, long muscular arms, short legs, and huge hands. Strong as an ox—in his prime he'd been a heavyweight Olympic weightlifter and gold medalist—Colonel Lemev was an ugly man.

Lemev was proud of his disfigured face and ugliness. To compliment his dour countenance, he had a heavy scar running diagonally across his face—a trophy from a Muslim woman who had tried to decapitate him in Kurtz Valley (the colonel later disemboweled her)—that turned his lips into a permanent sneer. He hated Muslims just a bit less than he hated Americans. However, he religiously kept that hatred to himself, especially in the present company of his own assassination team. Along with the disfiguring scar and his ruddy, pock-marked, weathered complexion, he had deep-set, piercing, alert gray eyes, all topped by a shock of gray hair. Most would think him very scary. But in his line of work, making people afraid was good, very good.

Colonel Lemev was not about to comment. He didn't have to answer to this particular Muslim idiot, no matter how high he was in the administration in Washington, DC, but no purpose was served by either argument or excuse. So he said nothing and continued to let Gravelly Voice rant. *Maybe he will spew the venom out of his system,* the colonel thought. He would be wrong.

"We're sending another team from Mexico City," Gravelly Voice paused to let that sink in. "They will take over your contract hit."

Lemev was stunned. His control of the situation had just evaporated. He was embarrassed before his own team and the Chinese Communists and seven professional assassins sitting around listening. "Who are they?" is all Lemev could manage.

Gravelly Voice was now suddenly calm. "You will find out when they contact your team." Ominous silence. "They are *real* professionals, and they will take over the operation, eliminate Steven Vandorol and his prosecution team, and actually derail the entire El Paso prosecution, which, if successful, will solidify all national public opinion against us."

"What about our team here in El Paso?" Lemev immediately regretted the question as it showed just how out of touch he really was.

Gravelly Voice was biting, "The señoritas in Juarez have you and your team much too distracted, Colonel. You are not on spring break."

The colonel said nothing.

"Your team will stand by, provide backup, and only act in accordance with their orders."

Lemev decided he would humor Gravelly Voice. "So, when can we expect them in El Paso?" He knew now that the corrupt American politicians were truly clueless as to their real mission: the takeover and invasion of America.

"Within the month, so try to keep the booze and women to a minimum. You're not on spring break," he repeated.

Total silence. One could have heard a pin drop.

"Well, Colonel Lemev, do you have anything to say for your team's pathetic performance?" Gravelly Voice was dripping with sarcasm and arrogance; hushed, muffled chuckling could be heard in the background from another person apparently listening in on the conversation.

Colonel Lemev didn't like the whip being directed at him and had had quite enough. Straightening himself defiantly for the sake of those assembled, he said, "I'm still assassination team leader, so back off. You can tell your stupid lies and spew your venom to someone else, but not to me. Do we have an understanding?" His English was now flawless, not the slightest hint of his heavy Russian accent to which he digressed when distracted by Powell's sexual profanity.

Gravelly Voice was silent.

Lemev was laughing to himself: *As a multi-millionaire, I don't have to take any der'mo from this particular Muslim fanatic anymore. All my money is safe in my secret account.* He was doing what he had wanted to do for a long time as he adamantly blurted out, "Our job was the initial assassination of Steven Vandorol, Eddie Egen, North Anderson, and Beth Barker, the entire prosecution team, which would decimate the special prosecution being watched nationwide, blow the case up in the faces of the current administration, and serve as a nationwide call to arms for the American people. I have been paid in full, and I will fulfill the contract. Do you understand?"

Suddenly, Gravelly Voice had a whole different tone. "So, does your team need any help in carrying out that objective?" His changed tone was almost sheepish. Powell noticed and gave Lemev a thumbs up sign.

Emboldened, Lemev answered, "We don't need any more bodies. Their security has tightened considerably. We're not dealing with a bunch of idiots here like those in Washington, DC." Lemev, further emboldened by silence on the phone line, continued, "We will corrupt from the inside, just like we have done since the Cold War ended." Lemev looked directly at Powell and nodded.

Gravelly Voice spoke again, "Any new intelligence on the ground there in El Paso prior to the arrival of the new team from Juarez to help yours?"

Lemev answered, "One critical difference is apparent. Steven Vandorol and Eddie Egen seem to have new leases on life."

"What's changed?"

"First, Ed Egen and his wife, Andi, are on their second honeymoon—both happy like *yeblya* newlyweds, and their previously filed divorced was dismissed. And Steven Vandorol has a new law partner."

"Oh, yeah? Who is he?"

Lemev knew he now had the entire American administration's undivided attention. "It's not a *he*. It's a *she*, Vanessa Carson. She has apparently been in El Paso since October of last year."

Gravelly Voice was apparently well informed: "Wasn't she married to Dudley Moore, a partner at Henderson Lane?"

"One and the same, she is smart and beautiful!" As he responded, Lemev glanced at his buddy, Powell, whose eyes now appeared glazed over. "Steven introduced her as his new partner, leaving out the *law partner* part. So, it seems to be a lot more than just work." Lemev was proud. He knew something Gravelly Voice didn't, as Powell had told him about her but wouldn't reveal his 'secret source.'

"Are they living together?"

"No, separate residences: she's in a Stanton Street high-rise; he's still on Golden Hill Terrace."

"They were good friends in DC and worked pretty close together then?"

Lemev was smiling broadly. "They're probably already sleeping together . . ."

Gravelly Voice clicked off abruptly, and the line went dead.

Momentary silence was followed by raucous laughter by all except Lemev, the target of the previous tongue lashing, who was smiling, thinking, *I put the arrogant Muslim in his proper place.*

Even General Xiangsui and Colonel Liang were quietly amused, smiling.

Powell was now especially jovial. Lemev noticed and thought to himself, *I'm sure glad I've got all my money in a safe place.*

Lemev was a satisfied, happy man as he looked forward to tonight's sexcapades along with Ward and Uri.

Now sitting in Vanessa's living room, young Jacob said, "Wow Vanessa, the view of downtown El Paso and Juarez just goes on and on like a sparkling nighttime light show. It's just awesome." Jacob was not only mesmerized by the view, but by the hostess as well.

"You should see the breathtaking views from Steven's home!" She smiled brightly at Steven, and winked.

It was Steven's cue to bring Jacob back to reality. "Jacob, did you get enough to eat?"

Jacob was sipping on a Coke, and Steven and Vanessa were sipping coffee after having the wonderful dessert. The two officers outside, Shultze and Cruz, were well fed also.

"I sure did!" Jacob turned to Vanessa. "The cake you baked, Vanessa, was to die for."

He apparently loves to say her name, Steven thought, but said, "Jacob, you're an intelligent, perceptive, and well-brought-up young man with your entire future before you!" Steven looked directly into Jacob's eyes. "The ultimate of human freedom is the God-given freedom of choice. An orangutan can punch the keys of a cell phone or keyboard, but only human beings can think, speak, read, and write."

Vanessa remained quiet but could tell Jacob was listening intently.

Steven smiled at Jacob. "It was Albert Einstein who jokingly said - before computers - that if you put forty monkeys on forty typewriters and let them type into infinity, they would eventually come up with the complete works of William Shakespeare."

Jacob laughed out loud, and an amused Vanessa nodded and smiled beautifully at both.

"The farther backward you may look . . . the farther forward you're likely to see."

Jacob was puzzled. "What? I don't understand. What does that mean?"

"That means you have to really look inward at yourself, where you came from, to understand who you are. Then and only then, with awareness and understanding, will you know where you are going." Steven took a sip of his coffee, and continued, "Knowing yourself is the beginning of all wisdom. That's Aristotle, the ancient Greek philosopher."

Jacob and Vanessa were listening in rapt attention, nodding slowly.

"It was Socrates, another ancient Greek philosopher—and the patron, almost saint, of lawyers—who said that people make themselves appear ridiculous when they are trying to know obscure things before they know themselves. Plato also alluded to the fact that understanding 'thyself' would have a greater yield toward understanding the nature of a human being."

"Man, that's pretty deep!" Jacob said.

Steven thought, *I think he's understanding,* but summarized, "You've been through a lot, my young friend. Concentrate on who and what *you* are right here, right now—blaming no one, just being yourself."

Vanessa interrupted, "Why, you're quite the philosopher." She was smiling radiantly at Steven, eyes wide open with love.

Jacob noticed as well, as Steven continued, "It was Charles M. Russell, the great American Western sculptor, who said, 'Spending that many hours in the saddle gave cowboys plenty of time to think. That's why so many cowboys fancied themselves philosophers."

Jacob and Vanessa both laughed out loud as Steven continued, "In the past, I had a lot of bad relationships and was not a happy man. But then here in El Paso, I had a lot of time to think, so I became a philosopher!" Steven looked directly at Venessa. "But now I'm a happy man since I have a partner."

Looking at them both together, Jacob changed the subject. "My dad had dual majors in computer science and philosophy. I think I'll do that as well, just like my dad!"

CHAPTER 14

Once the raucous laughter at Gravelly Voice died down, all sat in subdued silence.

Colonel Lemev, still smiling at his victory over Gravelly Voice, drank more vodka, as Ward Powell thought, *I've got me a new Russian slave!* He nudged Uri sitting beside him, who smiled as well.

Colonel Qiao Liang, planted as just an observer but the real leader of the assassination team hired to kill Steven Vandorol and his entire prosecution team, continued to sip hot tea from his delicate china cup and noticed the nudge and smiles by both.

Fat General Xiangsui, designated dictator and leader of all ground forces invading America, noticed as well and was the first to speak: "Obviously, gentlemen, the American administration had absolutely no clue as to the sirens they unleashed by contracting our Russian friends to assassinate Mr. Vandorol and his legal team just for political reasons, because it would coalesce public opinion against the American Democratic Party and other leftists.

"We Chinese will *not* destroy anything. We want to enjoy everything our 'collateral' has to offer. Other than a few dirty bombs in the major cities to create chaos, we will not destroy anything that America has. But regardless, the contract with our Russian friends in general and Colonel Lemev in particular is our cover for now." The general paused, licked his fat lips, and continued, "So we will complete the contract to eliminate Vandorol and his prosecution team and act as backup to whomever is coming from Mexico City."

The general already knew of the buildup of Muslim radical terrorists on the southern border of the United States in Mexico, which would walk en masse through the porous border from Juarez, Mexico. "And that day, America's nationwide electric power grid . . . and all mobile civilian and military communication devices will be interrupted!" The general finished with ice in his voice, proud of himself that he had turned the stupid, traitorous, and greedy American Jason Warren, though it took much more money than his chairman had authorized. Still, he worried because the son, Jacob Warren, was in complete protective custody.

"We need to be really careful," Powell finally said, having stopped smiling. "There're way too many Muslims coming across the southern border." Powell was looking directly at Lemev. "The Muslim radicals are our allies, right, Colonel?" Powell was grandstanding for the general and also very proud of himself now that he was in the general's favor since the Warren family was eliminated and the test succeeded. But he thought, *The fat slob screwed up big time with all his superior intelligence he keeps bragging about and didn't tell me about the Warren kid who was now in protective custody.*

Lemev didn't like to be berated, not by his own, especially after being on the short end of one Muslim's rant. "Ward, I'm in charge of this team; we'll handle them when it's time." Colonel Lemev didn't care if Ward did have friends in high places back in Russia, "You just do your job and stay out of mine, understand?" Burning fire was now glowing in his eyes.

Powell nodded and said nothing. *As soon as it's time, he's a dead man,* he thought. Powell knew that he had Lemev's enslaved life in his own hands. He would direct that kill himself, Powell thought and said, "I have a plan that will succeed."

Powell's giant menacing dog was again sleeping soundly right beside him, his huge head larger than a massive medicine ball, snout laying on his two huge front paws, like two catcher's mitts. He was snorting and occasionally belching loudly. Powell patted his huge head tenderly, and Ubiytsa, the killer dog, rolled over like a giant grizzly.

All were silent.

Lemev finally spoke again, directly to Powell, "How do we succeed, Ward?"

Powell answered, "Vanessa Carson is Vandorol's 'partner' now! I knew her in Washington, DC." He finally had the floor. "We succeed by kidnapping her."

"What will that do?" asked Lemev.

"It will draw Steven Vandorol out into the open." Powell smiled lasciviously. "He will try to rescue her, and we'll set a trap. When he comes after her, we'll kill him."

"How do you know he'll come after her?"

"Because he loves her. It's the only way. That's the only Achilles heel he still has left, so we'll capitalize on it."

"How are you going to do it?"

"I've got a plan, but then, when I'm done with both of them, I'll let Killer taste her as well!" Powell, the embodiment of evil, dead eyes reflecting Satan himself, was finished.

Lemev wasn't. "Wow, this I gotta see for myself," he said as Powell got up and abruptly walked out. His giant dog, Killer, dutifully followed behind as all the assassins watched.

───────────────

Steven Vandorol smiled at Jacob. "Your dad was, God bless him, probably a pretty wonderful guy after all, wasn't he?"

"I guess so."

Vanessa finished her coffee and said, "Well, boys, I've got to clean up and feed the cat. We have a busy day tomorrow, Mr. Vandorol." She stood, gathered their plates, and walked into the kitchen. "Caspurr, come on." She was followed by Caspurr and Jacob's eyes.

Steven smiled and refocused Jacob again. "Seriously, you're in a lot of danger. You've got to remain extremely vigilant and not be distracted by anything or anyone, understand?"

"What do you mean?"

"You're well protected now and relaxed, but you're a young guy." Steven paused and thought, *How do I say this to him delicately?* "You're gonna get lonely. Do you have a girlfriend?"

Jacob broke eye contact, looked down at his hands, paused, and slowly raised his head. He looked embarrassed. "Yes, but she doesn't know where I am."

Steven said nothing. Jacob continued, "Her name is Emily, and she's a freshman at UTEP. I called her on her cell phone and told her I was in hiding and in protective custody. Emily knew my mom and dad and sister had been murdered, and she was worried about me."

Steven was surprised. "When was it that you called Emily and from where did you call? Didn't they take your cell phone when the police and Chief Egen took you into protective custody?"

"Yes, they did. So, I snuck a call from a pay phone, right there at the westside police station. She was really worried about me," he repeated.

Steven still said nothing and continued to listen. He no longer smiled, his mouth closed, his lips a straight line.

Sensing Steven's displeasure, Jacob was apologetic. "Are you mad at me?"

"Jacob, I don't know you well enough yet to be mad at you. But you are twenty years old. You have to start thinking and not get distracted by *anything*." Steven accentuated that last word. "That's what I meant."

Jacob lowered his gaze back to his lap as Steven continued. "You are not just in danger; you are in extreme mortal danger! Extreme vigilance means that before you say anything or do anything, you should pause and think, 'What are the consequences, the collateral damage, as Chief Egan would say?' And if the consequences could be negative, someone could be hurt— *you* could be hurt, or worse, murdered—just don't say it or do it."

Jacob was listening solemnly.

Steven lightened up, smiled, and said, "It's like the old joke about the guy who walks into the doctor's office with his arm behind his back in an odd position with a contorted look on his face, saying, 'Doc, Doc, it really hurts when I do this!' And the doctor says . . ."

Steven pointed at his new friend, prompting him to fill in the blank.

"Don't do that," Jacob laughed.

He got it.

"Bingo." Both laughed out loud. "But, seriously, sinister, shadowy, evil forces could be planning your abduction and murder as we speak."

Ward Powell left the safe house, Killer following, walked to the Jeep Cherokee, and opened the back to let Killer hop in. He pulled out his cell phone, made a call, and waited, listening as seconds passed. When answered, he said, "What are you doing right now?"

Ward listened, then, "All by yourself?" He laughed. "Tonight, I'll do it with you, okay?"

"Yeah, sure you will!" Ward paused, smiling, then continued, "You need to check out our target's new girlfriend . . . okay, you do that, but be real careful . . . okay, okay, don't get all pissed off . . . yeah, I know you're a professional . . . all right, you know what you're doing. I'll see you tonight." Powell clicked off and thought, *Sometimes I just want to kill her, but sometimes not!* He smiled again as he got in the Jeep."

She clicked off herself and walked out to Mesa Street. Her car was parked at a meter two blocks away. The sun was burning hot. The street was almost deserted. Car windows were up in the few cars driving by. She walked to the stop light. It was red. She waited patiently, glancing all round. The light turned green.

She walked across the street leisurely, reached her car, got in, and let the windows down as she turned the air conditioner on full blast. Letting it run for a few minutes, she looked all around at the almost still-deserted street. She looked in her rear-view mirror: no cars were coming. So, she slowly pulled into the road and drove north on Mesa Street at the speed limit or below.

She drove slowly to her new killing field on Stanton Street. She had received those instructions as well. Instructions or not, she still loved the hunt. It was her escape, her aphrodisiac, her love. What that meant, she knew not. *It's just the thrill and lust for the hunt!* she thought.

Several miles from Sunland Park on the west side of El Paso on Stanton Street, four blocks away from Providence Hospital, a beautiful woman stared into binoculars. She was on a mission. She had her orders. She would carry them out with a vengeance.

She was on the roof of the seventeen-story high rise apartment building on Stanton Street. To her left, Providence Hospital was five blocks away, and to her right, the magnificent view of downtown El Paso and Juarez stretched into endless eternity. The sparkling blue, cloudless sky was starting to darken at six o'clock.

She was looking down from the roof, holding small but powerful binoculars, looking directly into a fourteenth-floor veranda where a man and woman were sitting in chairs next to each other, both holding glasses of wine, talking, and occasionally admiring the view. *That woman is truly gorgeous*, she thought with a tinge of jealousy. She noticed the small dog the lady held in her lap. She knew the man very well and disliked him intensely. He had a cat in his lap.

The assassin thought herself much more beautiful than the woman she was watching. She was wearing jeans, an oversized sweatshirt with the Coronado High School logo, and New Balance running shoes. In the small of her back, she had a 9mm Beretta with silencer attached.

She continued to watch, occasionally panning the surrounding neighborhood and writing notes on a pad she had nearby.

As the sun set in the western sky, she sketched out a diagram of the area on the pad, put the binoculars in their case, put both in the small bag, and proceeded down the empty stairwell to the open parking area over the secure parking garage. It was just turning dark, as she walked to the Providence Hospital parking lot a few blocks away.

CHAPTER 15

"I know how to stop a border blackout from happening again," Jacob Warren said, sitting at the head of the massive conference table in the district attorney's conference room. Eddie Egen sat beside Jacob, to his right, and Steven sat at the other end, drinking coffee.

Jacob was in a long-sleeve print shirt with button-down collar and khaki slacks. He was still depressed about losing his family, especially his innocent little sister, Michelle, and he continued to blame his parents for the events that led to her murder.

The conversation at their dinner had given Jacob hope and cheered him considerably, Steven thought as both Steven and Vanessa had decided to take him under their wings, not because of pity, but because Steven judged him to have a really good heart.

"Jacob, why don't you tell Chief Egen all you told me?" Steven picked up his coffee, looked at Eddie, smiled, and looked back at Jacob. "I trust Chief Egen with my life, and each of us would take a bullet for the other." Steven held his coffee high, as if to toast Eddie, and took a sip.

Jacob fixed his eyes on Eddie as Steven continued, "And I respect his judgment, love him like a brother, and he's my best friend here in El Paso, so anything—and I do mean anything—you tell him, like all you told me and Vanessa the other night, will remain between us. So why don't you tell your story just as you told me and Vanessa?"

"Well," Jacob said. "First, let me say that I think my dad betrayed our country by selling a computer security system back door code so the bad guys could cause a black-out . . . and he did it for a lot of money."

"Here's why I think that: I suspected Dad was having an affair and followed him out of anger for cheating on my mom. I confirmed that but also suspected more. That's when I discovered five thousand dollars in bubble wrap hidden in the garage.

"Later, I followed Dad to Gold's Gym and watched an Asian guy—I think he was Chinese—used some gadget to bypass Dad's Porsche alarm system, place a package on the passenger seat, lock the car, and leave. I was still hidden from sight when Dad came out of the gym, got in his car, and opened the package. It must've been a lot of cash.

"Then I came home late one night. It was right before New Year's Eve, and Dad was out in the backyard talking on a cell phone, so I went out back, hid close by, and heard Dad talking to someone who spoke very slowly and distinctly, different than when we Americans talk normally, and he mentioned the Year of the Horse and said something about an ancient Chinese proverb."

Chief Egen, listening with great concentration, said, "Tell me everything you heard—every word."

"They were talking about a test for something much bigger, and for the test, Dad had programmed the system or reprogrammed the 'back door,' as he called it. He said he would text the code—I think he said an eight-digit password—upon receipt of confirmation of the wire transfer into a Cayman Island account."

Eddie asked, "Did you hear how much?"

"Yes. One million US dollars."

After the safe house meeting, the two Chinese were dining at the Dome Grill, now the general's favorite El Paso restaurant.

Colonel Qiao Liang was a prominent name in Communist China among the ruling Chinese Communist leadership, the rulers of almost two billion people, all slaves to the ruling party. He spoke first. "My dear partner, and my general and co-author, Wang"—he called the general by his first name, which was only permitted when the two were alone together—"you seemed a bit distracted during our meeting at the safehouse." Colonel Liang paused, looked at this partner very tenderly and continued most deferentially, "Is there anything I can do to alleviate your distress?" He put his large hand on the general's meaty thigh.

General Wang Xiangsui, felt his partner's tender touch and said, "Your words and touch relieve my anxiety, and after our dinner, we can relax in my suite."

Both were having a sumptuous dinner at the Dome Grill in the Camino Real Hotel, the best hotel in El Paso. The general maintained an entire suite on the top floor under the name of George Hayakawa, Japanese businessman, based in Los Angeles, for Toyota Motors, Japan. He was presumably in El Paso and Juarez on Toyota business. He had a fake passport, driver's license, other credentials, and credit cards to prove just that.

The general continued, "Yes, I am distressed as I made a mistake and left an important loose end."

Liang said nothing but gently rubbed the general's thigh as he continued, "The traitor, Jason Warren's son, Jacob, is in protective custody and talking to the police and Steven Vandorol!"

Colonel Liang, shocked, removed his hand from the general's thigh, but the general put his hand on top of Liang's hand and said, "I have it well in hand."

"How so, my general?"

"I have already imbedded contacts at UTEP, here on foreign student exemptions, who are watching Jacob's young friend, Emily Blankenship."

Colonel Liang was impressed and squeezed his partner's thigh harder as the general continued, "At the first sign of contact, I will let you know, and you can lead the abduction."

Colonel Liang gave the general one of his infrequent smiles. "Can we go to your suite now and relax?"

———

"Where's the million dollars?" Eddie asked Jacob.

"It's in a secret off-shore account in the Cayman Islands, and Dad gave me the account number and instructions. He said if anything were to happen to him, I was to use it for Michelle's and my college education and not even tell Mom anything." Jacob teared up again. "And now they're all gone."

"Yes, but you're still alive and safe," Eddie said gently. "You just think, what would your dad want you to do?"

"Go on with my education and become a computer engineer, just like him. And stop his betrayers from carrying out their plans." Jacob was emphatic, as if the memory of this father gave him strength.

"How will you do that, son?"

"Dad outsmarted them! He gave them an eight-digit code that could only be used once and didn't tell them that after its single use to bypass the system and create the blackout, the 'back door' eight-digit code would erase itself automatically. It's worthless, and only I know the access number of the system, so another blackout more massive than New Year's would be impossible." He took a deep breath, exhaled.

Steven interjected, "Jacob, you know your life is in extreme danger. You must be totally vigilant about everything, at all times, thinking about what you're about to do or say and about the consequence, however slight, of what you're about to say or do. If it could have a negative outcome, then just don't do it or say it, okay? And promise us that you'll trust no one . . . absolutely no one!"

Eddie said, "That's really good advice, Counsellor. Listen to him, Jacob!"

"I understand, Steven. I'll do that. I promise." Jacob was finally smiling and said, as if he had a huge burden lifted from his shoulders, "I'm hungry. What's Vanessa making for dinner tonight?"

Emily Blankenship sat in front of a mirror in her robe, putting on make-up. She was in her room at the Chi Omega sorority house near the UTEP campus on Sun Bowl Drive, close to the student union and bookstore.

Emily was happy. Her boyfriend, Jacob, was safe, secure, and in protective custody. He told her, much to her relief, about needing to disappear, not as a criminal but as a star witness to some very big secret deal. Everybody in El Paso was relying on him. Jacob had also told her that he was very lonely for her and just had to see her. He was desperate for her and just couldn't be patient anymore. He said he was ready to get married.

Emily was ready as well. She couldn't wait.

Emily was just nineteen years old and a freshman at UTEP. She loved her boyfriend desperately. She had been ready to marry him from the first moment they met. But Jacob kept telling her he had to get an education first, to be able to support a wife and then a family, with lots of kids.

She couldn't understand all that because both their parents were fairly rich, and she protested that their parents could support them. Jacob wouldn't budge, though she continued to complain and complain about her own feelings, which he apparently didn't care anything about.

But Emily was happy today. When they talked on the phone, she told him she was lonely, too, and desperate to see him and spend a little time with him.

So, she talked to him about leaving, just for a little while, so they could be together. No one would be the wiser, and he could go back into protective custody. Jacob said he would think about it and how he could visit her. She smiled and almost laughed out loud at the prospect of being alone with him. She would think about it as well and maybe get her sorority sisters to help arrange the tryst.

Emily knew she was a pretty girl. She continued to look at herself in the mirror as she put on make-up and thought about the exciting feelings that lay ahead when she could be with him.

She smiled at her own reflection, as she admired her honey-blonde hair, long and down to the middle of her back, pouty lips, like rosebuds, she thought, and dimples. She knew she was pretty, had a good body, that she loved to flaunt, especially to the boys on the UTEP football team as a freshman cheerleader with a winning personality.

She always compared herself to Taylor Swift as Jacob said she looked like her. But Emily thought herself prettier.

"I can't wait to see him," she said to her image. "I just can't wait!" She laughed out loud, watching herself in the mirror as her hand eased past her navel.

CHAPTER 16

It was June, only six months since Steven Vandorol saw the brilliant sunshine in Vanessa Carson's hazel eyes and dazzling smile and fell in love with her all over again. The butterfly of happiness had landed on his shoulder, and after a lifetime of pain and hurt, the butterfly still remained. Steven and Vanessa's future was now intertwined and stretched into eternity.

Previously, Steven had looked backward an entire lifetime to see farther back than he had ever been able to look before, and now, together with Vanessa, they were looking forward to their future as one. Steven was so very grateful as he looked at Vanessa sitting next to him with tiny Harley curled up in her lap. They were sitting on her balcony drinking wine. She was knitting a warm blanket under which they could snuggle in front of the fireplace on chilly El Paso evenings.

Steven had a new sense of purpose to go along with his new-found happiness. It had been only six months since a leap of faith allowed each day to be seen as the next page in a truly miraculous story—a life filled with grace unknown to Steven but there, nevertheless, by the grace of the Lord, and the Lord's designated angels on earth. God had provided Steven with his brother in Brazil when he was young and his Uncle Ted in America, in south Bronx, when he was a teenager.

Steven was grateful for the ability to summon courage, persistence, and empathy, despite the very trying circumstances he was to face in the special prosecution. He was grateful, and he focused on coupling his gratitude with intention, focusing on the goodness in his life rather than the evils that had previously controlled and enslaved him.

He was grateful that the good Lord now completely filled his heart and the vacuum left from the previous pain, anger, and addiction of a corrupt and evil world. He was especially grateful for his two children, Josef and Karina. Steven was grateful for his true friends, Eddie and Andi Egen, Ray Ortega, and now Major G. Jack Reacher, who became Vanessa's good friend as well. Steven was especially grateful for Vanessa Carson. He was in love.

In a simple leap of faith, Vanessa came to him in El Paso to join an ever-decreasing circle of human beings Steven would gladly take a bullet for.

He was grateful not just for this moment now, but for all the moments past and, most important, for the moments coming in the future. His gratitude was boundless and timeless on this June 15, 2016, six months after everything changed.

At Steven's private law office, nothing changed but everything improved. Vanessa's calm perception, experience and boundless energy, and emphasis on structure and routine rallied Christina and Marce, the legal assistants, to renewed confidence and energy. Vanessa's professionalism, thoroughness, toughness, practical sense, and direction provided even better leadership than Steven could. He had acknowledged to Vanessa in private that both young women lacked the maturity to remove the male/female component from a working relationship and how he worried that Christina was much too tied to Ray, her father, and acted really weird around Vanessa.

Perceptive Vanessa sensed resistance and jealousy, especially from Christina, who she sensed had more feelings for Steven than just an employer-employee relationship. Rather than making an enemy, Vanessa sought to make two new friends. As he observed, Steven was inclined to agree with her assessment, with some reservations, but still didn't trust that relationship completely.

Steven was grateful for the emotional intimacy and happiness he shared with his two children. He was grateful for the intimacy and happiness he shared with his friends in Washington, DC, Courtney and Arlene, and in El Paso with Eddie and Andi; Ray and his wife, Jessie; and Captain Reacher and his ex-wife, Joan, with whom Vanessa had worked very hard to help the two rejoin. The Reachers were now also enjoying their marriage again and new-found real intimacy and love.

Vanessa worked earnestly with the captain, now Major G. Jack Reacher, brigade commander of 3rd Cavalry's Apache helicopter group, some one hundred fifty of the most powerful long-distance armed helicopters in the world. Each helicopter possessed enough armament and power to destroy downtown El Paso all by itself.

Major Reacher was not only a great friend and former client, but he had also joined the special prosecution as the prosecution team's liason with Major General John Nicholson, Texas Adjutant General, the Texas Attorney General's and Governor's office. In that position, Major Reacher would eventually coordinate the security of the Texas-Mexico border with the Texas Rangers, the Texas National Guard, and federal forces at Fort Bliss and Biggs Army Air Field. Steven remembered fondly when then Captain Reacher invited Steven to drive an Abrams M1A1 main battle tank one Saturday on the Fort Bliss North Range, as he knew Steven was a World War II tank buff.

As these thoughts ran through his mind, Steven looked at Vanessa. "I just want to compliment you for how you handled Jack and Joan's reconciliation!" Steven raised his glass to his precious angel and continued, "They were my friends before, but now they are also *our* great friends as well. To you, sweetheart, you really connected with both Jack and Joan, and in such a short time."

"Well, it was so easy. Jack just thinks you hung the moon, as they say. He loves you like a brother . . . a younger brother. How old is Jack anyway?"

"Well, let me think. When I was a first-year plebe cadet at West Point, Jack was a senior upperclassman, so I think probably in his mid-forties."

"So that's when you first met him, playing football at West Point?" Vanessa asked.

"That's right! I was a freshman at the academy and a second string running back, and Jack was the senior starting quarterback. His locker was pretty near mine . . . G. Reacher, his name plate said . . . I guess I was seventeen or eighteen."

"Steven, Jack is exactly five years older than you are." Vanessa was smiling.

"Wow, Jack is five years older than me . . . he sure doesn't look it."

"Is Jack just a nickname?"

"Yeah, I guess. All his army uniform name plates always show G. Reacher. I always wondered what it stood for, but everybody always called him Jack. "

"Did you ever ask him?"

"Well, the one time I did, he said, 'I'll tell you when the time is right,' so, I haven't asked again."

"You guys! The only question you ever ask each other is, 'Well, how about them Dallas Cowboys?'" She laughed.

Major Reacher and his ex-wife, Joan Carol Reacher, had been willing students when Vanessa confronted both, at Steven's urging, and counseled them as to their respective roles in the downward cycle that resulted in their divorce.

Vanessa recognized immediately that Major Reacher was Steven's really good friend. They had great commonality between them, especially their love for West Point, where Cadet G. Jack Reacher had graduated first in his class. But due to Steven's football injury to his knee, he was disqualified from further military service.

Steven, seeing what Vanessa was trying to do for the divorced couple, helped to counsel Major Reacher, just like he had counseled and prayed with his friend Eddie, helping the Egens in their marriage restoration.

Sensing success in the reconnection of their relationship, Vanessa offered to file papers to set aside the divorce that Steven had originally handled for the couple pro bono. Jack and Joan accepted her offer and reconciled, and in a quiet ceremony with only Steven and Vanessa present, they renewed their vows and recommitted to each other before their God. The couple was now Major and Mrs. G. Jack Reacher again, and Joan Reacher and Vanessa had become good friends as well.

In honor of their reconciliation and in gratitude for Steven and Vanessa's help, Jack piloted the two couples in his Command Apache helicopter named *Airship Genesis*, with Vanessa in the co-pilot's seat and Joan and Steven right behind them, all with headphones on. They spent the whole day above El Paso and Juarez at almost ten thousand feet. The highlight was coming within a thousand feet of Ranger Point; the top of the mountain was over a mile above sea level.

The rotor sound had been deafening, Vanessa and Steven had good reason to practice signing with each other all day and say, "I love you," several thousand times it seemed, as Steven was getting better and better at the silent language of signing.

Steven and Vanessa were now living each day, as Rush Limbaugh said, like it was their last, in peace, serenity, happiness, and joy, while the ROW boiled around them in chaos, sex, drug addiction, coming civil war, evil, corruption, radical Muslim terror, war, and death. Steven was thinking and looking out into the darkening downtown and Juarez stretching into the horizon before him.

The two now lived the Big Three, as Courtney and Arlene Wellington told him, that of having someone to love (each other), something to do (their law practice), and something to look forward to (a lifetime of peace, serenity, happiness, and joy until they would together be with their Lord).

In only six months, Vanessa's quiet, calm, and very practical manner easily took charge of an almost six-year law practice. Steven introduced Vanessa to the El Paso legal community, the El Paso judges, and command structure at Fort Bliss, and all were enchanted. Steven was grateful as her success and acceptance freed Steven to focus on the special prosecution.

In the last month, Steven had re-drafted the prior indictment to an almost forty-page amended and superseded indictment to be filed in the district court of El Paso County when Steven and Chief Judge Carbon were ready to empanel the El Paso County grand jury.

Steven was grateful for every moment, feeling the renewed energy and enjoyment of practicing law according to his own terms, rather than as dictated by clients or money. In the practice of law, Steven was now the organ grinder rather than the monkey with the tin cup. He was peaceful professionally and grateful personally for every moment of the day granted to him by the good Lord.

Most of all, Steven was grateful for the happiness and joy he felt every moment of every day through faith in God, which had sustained him in the past and was still sustaining him now, along with the love of his life put here by the grace of God.

These were his thoughts as they were sitting on Vanessa's balcony, fourteen stories up, drinking wine and watching the magnificent El Paso sunset over the Santo Christo Mountains of Mexico. And he finished his thoughts by saying out loud, "Always be yourself because the people who matter don't mind."

Steven looked at Vanessa and signed with his right hand, "I love you!"

Then, out of nowhere, Steven had a strange feeling in his gut. The hair on the back of his neck stood up, and he rose to scan up and down and in a 360-degree circle. "That's weird!"

"What's weird?"

"I felt like we were being watched!" Steven looked around again. "Probably nothing."

Vanessa put her knitting down, stood, and looked all around for herself. She didn't see anything out of the ordinary, but still wondered why he felt they were being watched. She shrugged her shoulders and sat back down.

"Steven, my love, in working on Jack and Joan's reconciliation, I realized that giving is the whole key to intimacy. In giving continually and not expecting anything in return, you keep receiving back. The more you give, the more you receive, all in an upward progression to a deeper and deeper level of love, forever and always."

"That's a really great insight. I also just realized that the special prosecution, win or lose, is just one battle in the civil war, which has already been lost."

So, Steven and Vanessa had to make decisions based in ROW reality, all the while having the time of their lives, living each day together as if it were their last.

Steven raised his glass. "To us, Vanessa, the love of my life!"

Vanessa smiled sunshine toward Steven. "I'll drink to that."

And just that moment, as if to accent the good Lord's grace, a brilliant shooting star arched across the star-filled Texas sky.

And two glasses clicked on the fourteenth floor of 4506 Stanton Street, El Paso, Texas.

"They have the kid in total protective custody," Ward Powell said to the assassination team assembled in the safe house on Piedras Street near downtown El Paso. "They chauffeur him around in an unmarked squad car, and two police officers are with him 24/7."

General Xiangsui glanced at Colonel Liang sitting on his right, then back at Ward. "Where do they have him living?" He knew Powell always exaggerated.

"On the Egen ranch, the Chico Gringo, which is more secure than Fort Knox . . . and get this: the kid is spending a lot—and I mean a lot—of time schmoozing with Vandorol and his 'partner,' Vanessa Carson."

Colonel Lemev interrupted, "How do you know this, Ward?"

Powell looked at Lemev directly, remembering that his use of foul language almost got him killed because Lemev, the hypocrite, wouldn't tolerate it in his troops in Mother Russia, so he only smirked and said, "I've got my sources. And that's not the important thing now. What matters is that the kid knows all about the Year of the Horse surprise, General." Powell paused, cleared his throat rather disgustingly, looked at the general, and thought, *What a fat, sloppy pig.* But he said, "I thought you had it all covered, General."

The general hesitated a second, then said, "How do you know this . . . about the Year of the Horse surprise, Ward?"

Powell would keep his 'secret source' to himself again. "Chief Egen's boys have been all over El Paso Electric and Energy, asking questions and concentrating on the "Star Wars" control room of the department Jason Warren ran. Jason designed the whole computer system and had carte blanche with the entire company. He was the executive vice president and member of the board of directors." Powell paused, thought, and now felt sure he knew. "General, Jason Warren *was* your insider for the Year of the Horse surprise New Year's Eve test black-out, wasn't he?" Powell was still smirking, eyebrows raised, almost laughing out loud.

The general's secret was out. "Yes, he was. The American fool betrayed his own country for money. With all these foolish, self-centered Americans, especially the politicians, it's all about the money." He was twisting a massive diamond pinky ring nervously around his fat finger while he talked.

The irony was *not* lost on Powell, who asked, "How much did it take to turn him?"

"One million US dollars."

Powell wasn't finished baiting the fat general. "So, was it worth it? Are we still on for the Year of the Horse project, which you told us would be the complete black-out of the entire Texas-Mexico border?"

For the first time, Powell noticed, the fat general was stammering. "No, Warren be . . . betrayed us as well." His eyes twitched nervously. "We have tried to check out the system through the back-door code he sold us, but it doesn't work. We can't hack back into the security system. Apparently, it only worked once and then ceased automatically."

"So, you were outwitted by an American, General?" Powell was grinning from ear-to-ear.

Colonel Liang sprang to his defense. "What do we do, General Xiangsui?"

The general looked at Liang. "We have to abduct the Warren boy and get the number of the Cayman Island account where the million dollars was wired and the new back-door code, both of which we hope the father shared with his son . . . in view of all the security around him! And we'll use whatever means necessary to get it out of him. No matter what. No matter what it takes!"

Colonel Liang smiled at the general most tenderly, which Ward Powell noticed as well.

CHAPTER 17

On the Chico Gringo Ranch, two powerful, very beautiful, and elegant thousand-pound beasts, one a white Arabian, fifteen hands, the other a smaller Paint, thirteen hands, gracefully loped across the West Texas desert almost floating like a mirage in the sunset.

Steven was sitting high and deep in the hand tooled, ornate trail saddle. He felt relaxed, holding the reins with his left thumb pointed toward snow white Pegasus's powerful neck and lush mane. His right arm was loose at his side, rocking seamlessly, hips moving perfectly with the rhythm of the horse, as if Steven and his horse were one.

Steven loved to ride horses and considered horses as friends, beginning with his childhood on the fazenda in Brazil. Back then, Steven and his older brother, Joey, would spend days on their horses, riding them mostly bareback through the endless steppes of the Brazilian cattle country, living off the land. Horses had been in their DNA dating back to Hungarian bloodlines from the Mongol hordes through the Huns who lived, fought, and died on their horses.

Steven was wearing boot cut jeans and a long-sleeve shirt, to guard against the cool El Paso evening, and his horn-back alligator boots. A white Stetson with leather strap pulled tight under his clean-shaven chin punctuated the outfit. Vanessa rode beside Steven, also sitting high and deep on her Western saddle on a beautiful black and white horse she had named Bozley after her favorite former Oklahoma University football star, Brian Bosworth.

The two loped along evenly just like the two dolphins riding a wave before the tramp steamer in the print photograph that hung above Steven's bed. Vanessa was an experienced horsewoman herself, having spent her own childhood on a horse farm in Oklahoma. She wore calf-high crimson riding boots over tight jeans and a western long-sleeved shirt. Steven thought she looked just gorgeous riding in the purple, blue, and white Texas sunset sky.

Bozley, the black and white Paint, was presented to Vanessa by Eddie as the attorney fee for handling the appeal of a lawsuit against Eddie, previously won by Steven at the jury trial, then appealed by the former owners of Adventure World Travel to the Texas Supreme Court.

"Vanessa, you did a really great job on the appeal, and to get additional attorney fees charged against the former owners . . . it's almost unprecedented. Way to go!"

"Thank you, sweetheart!" Vanessa directed her radiant smile toward Steven. "You did all the real work by winning the case for Eddie big time on the trial court jury verdict. I just did the blah, blah, blah on the appeal."

Steven laughed. "Yeah, but . . . finding the old precedent about attorney fees for an appeal of a case of conversion during the time when Texas was still the Lone Star Republic was positively brilliant."

"Well, thank you!" Vanessa said, signing "I love you" with her free hand, which Steven promptly answered with his. As they easily loped back toward Eddie's ranch, Vanessa added, "Plus, Eddie giving me this wonderful horse was a nice attorney fee present!"

Ever since Vanessa told Steven of how she had learned American Sign Language, Steven and Vanessa had adopted signing as their love conversation. It was their very own private love language, like telepathy. The signing served them well in court but worked best riding horses, galloping with the wind and signing, "I love you," back and forth.

That also fit in with what Steven's first senior law partner used to tell him when he was a young lawyer. He told Steven these were the only things that mattered in the practice of law and in life:

Never waste the opportunity to tell someone you love them.

Never take credit or blame for something you didn't do.

Always tell the truth.

Steven, as a lawyer, had previously been a bit fuzzy on the "truth," but now he considered being truthful an absolute imperative.

Since being introduced to signing by Vanessa, Steven had worked hard to learn sign language. He had practiced with Vanessa and in front of a mirror when by himself, so they had a shorthand sign language all their own, where even glances, slight hand gestures, and rapid eye movements spoke volumes for them alone, to the exclusion and great disadvantage of all others.

"Are you going to declare Bozley as income to the Internal Revenue Service?" Steven laughed.

"Not unless Eddie takes an expense deduction."

"He's not! He already told me so. He knows what a wonderful 'do the right thing' person you are!"

Steven smiled back until both horses, suddenly threatened, separated, Pegasus veering left, Bozley right.

Steven saw a massive rattle snake ahead, coiled, its rattler vibrating and about to strike, approximately ten yards ahead.

Steven calmly directed Pegasus farther left, pulled out his Colt 45 like a gunfighter in one smooth move, and fired. The rattle snake's head exploded in the desert sand and brush, splattering blood on the plants and cacti all around the snake.

"Incoming gunfire always has the right of way!" Steven laughed and holstered the weapon. "That's why we're always armed while riding horses in the desert!"

Vanessa, startled initially by the gunfire, laughed.

Pegasus, well trained, didn't even flinch. Bozley, younger and untrained, did, rearing up on hind legs, but Vanessa handled the skittish horse very well. She put her hand to her heart. "Jeez, Steven, that scared the daylights out of me!"

Steven stopped Pegasus and patted him on his flank, calming the horse further. "Good boy, you did well. And you, too, honey. You handled Bozley very well . . . are you okay?"

"Yes, I'm fine now. Just don't tell me we're having rattlesnake meat for dinner!"

They both laughed.

"I guess we'll have to take him out on the firing range to accustom him to gunfire."

"I'll get you a nice little gun, Vanessa!"

"Little?" Vanessa smiled. "If attacked, you can say 'stop,' or any other word, but a large bore muzzle pointed at someone's head is pretty much a universal language."

They were still laughing.

Steven said, "Just like Eddie says, 'Make your attacker advance through a hail of bullets. You may get killed with your own gun, but he'll have to beat you to death with it 'cause it'll be empty.'"

"Yeah, and always remember this quote from our premier Founding Father, Thomas Jefferson: 'Peace is that glorious moment in history when everybody stands around reloading!'" Vanessa paused. "Thank you, Steven, for all that you've done for me and for us. Thank you! You're my gift from the Lord. You know, life without you would be like trying to color with only a black crayon."

Steven smiled at the love of his life, felt warm all over, leaned across, and interrupted Vanessa with a kiss right on the lips. They lingered.

When Steven drew back, Vanessa said, "Here?" and arched her eyebrows, remembering that time at Café Central on their first El Paso date.

They both laughed as they saw the others in their riding party come over the rise almost two hundred yards away.

Jacob Warren was having the time of his life. He was riding a yellow-brown Paint named Lucky, riding high and coming up behind Steven and Vanessa, now just a few yards ahead, waiting for him to catch up. Jacob's new friend Officer Jesus Cruz was lagging behind.

As Jacob approached, Steven thought, *Being in protective custody has been good for him. His many conversations with Eddie and the Christian counselor Eddie arranged for him have really helped him in the grieving process.*

Jacob was still sad and missing his family but now less angry at his parents. Due to many conversations with Steven and Vanessa, Jacob realized that no matter what, both his parents had loved him dearly and cared for him well.

Steven and Vanessa were resting the horses. He rode up alongside of them and asked, "What was that gunshot?"

"Steven just blew up a rattler that was threatening our horses!" Vanessa replied.

"Wow," Jacob managed.

Steven asked, "Having fun, Jacob?"

"OMG, am I?" he answered. "I've never had this much fun in all my life."

"In all of your twenty . . . oops, twenty-one years?" Steven chuckled.

Jacob just had a birthday party. All of their close friends had attended on the ranch, including the ever-present Officers Schultze and Cruz. Officer Cruz, just a few years older than Jacob, was developing quite a friendship with Jacob. He was lagging behind on another Egen Ranch loaner horse.

Jacob laughed, "We never did this . . . as a family. Oh, we went to Six Flags and stuff, but all we did was spend a lot of money and bought a lot of fricking trinkets." There was anger in his voice again.

"Didn't you tell me that your dad paid for horseback riding lessons for you when you were seven?"

"Yeah, why?"

"Because you're a really good rider!"

"Thanks, I love horses!" Jacob said patting his horse.

Vanessa looked at him. "Jacob, why don't you and Steven go and have lunch soon? We talked yesterday, and I told Steven that you wanted to talk to him about guy stuff." Vanessa looked at Steven, who was nodding. "It could be a guy's day out!"

"That's a great idea, Vanessa." Steven looked at Jacob. "I'd like that. How about it, Jacob? I could ask you, 'How about those Dallas Cowboys?'"

Jacob, laughing, said, "You bet. I'd like that very much."

CHAPTER 18

Steven and Jacob were sitting opposite each other in a red pleather booth at 'AJ's Diner on North Mesa Street waiting on two of the biggest cheese burgers in El Paso, French fries, and onion rings.

Opened in 1986, this true 1950s-style diner brings back the good old days for new generations and those who want to remember the past with fondness. It was one of Steven's and Vanessa's favorite casual hangouts.

Even though the restaurant was in an unremarkable strip mall on Mesa Street and didn't look like much from the outside, the inside was alive with nostalgic 1950s décor. The rows of red pleather booths were overseen by numerous photos of antique cars, old pictures of Elvis Presley, Ricky Nelson, and Mickey Mouse memorabilia.

The counter took up the other half of the restaurant; stools with red pleather padding to match the booths were cozied up to the silver bar. Behind, a number of servers were busy making shakes and malts at one of the true soda fountains left in El Paso from that bygone era. An old jukebox stood as a centerpiece in the diner, crowned by painted musical notes and the word "music" written in red neon lettering shining and pulsating, giving the restaurant a festive glow. Elvis Presley's "Jail House Rock," which Steven had selected, was playing.

The menu, not as interesting as the décor, was full of 1950s greats: burgers, sandwich platters, onion rings and fries, tuna melts, and pizzas. The burgers were named after music icons, like Little Richard, Fats Domino, and Buddy Holly.

The sights, sounds, and delicious aromas reminded Steven of a time when he was a teenager in south Bronx in the early 90's, after he and his mother left Brazil to join Steven's Aunt Helena and military man, Uncle Ted, in New York City, leaving Steven's brother, Joey, behind in Brazil.

Steven and Jacob were both sipping on thick strawberry shakes, waiting for their order.

Jacob asked, "Was it just like this when you were a kid, Steven?"

Steven answered with a laugh, "I'm not quite that old, but we did have cool hamburger joints and great Jewish delis when I lived in South Bronx. The music was very different. We were listening more to Savage Garden, Whitney Houston, and Celine Dion. The movies, *Goodfellas* and *The Unforgiven*, with Clint Eastwood, were all the rage."

"Clint Eastwood's still really cool."

"Yeah, he is." Steven continued, "South Bronx was going down fast . . . like the movie, *Bronx Battlefield*, but that's another story for another time."

They were interrupted by a waiter dressed like Buddy Holly. "Who gets the Little Richard?"

Jacob said, "That's me . . . and the fries."

"There you go." He put the burger down by Jacob as he continued, "And the Fats Domino and onion rings for you, Mr. Vandorol." He put the burger and rings in front of Steven. "Where is Ms. Vanessa today?"

"Just the guys today, doing guy stuff!"

"Tell her Buddy Holly said hi."

"I will, Buddy. We'll probably be in next week." Steven bit into his burger.

Jacob was digging in himself.

While they ate, they talked about sports, girls, TV shows, movies, and other "guy" things. Steven sensed Jacob wanted to talk about something important, but Jacob never let on what it was.

———

After finishing at AJ's Diner, Steven took Jacob to his office to talk more "guy stuff." He drove them to the office not far away on Shuster Street and Sun Bowl Drive as Jacob sat beside him patting his stomach. He looked over to Jacob. "Well, did you get enough to eat?"

Jacob appeared relaxed but thoughtful. "More than. I'm stuffed. Old Buddy Holly sure likes Vanessa, doesn't he?"

"We all do. Right, Jacob?" Steven winked at him.

"Vanessa is one of the most beautiful women I've ever seen! You really like her, don't you?"

"No, I don't like her, Jacob. I love her!"

Steven pulled in to the office parking lot off Sun Bowl Drive and parked his Taurus but stayed in the car. He looked all around, wary. *After all, I've got a contract out on me,* he thought, smiling ruefully to himself in the rearview mirror.

Officer Shultze had followed them and covered the parking lot and second floor entrance. Steven was well armed, as usual. Since it was Saturday afternoon, the lot was not very crowded. He thought Jacob would be more relaxed at his law office on Sun Bowl Drive.

While driving from AJ's to his office, Steven noticed Officer Shultz, in plain clothes, driving a nondescript white Toyota Camry with another man in a T-shirt, whom Steven didn't know, in the passenger seat.

Steven thought, *Eddie's got us covered! Looks like we have El Paso Police Department muscle covering us.*

Jacob noticed but remained silent.

The small parking lot was on a bluff facing I-10 and was concealed from the highway below by acacia and mesquite trees and six-foot shrubs. Steven noticed six cars, all familiar, belonging to office building tenants. Ray's four-wheel-drive Ford SUV with dark windows and Chris's small red Toyota pickup were both conspicuously absent. *All clear*, Steven thought. Out loud, smiling, he said, "No bad guys lurking about!" Steven had learned the 'situational awareness lesson,' as he called it, over a lifetime of vigilance and observation.

Jacob was silent but looking all around as well.

Steven got out and locked the doors from the inside. He didn't use his key fob as he had heard somewhere that bad guys could override the clicker by using their own from another car. He warily looked around again and went up the concrete stairs to the street-level stone walkway to the building's entrance. Jacob followed.

The midday late August sun was still brilliant, and Steven could feel its warmth on his shoulders as the temperature was rising. The building was a two-story Frank Lloyd Wright-style office building with mirror-glass sparkling windows nestled among the trees on a bluff overlooking the Rio Grande, and Juarez slums.

Steven could smell the aroma of the trees mixed with the exhaust fumes from the highway as the two walked up the concrete walkway leading to the front of the building.

Jacob liked what he saw. "This is sick for a law office, Steven! I always thought they were going to be 'stuffed shirt' type places!"

Steven laughed, "We think so." Steven emphasized the *we* as he continued to look around. Officer Schultz had pulled in behind them. "Vanessa and I think it's very cozy and secure."

Steven used his card to open the front door entrance, nondescript double glass doors, and into the lobby with an elevator straight ahead and staircase to the left. A lobby building directory with various names showed "Vandorol and Carson, Lawyers," with their full names below: Steven J. Vandorol, Esq. and Vanessa R. Carson, Esq., Suite 205." Then Steven and Jacob walked past the elevator and up the stairs to a deep-pile carpeted second floor.

Jacob continued to observe as they walked soundlessly down the oak-paneled hallway, past two other office entry doors on the right and windows on the left. Suite 205 was on the end, the fifth suite on the second floor. Outside the office, the suite plaque was the same as on the directory.

"What's the *J* stand for?" Jacob asked.

"Josef with an *F*; it's the Hungarian spelling," Steven answered as he unlocked the door. Both walked in as Steven flicked on the suite lights, closed the door behind them, and locked the deadbolt from the inside.

"Was that your brother's name?"

"Yes, it was! But I always called him Joey."

Steven and Jacob were alone in the reception area waiting room.

"Is this where the bad guys tried to blow up your office, Steven?"

Apparently, he's been talking to his new friend, Officer Cruz, Steven thought. "Yep, last December, just before New Year's. These are our KISS Doctrine offices."

"Huh, what's that?"

Steven was a firm believer in the KISS Doctrine. "Keep it simple, stupid!" he would wryly say to clients, jurors, and litigants. "That's me, and that's what you should do: keep it simple. The truth is always the simplest." Now, Steven really believed that. Before, he had not. "Simple but true is always best! I've now simplified everything in my life, Jacob!"

The entire office was carpeted with the same deep-pile carpet. The waiting room had two straight back leather armchairs in each corner, left and right, with small magazine tables by each. The *Wall Street Journal* and *Washington Examiner* were placed on one, with the *El Paso Herald-Chronicle* and *Dallas Morning Clarion* on the other. Two plain leather couches sat against the other wall. No paintings or diplomas were on the tan walls; bright overhead lighting, with two lamps on end tables, made the area subdued yet elegant and comfortable.

Jacob seemed to be noticing everything.

The front door led right to a sliding glass opening for reception, and the whole left side interior wall was mirror glass that, unknown to clients and persons coming into the reception area, was two-way glass into Ray Ortega's office. That was Steven's accommodation to his friend and investigator, who was also a student of humanity and human behavior, not unlike Steven himself. Steven respected Ray's opinions and instincts about people in general and his clients in particular, both in the office and especially during jury selection in both criminal and civil trials.

Steven unlocked the inside door to the offices, entered, closed, and locked the door behind him, while Jacob followed behind. Double security was in place to protect the inside offices. To Steven's left was a glass divider leading to the reception area. It contained a built-in fax machine, telephone, message lights, credit card machine, and now a teletype Steven had obtained for the special prosecution, since that was *still* the most secure form of private communication in this internet age.

Steven walked down the ten-yard hallway. Ray's office was to his right, also with a glass divider. Inside the office sat a desk chair, desk, computer desk, gun rack with his in-office arsenal, and one-way glass out to the reception area.

"Wow, your investigator has a lot of weapons right here in your offices!"

"Right! We're what the liberals and leftists call 'gun nuts!'"

"Yeah, I know! There's a lot of those at UTEP."

Past a closed door to their left was the small conference room. To their right was the closed door to Marce's office, then an office restroom. The smaller empty office to his right was Vanessa's.

"That's Vanessa's office," Steven said and pointed.

"Right next to yours?"

"That's right! With both of our doors open, we talk and work, sharing everything. We planned it this way so we'll always be singing out of the same hymnal, as the old expression goes."

Jacob laughed. By his expression, Steven could see that the message of oneness had been understood.

Steven opened the hallway door to his own office and walked in, leaving the door open. He took off his jacket, put it on a hanger, and hung it on the rack against the wall. He didn't turn on the light as the sun of Sun City, still high in the western horizon, shone brightly and made his small, simple office sparkle. He said, "Have a seat, Jacob. Would you like something to drink? Coke, water, coffee?" He got up, stating, "I'm going to make a pot."

"No, thanks. I'm still full from lunch."

Steven walked to the coffee area, turned on the coffee maker, then returned to his desk chair. He smiled at young Jacob, who exclaimed, "Nice space, Mr. Vandorol . . . er, Steven!"

"Thanks, it's very comfortable!"

Steven glanced around his own office, at the built-in oak credenza and full plate glass windows that revealed a magnificent view. He looked down to Interstate I–10, Paisano Drive right below, and the Rio Grande ambling by. The river was the designated Texas-Mexican border. Another open door in his office led to the small conference room, and two wingback client chairs sat in front of his desk.

Pointing, Jacob said, "That's a really cool statue. What is it?"

To his right was a low cabinet. On top of the cabinet was a very beautiful and ornate bronze statuette of the good Lord's blindfolded messenger archangel Gabriel holding the sword of righteousness in his right hand and the scales of justice and reason in the other.

"It's the messenger archangel Gabriel. It's the only remnant from my law practice back in the Sunbelt and then in Washington, DC, that I really cared about, so I brought it to El Paso when I opened my law office here."

Steven picked up his phone to check messages. He listened, saved all for Christina to handle Monday, hung up, and turned toward the magnificent view that he enjoyed every day. It had a calming effect all its own. He glanced down to the parking lot below just in time to see a strange car—one he had never seen before in the parking area—pull into a space right next to his own but almost fifty yards from Officer Shultze's car.

Steven immediately picked up his cell, punched in a number, and waited. Ray answered, "Steven, what's up?"

"Where are you right now?"

"Just leaving the courthouse garage. Why?" Ray Ortega, Steven's investigator and friend, always worked on Saturdays.

"You coming to the office? I'm here already."

"Yep," Ray answered. "What's up?"

"I'm with Jacob, just chatting after lunch. The parking lot was pretty clear when we arrived, but when we got to my office, I noticed a strange SUV in the lot below . . . smoked windows . . . I can't see if there is anyone in it . . . or how many. Officer Shultze is too far away. It's a late model black Suburban, Texas license number XYZ666."

"Got it. Why you interested?"

"I'll tell you when you get here, and I'll let you show off your office arsenal. We got a lot to talk about and a lot to do."

"I'll call my Texas Ranger bud and get a make on the Suburban." He clicked off.

Jacob had taken it all in. "Ray is really a good Bro, isn't he?"

"He's a great guy, a good family man and father, a moral Christian with the good Lord in his heart. We've been through a lot these last five years."

Steven sat back in his chair and looked around. He really liked his small office. KISS Doctrine again. Simple. He loved the view into Mexico and of the Rio Grande and mountains to the west, especially the wonderful sunsets in the evening, which he looked forward to daily. "Isn't this a great view, Jacob?" Steven sighed and looked out at the brilliant sunshine and wondrous sparkling colors dancing in the Sun City sky that always reminded him that the good Lord was the Ultimate Artist. "I just love El Paso!"

Jacob said nothing.

Steven opened the doors below the plate glass of the built-in oak credenza, revealing the Persuader shotgun Ray had given him as a present last Christmas as a substitute for a gun that had been taken during the bombing at Steven's home. *I think I'll take it home. Ray's got his arsenal here,* Steven thought.

"Wow!" Jacob said. "Can I see the shotgun?"

"Sure." Steven handed it to Jacob.

Steven glanced down into the parking lot. The Suburban was still there, stationary but idling.

Steven spun around and remembered the throwing knife concealed in his right boot. So, he leaned down and slipped it out of the thin sheath where it was concealed in his right boot and put it on his desk. He also unclipped the holstered Glock 22 and put it right beside the knife.

Holding the shotgun, Jacob said, "Jeez, Steven! Can I see the knife, too?"

"Of course."

"We're ready for an office invasion!" Steven said out loud. He looked at Jacob sitting across from him holding the shotgun and knife. "You look like the "'Frito Bandito,'" young Jacob!"

Jacob laughed as well. "You're kickass, Steven!"

CHAPTER 19

"Well, my young friend, Vanessa said you wanted to talk." Steven was looking at Jacob intently, ready to listen.

"Yes, I do." Jacob paused, gathering his thoughts. He took a deep breath and began, "I think I've made a terrible mistake. When they first picked me up to place me in protective custody, they asked me for my cell phone. I handed it over to them, but I didn't tell them that I also had my father's old phone."

Steven, shocked, listened.

"As I told you, I called Emily from the police station, but when they moved me to Chief Egen's ranch, I felt I just couldn't allow Emily to wonder why I disappeared from this earth. So, I called her again and we talked, and I told her we couldn't talk anymore until all this was over. Am I going to jail? Am I in big trouble now? I'm really scared, Steven. Please help me!" Jacob started crying.

"Gosh, Jacob, this is a surprise that you're just now telling me this. Yes, you could be in serious trouble, because if the phone call was traced back to Emily, they'll know where she is. And they may find her and pick her up. And lying to the police is not good."

"Oh jeeze, Steven. Now I've put Emily in danger. I'm so stupid." He was still crying. "I'm so sorry. I wasn't thinking and it's been making me crazy. Here's my dad's phone that I used." He put the iPhone on the desk as if it were burning hot. "Can you just throw it away and not tell Eddie?"

"Jason, you know I'll have to tell them because now you and Emily are both in extreme danger. As a matter of fact, let's call him right now. We need to turn this phone over to them right away."

Jacob was nodding, wiping his eyes and sniffing.

"Jason, I'm glad you finally came clean and told me. Is there anything else you haven't told me or the police that we should know?"

"No. It was just the phone and the call."

"What did you guys talk about?"

"Just that I'm safe and that we still love each other and that this will all be over soon."

"And that's it? That's all?"

"Yes," Jason replied. He hated lying to Steven, but he just couldn't tell him that they had planned to sneak away to see each other for a few minutes next weekend.

"Well, thank you again for letting me know, and let's call Eddie right now and get this part over with. Okay?"

"Yes, please, Steven," Jacob replied.

Steven picked up his phone and dialed, "Hey Eddie, Steven, got a minute?"

After talking with Eddie, Steven said to Jacob, "My young friend, you can't really trust anybody in the ROW, rest of the world, as I call it."

"Not even Vanessa?"

"I told you that I trust her implicitly—because I love her first—and because in my heart, mind, and soul I know that I can!" Steven looked at Jacob. "Can you say that about anyone on this planet?"

Jacob nodded, listening intently. He thought, *I can trust Emily—she loves me,* but he said, "I trust you, Vanessa, and Chief Egen!"

"Anyone else? Probably not so much. And you, especially now, until this whole deal is over, cannot trust *anybody!*"

"So, what do we do?" Jacob asked, really uncomfortable. "Who can we trust?"

"'Some trust in chariots, and some in horses, but we will remember the name of the Lord, our God.' That's Psalm 20:7. I was just reading it again yesterday, trying to get guidance for my task ahead in the special prosecution. I have to be careful with that as I've had a tendency to trust my own abilities and street smarts, just like all young guys—who think they know everything about everything—rather than turning it over to the Lord. For as long as we continue to trust in our own abilities and activities, we gain nothing."

Jacob could hardly speak but finally said, "I know what you're saying is true. I always thought I knew better than my parents . . . about everything. But there's got to be an alternative."

"Yes, what you're saying is true. But, only to a point. It happened to me, and it happened to Chief Egen, so I know it can happen to you, but I also feel that while there's salvation for the individual, there's no salvation for humanity as a whole."

Jacob looked quizzical, so Steven continued: "The best example of that in our contaminated pop culture is the movie *Pulp Fiction*. Have you seen it?"

He nodded. "Yeah, it was great, and funny, too. A little raunchy, though. I laughed a lot!"

"Yes, it was! It sure showed all the filth and corruption that evil ways bring to humanity. But then remember the Samuel Jackson character, the hit man, Jules Winfield, and his partner, the John Travolta character?"

"Vincent Vega."

"Right! When the two were fired at by the fourth drug dealer coming out of the bathroom, with a 44 Magnum, a real hand-cannon, all six shots all of them missing! Why did that happen?"

"One guy said it was just luck," Jacob answered.

"Right again. But Jules, on the other hand, said it was a miracle. And that was the right answer . . . it was the grace of the Lord!"

It seemed Jacob was beginning to understand.

"The Vincent Vega character was the doubter who thought it was only luck that they survived. But Jules knew that it was a miracle and the grace of the Lord. It changed him just like grace changed me when my so-called friends in Washington, DC, were trying to destroy and enslave me!"

"Do you remember Jules quoting the Bible, Ezekiel 25:17?" Steven asked. "I've memorized it: 'The path of the righteous man is beset on all sides by the inequities of the selfish and the tyranny of evil men. Blessed is he, who in the name of charity and goodwill, shepherds the weak through the valley of darkness, for he is truly his brother's keeper and the finder of lost children. And I will strike down upon thee with great vengeance and furious anger those who would attempt to poison and destroy my brothers. And you will know my name is the Lord when I lay my vengeance upon thee.'"

"Wow," was all Jacob could say, cringing.

"And that's how you need to handle your embarrassing feelings about your mom and your dad, your anger, all the evil in your own heart and soul. It's what I did with the people who ultimately betrayed me in Washington, DC. It's what I have said about dealing with the rest of the world, ROW. Sometimes, with righteous anger . . . you have to drive the archangel's sword of righteousness into evil, so it comes out on the other side . . . bloody and showing steel!"

Jacob was looking at Steven, eyes wide open, taken aback by Steven's intensity.

Steven continued, "And that's exactly how it is in ROW! To a Vincent Vega, the sleazy, corrupt evil in the ROW all happens by chance, but to Jules, the good in the ROW, everything happens by choice, the ultimate of human freedoms, and by grace and the miracle of faith."

Jacob took a deep breath. "I think I understand now, Steven. Thank you! I understand the concept . . . but how do I do that? How do I make the change in my heart, mind, and soul?"

Steven replied, now smiling, "I don't want to get too deep for you, but when both of my so-called friends tried to destroy me, Jacob, I was saved by grace and had been all my life . . . I just didn't know grace. I do know it now! The evil and addiction ultimately destroyed those so-called friends. One committed suicide and the other, a woman, became irrelevant like a puff of smoke. Jacob, you can do it! You might not cure those enslaving feelings, but you can control them . . . and find happiness and joy in your life!"

"So, how do I do that, Steven? I need your help."

"No, you really don't. You now have it within you. I think and hope that now you have grace in your heart. I pray and hope that by your experience in losing your family and being spared, you've been washed by the Blood of the Lamb . . . and have the good Lord and Jesus Christ in your heart! You are just now recognizing it."

"We, you and I, all of us, through our faith have constant access to God's presence because of what Jesus did for us on the cross. He bridged heaven and earth, and by His death and resurrection, we're reconciled to God through His blood. We can say, 'Surely the Lord is in this place,' even when we can't sense His presence. We know by faith that He is near."

Jacob was gaining strength, Steven could tell. He finished with this admonition: "Just remember, only Christ could build a bridge to God with two pieces of wood."

Jacob was humbled. "I know now that the good Lord's grace is in my heart. It's saved me many times in the past and has given me humility and gratitude, without me even knowing it. I see that now, and I see . . . and feel . . . the good Lord catching my attention by showing me what true friendship is, Mr. Vandorol. You and Vanessa are showing me what a good relationship can be like." Jacob paused, then changing the subject, he asked, "So, when are you and Vanessa getting married?"

CHAPTER 20

"Sweet angel," Steven said to Vanessa, both seated on the big leather couch facing the panorama of downtown El Paso and Ciudad Juarez at dusk. Rommel was sitting right beside her with his big snout in her lap. "I want to talk to you about our future and have a question for you."

It was the end of the week, and after a long day at the district attorney's office, Steven stopped for Chinese food before meeting Vanessa at his house. Vanessa had an equally long day at the law office, and she was already at his house when he arrived. They still had separate residences with keys to each other's place as they had agreed to work on their relationship.

They felt no rush. It was in the Lord's hands completely, and it was in an upward progression proceeding well with the good Lord's grace, and Steven's and Vanessa's choices as to their loving intimacy.

Vanessa took a sip of her wine, smiled sweetly, and said, "You've been reading my mind again. I've been thinking about our future as well!" She chuckled softly. "You go first, my love."

"I'll start with a question." Steven moved closer to Vanessa. "I think better when I'm feeling your warmth."

Vanessa smiled, kicked off her slippers, and put her small feet with manicured toenails across his lap. "I think better when you're massaging my feet. As a matter of fact, I just love it when you massage my tired, aching feet in the evenings, especially when you do it with lavender vanilla lotion . . . uhm, uhm." She was purring like her cat, Caspurr.

"Well, my angel . . . have you seen the movie *Pulp Fiction*? It's one of my favorite movies of all time."

"As a matter of fact, I have!" Vanessa answered. "It was pretty disturbing, but really well done!"

"Do you remember the character Jules, Samuel Jackson, when he gives a really funny speech about foot massages?"

"I remember. It was hilarious."

Steven laughed. "Well, like Jules, I'm the foot massage master. And I love to massage your cute feet, all your toes, especially the one that's a little longer than all the others . . . and I think it's definitely a part of our passion, don't ya' think?"

Vanessa was smiling. "I don't know about all that . . . I just enjoy your massages tremendously."

Steven bent down and kissed her toes, one at a time, and smiled. "You've got the cutest little toes. You wanna play 'this little pig went to the market?' "

"No." With a big smile, Vanessa settled back and wiggled her toes. "You were asking a question?"

"I love you, sweet angel. Okay, are you ready to spin ourselves out of the system . . . are we done with the ROW?"

Vanessa knew exactly what Steven meant. Steven had shared the tip of the iceberg, the special prosecution, with her almost daily. They both saw all the signs of a futile second civil war, in which there would be no possibility of salvation for America as a constitutional republic built by the Declaration of Independence and the Constitution.

But there would be salvation for Vanessa and Steven.

Vanessa, now turning serious, said, "Yes to both questions, Steven." She took her legs off his lap, hugged him, and kissed him hard on the lips. As her lips left his, she said, "It's just you and me together. We cannot trust or rely on anyone else."

"You're right, and we're *not* going to rely on anyone else . . . or trust anyone except each other. All that I know absolutely is that I love and trust our Lord; you, my sweet angel; my kids; and selective friends. We have a pretty narrow and tight concentric circle."

"So, what are we gonna do?" Vanessa asked and put her feet back in his lap.

"How about a secret withdrawal plan?"

"My thoughts exactly. How, when, where?"

"Okay, let's think of where first. Any suggestions?"

"Baja, California?"

Steven frowned. "Kinda hot . . . how about Cloudcroft, New Mexico?"

Vanessa said, "Let's stay in Texas."

"By a beach . . . okay?"

"When?" Vanessa asked.

"When the special prosecution is over and arrest warrants are issued for all the criminals. Is that okay with you?"

Vanessa was nodding and directing her dazzling sunshine smile at him.

"Done. As to how, if it's okay with you, I'll start working secretly, keeping all appearances in place like I did with my secret DC withdrawal plans five years ago and using the KISS Doctrine. As I'm going to do with the how and where, I'll keep it all our secret and keep appearances all the same."

"That's one of the reasons I love you so much, Steven!"

And they talked and planned far into the night . . .

Vanessa had left, and with dawn not far away, Steven sat looking out at the magnificent electric light show of El Paso-Ciudad Juarez below, with Rommel on the floor within reach. He was having a small glass of Courvoisier and thinking about his earlier conversation with Vanessa.

The barriers to our freedom are the ones we build ourselves, and in order to break down those barriers, we must do it by ourselves with the good Lord's help, sometimes with the help of the good Lord's appointed angels and God's grace.

With chaos, breakdown, and evil permeating the culture and the world, there is no salvation for humanity as a whole, but there is salvation for the individual. Steven thought, *Vanessa and I will do a 'John Galt' as Ayn Rand wrote in* Atlas Shrugged *. . . on this, our Independence Day, 2016.*

CHAPTER 21

"Good morning, all, " Gravelly Voice intoned to the assassins at the safe house in Sunland Park. "Well, Colonel Lemev, it has been several weeks . . . have you been ignoring me?"

Only Powell and Lemev were actually at this safe house today.

General Xiangsui, Colonel Liang, and the rest of the assassination team were at the other safe house near Steven's home planning the 'Big Event,' as the general called it. Even Uri, Powell's driver, was there with them. Powell and Lemev were the only ones listening to Gravelly Voice today.

The colonel had been renewed. He now knew with absolute certainty that the United States of America was dying. He was ready to speed that process along by fulfilling his mandate: kill Steven Vandorol and the entire prosecution team and eliminate the threat that the special prosecution presented to the take-over of America.

"Not at all, we have just been planning to execute another person, thereby eliminating Steven Vandorol by breaking his spirit and rendering him completely useless."

"And how do you propose to do that, Colonel?" Sarcasm was dripping from Gravelly Voice. "The mainstream media created a national hero in Steven Vandorol. Didn't you read the *Dallas Morning Clarion* article carried nationwide?"

"Yes, we have," Lemev replied with Powell listening. "That's why we have added to our plan." He paused, then said dramatically, "By killing Vanessa Carson."

"What's that going to do?"

"Steven has put all his emotional eggs in one basket. It seems she has given him a new lease on life. Before her, his only real emotional attachment was his dog, that stupid animal we almost killed. By the way, we have a plan for that Great Dane also. Now that Carson is in El Paso, he is completely bullet proof. He has a partner and confidant and seems to be invulnerable. With Steven like that, a win in this case will coalesce that majority of America."

Gravelly Voice interrupted, "Against us and our infiltration and transformation of the big Satan America and all that we have accomplished so far."

The colonel shot right back, "So you agree with this change?" But he was thinking, *I really don't care if the stupid Muslim agrees or not.*

"I agree. Your new plan is brilliant! Earn all the millions you've been paid, Colonel Lemev," Gravelly Voice said as a parting shot.

The line went dead.

Colonel Lemev was laughing. "I guess our replacement assassination team is not coming."

Now Powell interrupted, "They are *not* coming! General Xiangsui's killers in Juarez intercepted and eliminated them." Ward paused, his eyes almost demonic. "All of them, every last one of the dozens of them, and he had it done in the bloodiest and ugliest way!" Powell's face was flushed with excitement, eyes glazed over and blood red.

Colonel Lemev was stunned. "How do you know?" Lemev inhaled and continued, "You have proof of this?"

"Because General Xiangsui told me." Powell imperceptibly changed the subject: "The Gravelly Voice Muslim doesn't know my full plan, does he?" He looked directly at Lemev, eyebrows raised questioningly. Powell didn't say that his own insider, Vladimir Gorki, a Russian Muslim as well, had witnessed it all and had recounted it to Powell, every bloody detail.

Lemev shook his head. "Of course not, Ward!" Lemev paused, put his hand on Powell's arm, and asked, "What *is* your plan?"

"First, I'm gonna kidnap her, torture her, then tell Steven I've got her and trap him. Then I'll kill him and make her beg me to stop hurting her." His eyeballs were bouncing like pinballs on a scarlet screen.

"How're you going to do it?" Lemev asked. "How are *we* going to do that, Ward?" he repeated.

"I know exactly where she's going to be that Friday night. She herself has been betrayed by people she least suspects." Powell was really smug.

"Who is that, Ward? Another one of your conquests?"

"Yes," Powell boasted. "And you and I are gonna grab Vanessa while the ranch is under attack. And they're gonna grab Steven and kill Ed and Andi Egen."

"The wife too?" Lemev asked.

"She's just collateral damage."

"So, when are we gonna do this, Ward?"

"I've got the boys working on it." Powell paused, his handsome face was contorted in an ugly snarl, his eyes dancing and flashing. "I'm planning on becoming a full member of the all-American mile high club."

Both were laughing hard. "How is it going to be done?" Lemev asked.

"Standard military maneuver. We'll have plenty of help!"

Lemev asked, "When?"

"I'm going to do it as General Xiangsui's Chinese and Muslim forces pour across the main bridge from Juarez into El Paso by the thousands." Powell was grinning.

"Will the courthouse and city hall be secure by then?" Lemev questioned.

"Yes, sir. Colonel Liang and General Xiangsui are handling that deal."

"Do they have enough for that?"

"Yes, they do! More than enough . . . twelve for city hall and another twelve for the courthouse. Both groups have been infiltrated and will be wired . . . before the big event. They'll all just march in after the explosions, kill everybody, and secure both."

"What about the federal courthouse?" Lemev wanted more details; he was really having fun. "This is like we're on spring break, Ward!" He was laughing.

"The Muslim plants in the US attorney's office will take care of all the infidels in there." Powell said with an evil grin on his face.

"Who are these infidels, Ward?" Lemev was looking directly into Powell's eyes. "Are you one of them?"

Powell deflected. "Naw, I'm just gonna make sure we wipe all of them out . . . the stupid Muslim morons."

"I guess that Muslim Manchurian candidate in DC's got all the US attorney's offices infiltrated?" Lemev asked, seemingly satisfied.

"They've had almost eight years since the head Muslim got elected to do it. So, what do you think?" Powell was finished—for now. He thought to himself, *Vanessa Carson, I want just for myself, and I'm not going to share her with anybody. I'm not waiting for the 'Big Event' either, as the stupid fat slob calls it!* He started laughing hysterically.

Colonel Stanislav Lemev frowned, looked at Powell, and thought, *He is insane.*

Powell continued to laugh.

CHAPTER 22

It was eight in the evening. She was again on the now familiar roof of the sixteen-story high rise apartment building on Stanton Street. To her left was Providence Hospital, just five blocks away, and to her right, the magnificent view of downtown El Paso and Juarez, Mexico, stretched into eternity.

It was a clear evening and starting to darken. Everything was the same as the last time.

She was looking down from the roof, holding her small, powerful binoculars to view the fourteenth-floor veranda. A man and woman were sitting in chairs, each holding a glass of wine and talking. This time, the woman appeared to be crying, and the man seemed to be trying to console her. She thought about how much she hated the man.

Putting down the binoculars, she adjusted the 9mm Beretta with silencer attached that she had tucked in the small of her back. She panned the whole area below and continued to watch, occasionally panning the surrounding neighborhood and writing notes on her pad.

As the sun was setting in the western sky, she carefully sketched out a diagram of the area on the pad. She put the binoculars in the case and put both the case and pad in the small bag. She then walked to the roof door, down the empty stairwell, and out into the parking lot, just as it was turning dark. When she got to her car, she looked all around and got in. She pulled out her cell phone, hit one number, and listened, waiting.

"Yeah?" A man answered.

She said, "All done." Then she clicked off, paused, and searched in her contacts for another number. She touched the keys and heard it ringing.

"Hello?" A very nervous and tentative voice answered.

"Do you have her schedule again for Friday?" she asked.

"Yes, I'll text it to you again, okay?" Then, in a soft and tentative voice, the contact continued, "I can't do this anymore!"

"Do it . . . or else." She ended the call abruptly as a couple approached her car.

Ward Powell's face was a mess. He thought, *I certainly don't want this idiot to know a woman's husband kicked me from here to kingdom come. How was I supposed to know she was married,* but said, "What's going on, Lemev, did you miss me?" Powell had been gone for almost a month and had just returned to the safe house.

Spetsnaz Colonel Stanislav Lemev looked at Spetsnaz Major Ward Powell and laughed, "What happened to your face, Ward?" He was smiling, something he didn't do very often. "Did you stick your face into a meat grinder?"

"Screw you," Ward growled and wiped his tearing eyes with tissue. His face was swollen and looked like someone had hit it with a baseball bat. His nose seemed to be broken, and he had white tape across it. Ward continued to look at Lemev with a sly smirk on his face, daring him to chastise or threaten to kill him when he used foul or sexual language.

Ward Powell, General Xiangsui, Colonel Liang, and Colonel Lemev remained at the safe house after all the others, including the three radical Muslim assassins in their midst, had all left.

The General had the floor. "My friend Colonel Liang will lead the abduction!" He smiled at his friend and asked Colonel Lemev, "Who will help him, Colonel?"

Powell, proud of his new power position with the general, interrupted, "Get the Muslims on it now, they're all vicious little spiders!"

Colonel Lemev answered Powell immediately, "I'll get Atta to do it!" He paused a second then said, "And Vladimir, my driver, will help him!"

"Good, they are both just a couple of moron killers and love to kill . . . anything!" Powell said and thought, *Atta, I get, but why did he include Vladimir?* Ward continued to smirk at General Wang Xiangsui. *Future Emperor of the World,* Ward thought and almost laughed out loud.

The general noticed but controlled his own emotions. "Powell, we have two students at UTEP, whom I have placed there, and we have Emily

Blankenship already under surveillance." The general smiled enigmatically and looked at his co-author, partner, and dear friend.

Powell was surprised. "How did you know Emily Blankenship was Jacob Warren's girlfriend?"

"Because we've intercepted a cell phone conversation when he called her!" The general took back the power, paused, and then said, "Young Warren will attempt to see her next weekend, and I'll let you know the location!"

"Will the kid shed his protective bodyguards?" Powell asked. "I don't think the kid is smart enough to do that . . . but little Emily might be!"

———

"Steven, my love, I fell in love with you the first time I saw you at your reception at our house in Chevy Chase. And my love continued to grow . . . I wanted so badly to call you . . . and not just as friends."

Steven and Vanessa were again sitting on the balcony at Vanessa's apartment. They were sipping wine, the cat at their feet and little Harley in Vanessa's lap. Steven had an eerie feeling in his gut, the same feeling as before that they were being watched, as Vanessa was talking. He looked up and all around but didn't see anything suspicious, so he continued listening.

"What's wrong?" Vanessa asked, noticing a strange look on his face.

"Nothing, I guess," Steven answered. "I got that eerie feeling again that someone was watching us. Why didn't you call me back then?"

"I didn't want to have a relationship with you at that time. I thought you weren't ready to have one. Anyway, I was married to Dudley."

Steven's eyes widened. "Maybe you knew me better at that time than I knew myself . . ." His voice trailed off.

"You tackled everything in life, including the practice of law and all your relationships, with a smothering desperation. You frantically clung to whatever you could . . . you really didn't know what you wanted. You were chasing an impossible dream. Your addictions were controlling you, forcing you through escapism to chase that impossible dream."

"Including our friendship!"

"Yes, including our friendship. You chased it not because we had made that connection, but because you were afraid of losing more than you already had."

"I knew I loved you even then," he said.

"I know. I'm not going to put this all on you. It was really hard for me not to call you back in DC. That was my fault. I admit that. But your love back then bordered on the desperate. You channeled a lifetime of grief of never having a real childhood and losing your brother, who meant everything to you, into a grasping need. You needed to mourn, not suppress it. At that time, you weren't ready to face it; you weren't ready for *us*. "

"You thought solitude would make me face it?" Steven asked.

"It did, didn't it?" The dazzling sunshine of her smile was back.

"It's not like it was a cure-all."

"I know," she nodded. "But it helped you let a lot of the pain go and start to see yourself, right?"

"That's why I think you're ahead in letting your prior pain go."

"You'll catch up . . . I know that now," Vanessa said, and in sign language, she signed, "I love you, Steven!"

CHAPTER 23

Saturday morning Steven was working in the office on a draft of the superseded and amended indictment. He was by himself. Vanessa was at her apartment sleeping in. It had been an emotional Friday evening when the two had discussed the good, bad, and ugly in the sharing of their love and had made a mutual commitment to their future.

Steven was exhausted himself. It had been a long and arduous week, but he thought he handled it well. He glanced at his Rolodex, picked up the office phone, and dialed.

"Hello?" Courtney Wellington answered.

"Courtney, it's me . . . how are you? I'm glad you answered. How is Arlene?"

"I'm good, Steven! Arlene is great as well! I take it this is not a social call?"

"It's both really. I wanted to find out how you guys are doing and also any news that I should know about."

"What I do know is that there is a lot of chatter coming in . . . just like before September eleventh, 2001, just before the Twin Towers came down."

"Oh no," is all Steven could say.

"And it gets worse. September fourth of last year, at 1:50 a.m. at the Manitoba United States border crossing checkpoint, which is some twenty-five miles from Carrington, North Dakota, surveillance cameras recorded the execution of a Royal Canadian Mounted Police Sergeant, Trevor Colington, and his checkpoint partner, Mounted Police Constable Jack Ryan, when he came out of the guard house to replace him." Courtney paused, then with some sadness, he continued, "Both had families, each with two kids . . . just youngsters. Steven, it was a particularly vicious overkill on Constable Ryan. He was killed as he walked out. He fell to the ground, but the killer put three more shots in his heart!"

Steven was stunned. "Did the cameras record the killer?"

"They sure did, but . . . the car windows were darkly tinted, and even with image enhancement software, we could see only a shadowy figure with long hair, could've been a man or a woman. On Colington, we found two shots right in his face with a 9mm Beretta, with silencer."

"How about plates?" Steven asked.

"YZ3242, Nevada plate," Courtney answered. "It was a Hertz rental from McCarran International Airport in Las Vegas . . . bogus application and fake driver's license . . . dead end. The car was never turned in. It was a well-planned professional hit, Steven."

Steven shuddered. "But why hit a border crossing?" he asked, really tense. A thought snuck into the back of his mind, but he couldn't put a finger on it.

"My contacts think the hit was carried out so that something big, coming across from Canada to the United States, would not be recorded by the cameras. The cameras were all shot out immediately after the killings. Speculation has it that it could be a dirty atomic device." His voice trailed off.

"Oh my God," Steven repeated. "As you know, a lot of fake news about the Russians is circulating now. Remember what the president said to Russian Prime Minister Medveb: 'Tell Vladimir that when elected again, I'll be in a better position to deal'?"

"With the godless communists."

"Yeah, that's right," Steven said. "Anything else?"

"Steven, before you sign off, I've got some interesting info for you in the special prosecution." Courtney paused. "I was just about to call you."

"Yes? What is it?" Steven was always interested when Courtney had something to say.

"Well, it's stunning news, really."

"Come on, Courtney, the suspense is killing me." Steven chuckled.

"The president's wife left the White House with her entourage."

Steven was shocked. "Wow! That is interesting. What's the deal?"

"Rumor has it that she'll be divorcing him . . . my sources tell me she is in contact with the top DC divorce lawyer."

Steven, aghast, interrupted, "Who is he? If you know and can tell me."

"It's a she! Leslie Abrams."

"Yikes!" Steven exclaimed. "I heard about her when I was in DC. She has a reputation for being a 'nutcracker,' I heard. I think that was her nickname: 'Nutcracker Abrams.'"

Courtney laughed. "I think that's right! Steven, seriously, my source also tells me that she might be helpful to your special prosecution right there in El Paso."

"Really?" He didn't want to know if by 'she' Courtney meant the lawyer or the president's wife. He'd have to think about it. "Thank you for that, Courtney! I'll keep it in mind! Say hi to Arlene . . . and we love you guys."

"Love you two as well." Courtney hung up.

Steven leaned back in his chair, looked out at the magnificent view, and prayed to the Lord. Steven thanked Him for his faith and His grace, for Vanessa, for the Lord placing her into his life, for their love, his kids, his family and friends, their health and mutual survival. He ended with the Lord's Prayer.

After several minutes looking at the horizon before him, Steven thought, *I've got to get Vanessa some self-protection.* He picked up his cell phone and hit a number; it was ringing.

"Hey, Steven," Ray said.

"Good morning, my friend," Steven said. "I'm at the office, and I just talked to Courtney Wellington." Steven had told Ray all about Courtney and his work with the CIA. "He told me about a double killing on the Canadian-US border checkpoint some twenty-five miles from Carrington, North Dakota."

So, Steven told Ray all about the vicious killings of two Royal Canadian Mounted Police officers. He noted, "Surveillance video suggests it might have been a woman, but they're still checking. Also, the rental car folks in Vegas think it was a woman, but that doesn't necessarily mean it was a woman who killed those border guards."

As Steven finished telling Ray what Courtney had said, the thought that had snuck into the back of his mind was still nagging him, but this time, alarm bells were ringing. "The speculation at the CIA is that it might have been a dirty atomic device that was coming into the United States via Canada, and they—whomever they are—didn't want it to be recorded. All the security cameras were shot out immediately after the killings. What do you think, Ray?"

"Could be! I'd heard internet chatter that at least three dirty atomic devices were already in major US cities."

"Who's doing the chatter, Ray?" Steven asked.

"Islamist terrorist groups . . . or at least that's the word around the internet campfire," Ray answered.

Steven turned serious. "Another September eleventh, Ray?"

"Could be."

"Well, keep checking around the campfire, okay?" He smiled at the "around the campfire" reference from *Pulp Fiction*. "On another subject, I think Vanessa needs some personal protection. What would you recommend?"

Ray thought for a minute. "I've got a small Bauer 25 caliber automatic she can have, my gift to Vanessa!"

"Great, she'll really appreciate it! Is it pretty reliable and easy to use?"

"You bet, Steven. Both!" Ray said. "And it really packs a wallop! And you can tell Vanessa it's got a cute pearl handle." Ray was chuckling.

Steven hung up, yawned, and leaned back on his large desk chair. Before he knew it, he was fast asleep . . .

The brothers were on their way. Eight-year-old Steven and his thirteen-year-old brother, Josef, who he always called Joey, had been inseparable since back in Germany. They were having the time of their lives on the fazenda, a mega Brazilian ranch in Matto Grosso, Brazil, where two hundred and fifty thousand acres of the Brazilian plains and jungle were their playground.

The brothers were on their way. Their Uncle Bach and Uncle Sandor had made them a swimming pool about a hundred yards inside the velour curtain of green of the jungle where a little stream ran.

They came to an opening in the lush, green curtain into the dense, dark jungle that was like an entrance to a dark cave. They went down a little incline, and at the bottom ran a little stream. It was lit by sunlight for at least ten steps, but then it grew darker as vines and foliage went straight up and touched the clouds. After fifteen or twenty more steps, they came upon a small clearing with sunlight laser beams filtering through only in spots. It was a mystical and magical place in the dark jungle.

A dug-out fifteen-foot swimming hole was in an almost oval clearing, courtesy of their uncles. The bank around the swimming hole was a path about two meters wide, and the silt and mud had settled around the rocks, clearing the pool to crystal clear.

This was the most beautiful place young Steven had ever seen in his short lifetime. Almost pristine virgin jungle foliage, acting like a prism, filtered the sunlight, creating an explosion of lavish colors: greens, purples, oranges, and bright, bright reds.

Steven was walking along the rocks on the bottom of the pool with his arms flailing in a swimming motion. "Look, Joey, I'm swimming."

Joey was really swimming and gliding across the pool. Joey looked up. "Bull crap! Come on. I'll show you how."

Perceptive Steven thought his brother was getting angrier all the time and wondered why, but only said, "Okay, Joey. Show me how."

Tiring of their wild activity, both were resting quietly in one corner, leaning against the bank, preparing for yet another whirlwind of activity coming up. They were breathing hard but noticed that in the stillness even the birds held their breaths.

In that moment, they both looked toward the other end of the clearing, and suddenly saw the sparkling black eyes of a shining black panther slowly moving to the water for a drink. They froze in horror as the panther, on the other side of the pool, stood coiled, looking directly at them.

At the slightest motion, the panther snarled and let out a scream, which chilled them even more than the icy cold water had.

Joey mastered his fear quicker than Steven, who was still frozen, almost petrified, stuck to the rocky bank. Gently but surely, Joey started easing up backward on the bank, pulling his little brother with him. Luckily, their clothes were right behind them.

As they eased out of the water, the panther sprung around the pool in long, graceful bounds. They grabbed their clothes, and two naked boys, holding their clothes as best they could, ran wildly out to the mouth of the cave of the jungle with the black panther, snarling, screaming, and pouncing behind them.

The longest hundred yards in the world lay before them. They ran in horror, the black panther bounding after them. They headed for the opening, running like two Olympic sprinters. They had never run that fast in their lives. They covered the hundred yards in mere seconds, though it seemed like an eternity with the panther still right behind.

They hit the opening and continued running.

The panther, on the other hand, stopped. The animal would not come into the clearing, having learned long ago that the danger of mankind lay on the other side of the jungle cave's mouth. The animal stopped, but the boys continued running, both naked, waving their arms.

They didn't stop until they reached the house and were safely in their room, under the beds, where they lay crying. Their mother came running in behind them. Both were still shaking with fright and terror but were suddenly crying and laughing at the same time.

It had been close, much too close.

Steven woke with a start when his phone rang.

"Yes! This is Steven Vandorol."

"Hi, honey, when are you leaving there?" Vanessa asked.

"Oh, in just a few minutes!"

"Okay, come on over now. I'll see you soon. I love you!"

"I love you, too."

When he hung up the phone, he noticed he was sweating. *That dream seemed so real, just like it happened yesterday,* Steven thought.

He yawned, stood and stretched, turned out the light, and left.

CHAPTER 24

Jacob Warren was a bloody mess: eyes dark and puffy, red, watering, almost swollen shut. His face was bruised and bleeding, and his nose broken and listing to one side.

He was hog tied to a wooden straight-back chair, arms behind him zip tied tight, the ties cutting into his flesh. His shirt was ripped and stained with blood. He was still bleeding from his nose and mouth.

He slowly raised his head from his chest with great difficulty. He had passed out from the brutal beating and agonizing torture he had received at the hands of Colonel Lemev; Vladimir Gorki, the Russian Muslim; and Muhammed Atta, the Muslim Hezbollah operative Lemev had himself trained in Afghanistan.

Ward Powell, Colonel Liang, Uri Gagarin, Mohamed Atta, and Ussef Hammadi, both Muslim terrorists, and even the dog, Ubiytsa, "Killer," all watched with great interest and stood by the "festivities," as Powell had called it.

Muhammed Atta, Hezbollah operative, now in the US for three years and leader of the Muslim terrorist cell operating in Juarez and El Paso, was getting especially agitated. Dark skinned, barrel-chested, and stout with dark dead eyes. He was a coiled hyperactive cobra.

General Xiangsui, although invited by Colonel Liang, didn't join them, electing to stay in the lap of luxury, dining at the Dome Grill with another friend, he had announced to all. He found all types of violence distasteful and abhorrent. Colonel Liang was wondering about the new *friend* as the general was growing more distant and seemed to be less desirous of Liang's attention when "they were relaxing alone." Colonel Liang watched the festivities without interest, too distracted to care.

"Looks like he's waking," Powell said as he walked over to Jacob and stared at him as he opened his swollen eyes. Putting his hand on Jacob's bruised, swollen, and bloody face, Powell raised it higher and said, "Ready to tell us what we want to know?"

Jacob said nothing.

He had been abducted when he met his girlfriend, Emily, as they secretly agreed to meet at a deserted parking lot, planned during the last call he made to her. Jacob wasn't vigilant enough and did not consider the consequences of the evil people in this world, so he succumbed to his girlfriend's pleading that she was *so* lonely. He waited until dusk, got a key to a ranch jeep from the bunkhouse key-board, avoided the patrol car with officers Shultze and Cruz, slowly left through the back gate leading to Canutillo, and headed to El Paso on Interstate I-10.

After a short drive to the parking lot near the university, he got out of his car. He didn't see Emily's car. Seemingly out of nowhere appeared Atta, Lemev, Liang, and Powell. They had been waiting.

"Are you ready to talk? I will not ask again."

Jacob still said nothing.

"This is not getting us anywhere." Atta, like a coiled cobra ready to strike, was getting very agitated, especially after Jacob's torn shirt revealed a silver crucifix on a silver chain around his neck.

"You stupid little infidel! I've cut the heads off hundreds just like you." Atta grabbed the chain with the silver crucifix and brutally ripped it from Jacob's neck, slicing into the flesh of his neck and drawing a spurt of his crimson blood.

But still Jacob said nothing, although in horrific pain. He thought of his Lord and Savior, Jesus Christ, opened his heart, and prayed.

With eyes darting in their sockets like pinballs, hyperactive Atta, now in a blind rage, ripped off Jacob's shirt all the way, grabbed his razor-sharp steel machete, jumped back to the chair where Jacob was tied, pulled his head up by his hair, stretching his neck to its limit, and raised the machete up high . . .

None of the others said anything. All just stood by, watching.

Jacob opened his swollen eyes, mere slits, and felt more than saw, as the machete started its descent from the top of its arc. He thought, *I'm on my way to my Lord Jesus.*

A sickening thud, like a watermelon splitting open, echoed in the now totally silent room.

Mohammad Atta, eyes flaming red, picked up young Jacob Warren's head, now dripping blood, and held it high in his left hand triumphantly. His bloody machete was in his right, blood running down his arm.

And Jacob Warren saw the face of God.

CHAPTER 25

Steven and Vanessa had been having lunch at Vanessa's apartment.

They arrived separately as they both had been downtown at the court house, Vanessa at the court master's divorce docket, and Steven working with North Anderson on the superseded indictment at the district attorney's office. They had agreed to have lunch at Vanessa's apartment on the way back to the office.

Both were solemn, downcast, and somber. Jacob was now with their Lord and Savior, Jesus Christ, and with his family. "All must have been waiting for Jacob so the family could be together again," Steven had said to Vanessa.

For too short a time, Steven and Vanessa had been disciples and designated angels of the Lord and almost surrogate parents to Jacob Warren, helping him through devastation, agony, and loneliness with friendship, love, intimacy, and caring. Steven and Vanessa knew in their hearts that Jacob was in paradise.

Jacob's decapitated body was dumped at the main entrance of the Chico Gringo Ranch between two and three o'clock in the morning, Eddie had told Steven. He had been mercilessly beaten and brutally tortured by at least three people; forensics speculated by the multiple blunt force trauma all over his young body.

Jacob's head was found a short distance away, eyes wide open, blue eyes shining as if he were still alive. "He had the most peaceful and serene look on his face," Eddie had said.

It was twelve thirty in the afternoon, Monday, July 11, 2016, and the two partners were sitting on the shady veranda having coffee. The cloudless sky was a brilliant electric blue spectacle shimmering with light from the very bright midday sun above them. Downtown and Juarez were like shining, multi-colored Lego pieces growing smaller and smaller, stretching all the way to eternity in the haze of the horizon. The air was dry and the temperature in the eighties, cool for mid-July.

"Thank you for showing me how to handle my new twenty-five caliber automatic that Ray gave me when we rode our horses yesterday!" Vanessa said and took a sip of coffee. "I really like my little gun. I called Ray yesterday to thank him; the pearl handle is so *elegant!*" She was smiling sunshine at him, but poisonous snakes and snarling black panthers were on both their minds.

Neither Steven nor Vanessa had smiled in the last five days since Jacob's funeral in a special grave on the Chico Gringo Ranch. Both were still serious, downcast, and sad. But her last comment of "elegant" for a gun did bring smiles to their faces.

"You're most welcome, my love! Ray said he thought you'd like it since, as he said, 'It was really a cute little gun'!"

"It *is* a really cute little gun. And I'm gonna keep it with me all the time in my purse now that I know how to use it. Thank you again!"

"You're welcome, again!" He went to give her a hug. "I really worry about your safety, my love, especially now that they got Jacob—in spite of all the security and vigilance!"

She hugged him back, kissed him, and said, in a serious tone, "I'm a big girl, Steven!"

"I know you are, but you don't know the ROW as well as I do. It's the rest of the world that worries me. In your goodness, you tend to be a little naïve about the ROW . . . or if you are a little distracted, unintended consequences will get you. Now that the good Lord put you into my life, I couldn't bear for anything . . . anything . . . *anything* . . . to happen to you. I couldn't bear to lose you. You're now my life, Vanessa Carson!"

"And you are mine, Steven Josef Vandorol!" They hugged again and kissed for an endless moment into forever and always.

Steven broke the embrace first and spoke, "Please promise me you'll be very careful and always situationally aware about your surroundings as we have discussed numerous times. Vanessa, say, 'I promise.'"

"I have been, and yes, I promise to be more so now since Jacob was murdered." Vanessa shivered, paused, and then said, "Sadly, Jacob is with the Lord." She started crying but caught herself. "I wish I didn't, but I've got to get back to Judge Paxton's court; it's almost one thirty."

"I wish you didn't have to either. But I've got to go back to the office myself and finish working on the amended indictment."

"How is it going?" Vanessa asked, getting up.

"Labor intensive, but it's almost finished and is now almost a fifty-page monster." Steven chuckled. "I'll be glad when North and I get it filed . . . I'm pretty well done with all this ROW crap."

"I know you will be! Me, too!" She kissed Steven again and walked into the apartment.

"I'm going to finish my coffee, relax a few more minutes, and enjoy the view for a while. Then I'll head back to the office. I'll see you back here for cocktails around six?"

"See you then, Steven. I love you!"

"I love you, too, my Vanessa!" Steven said as she slid the glass door shut behind her. And she was gone.

Steven finished his coffee, got up, and went to the side of the balcony where he could look down on the visitor parking that was above the parking garage. Vanessa had a secure space there, but she had parked next to Steven when they came from downtown for lunch.

Steven grasped the balcony railing and looked down, waiting. He wanted to wave to Vanessa as she walked to her little Kia Soul parked below.

In about three minutes, Vanessa came out and was walking to her car. Steven saw her, whistled real loudly, and she looked up. She signed "I love you" to Steven, and he signed back the same and started to turn away. Just then, Steven heard tires screeching and went back to the railing. He looked down, and a black Suburban was right beside Vanessa. Two men with hoodies and black ski masks on jumped out and threw a blanket over Vanessa. One of the men grabbed her roughly and threw her in the back seat and went in with her. The other jumped in the driver's side and drove out of the lot in mere seconds, tires spinning, burning rubber.

All Steven could do was watch in horror as desperation, anguish, and despair washed over him, making it hard to even breathe.

CHAPTER 26

Steven was crying. The tears streaming down his face communicated the complete desperation and despair he felt in seeing his love being taken right before his eyes. He managed to take out his cell phone and punch the number.

"El Paso Police Department, how may I help you?"

"Listen carefully," Steven said. "This is Steven Vandorol. I'm on the fourteenth floor of the Stanton Street high rise apartments . . . 4506 North Stanton. I just witnessed my law partner Vanessa Carson being abducted by two masked men with black hoodies . . . and ski masks driving a late model black Suburban, smoked windows—I don't know the license plate—from the visitor parking on Kirbey Street. The Suburban was headed north on Stanton Street! Got all that?"

"Yes, I got it! Chief Egen is not in, but I'll contact him immediately. This is Officer Trent McGuffin speaking."

"Thank you, Officer. I'll stand by right here on the veranda. I'm on the fourteenth floor in Ms. Carson's apartment. Please hurry."

"I'm on it." The line went dead.

Steven dialed again.

"Steven, what's up?' Ray answered.

"Ray, I just watched Vanessa get abducted by two guys in black hoodies and ski masks, driving a late model black Suburban, unknown license plate, headed north on Stanton." Steven, trying to control his breathing continued, "I called El Paso PD . . . Eddie wasn't in, but Officer McGuffin got it all . . . and was contacting Eddie right then."

"I know Trent . . . I'm on it." Ray was gone.

Steven dialed again.

"Law offices of Vandorol and Carson, may I help you?" Marce answered.

"Where is Christina?"

"She's not here."

"Where is she?"

"I don't know. Probably at home," Marce answered. "She left about ten, said she was going home sick. She'd just thrown up, she told me!"

Steven had a bad feeling about Christina not being in the office. *She's been very distant lately and weird around Vanessa,* he thought. "Stay on the front desk phone until I call you, okay?"

"Steven, what's wrong? Are you alright?"

"I'll tell you later. Just stay on the front desk and lock the front door!" Steven hung up.

Steven slumped down on the cold, concrete balcony floor as tears streamed down his face. He inhaled again, wiped his face with the back of his hand, exhaled slowly, trying desperately to calm himself, and started praying out loud: "Dear Lord, please protect my Vanessa, please, please." His head fell to his chest.

Caspurr came out and rubbed against Steven's leg, purring. Next, little Harley also came out, jumped on the chair, and licked Steven's face as Steven said the Lord's Prayer out loud.

Eddie Egen's cruiser screeched to a stop right below. Eddie jumped out, looked up, saw Steven waving above on the veranda, and screamed, "Vanessa is okay . . . we got her. She's safe and I'm coming up." He was already running for the second-floor entrance.

Steven left the balcony and ran to the front door intercom and pressed the button to let Eddie in. He could hear the door open. "I'm in . . . coming up."

Steven waited.

The elevator door opened, and Eddie burst out and came down the hall in a rush. "She is okay . . . she is safe." Eddie repeated as the two hugged.

Steven started crying again. The two friends hugged each other. "Thank God, thank God," Steven kept saying. "Thank you, Eddie." He collapsed to his knees in relief. Eddie helped Steven up and to the couch in Vanessa's living room. Eddie made his friend sit down and got him a drink from the fridge.

Steven and Eddie sat. It was four thirty, almost four hours since Vanessa had been abducted.

"Where is she, Ed?"

"She's at Providence Hospital right now. She was pretty shaken up, but she's unhurt. Groggy . . . but *not* hurt, except she was jostled around in the car chase. She was asking for you."

Steven jumped to his feet. "Well, let's go."

Eddie was firm as he pulled Steven back down. "Steven, calm down and listen. You're not gonna do her any good like you are now . . . so calm down and listen . . . just calm down!"

"Okay, I'm okay. Tell me what happened." He took a deep breath, exhaled, and looked at his friend. "I'm listening."

"Well . . . as I said, Vanessa is okay . . . still a little shaky but completely unhurt. She just has a bruise on her forehead where she bumped her head during the chase."

Steven interrupted, "There was a chase? What chase? Did they crash?"

"Yes, there was a chase, and, no, the Suburban did not crash, so . . . please calm down, my friend. She's been sedated and is resting well, sleeping."

Eddie told Steven the whole story: that Sergeant Wilson, assigned as Steven's security surveillance, was parked on Kirbey Street and had followed Steven from the courthouse to the apartment. He was sitting in his unmarked car having lunch, listening to the radio. He saw Vanessa walk out and wave to Steven when, suddenly, the black Suburban pulled up, two guys in ski masks and hoodies jumped out, abducted Vanessa, and left. They went past him in seconds, burning rubber, tires screeching. Wilson spilled his coffee but recovered and was right after them and, on his radio, calling for backup.

"The call from Wilson came into the station just about the time you called it in, Steven. Officer McGuffin got a hold of me!"

Steven was nodding, calming further. "So, what happened?"

"Just listen, okay? The Suburban was going about eighty miles an hour up Stanton Street with Wilson right behind, when it cut over to Mesa and headed north and out of town, again with Wilson right on his tail. A backup unit joined him around Sunland Park Mall, and the two cornered the Suburban at the road block already set up on I-10 toward Las Cruces. And that's it!"

Eddie put his arm around his friend's shoulder. "The Suburban was surrounded by five officers, all with guns drawn. The two thugs were yanked out of the car. Then officers saw Vanessa still in the back, covered with a blanket. She was okay but crying and really dazed. The suspects are in the hospital, in comas, I hope . . . they were pretty beat up." Eddie winked at Steven. "You know, they were probably resisting arrest and had to be subdued."

Steven finally smiled. "Okay, I've got it! I'm fine now. Thank you, Eddie, my friend, and thank the Lord she is okay!"

"Amen," they chimed in together.

"Now let's go see Vanessa!"

CHAPTER 27

Ray and Christina where sitting quietly at one end of the conference room table at the office when Eddie and Steven walked in. Christina was crying softly and Ray seemed angry and distraught.

"What's wrong?" Steven asked Christina. "Marce told me you went home sick. Why are you crying?" They both sat down at the other end. "How are you feeling?"

Earlier, Steven told Ray when they talked after the abduction that he best check on his daughter, because she went home sick.

Ray spoke first, "After we talked, Steven, I did go home and found Christina in her room crying. She wasn't really sick and she told me everything." Ray put his hand on his daughter's arm and said, "Chris, tell Steven everything you told me, just like you did at home!"

Christina looked up at her father, hesitated, wiped her eyes, looked at Steven, and words began flowing out of her mouth at a break-neck pace. "I was given five hundred dollars to text Vanessa's schedule for Friday to a number, and I told some lady when she called that Vanessa was at her apartment having lunch with Steven and would be going back downtown for Judge Paxton's divorce docket. That was the second time she called me. The first time it happened, I had sent the woman a layout of the office by mail to a post office box in Sunland Park." She started crying again.

"Why did you do it?" Ray asked. "Stop crying and tell us . . . *now*."

"I don't know," she said between sobs. "I guess for the money? I may have been the cause of Vanessa's abduction. I didn't know, I thought five hundred dollars was a lot of money. I'm so sorry. Please don't be mad at me . . ." Her voice trailed off; she was crying again.

Steven said, "Christina, you betrayed us, Vanessa and I . . . and your father as well. You are fired!" He looked at Ray, who was nodding, somber and serious. "I'm not going to file a complaint with Eddie . . . because of my friendship with your dad, but I would like to know why you did it, and how five hundred dollars would be enough to betray us when you have everything you need!" Steven looked directly into Christina's tearful eyes.

Christina wiped her eyes and looked directly at her father. With a sharp glint of defiance in her eyes, she said, "Dad, you pay more attention to Vanessa . . . and Jessie . . . than to me." She was still crying.

Ray put his hand on hers and said, "Chris, I love you! You're my daughter, and I will always love you, but my wife, Jessie, comes first. You're going to have to take responsibility for your actions and live with them." Ray paused. "Let's go home."

After Ray and Christina left, Steven and Eddie sat in the conference room, both serious and sad, drinking coffee. Both silent.

Eddie spoke first, "We impounded the black Suburban, Steven, and checked it all out. Stolen Alaska plates and bullet proof windows and chassis and get this—the engine block had Russian markings."

Steven was thinking about what Christina had said about Vanessa's abduction and betrayal. Suddenly, the thought that had been sneaking in the back of his mind crystallized. He looked at Eddie, eyebrows raised.

Eddie looked at Steven. "What?"

"Christina said it was a *woman* on the phone. The killing of two Royal Canadian Mounties at the border was proved to be a *woman* who had driven from Las Vegas, from McCarran International Airport, in a Hertz rental."

"So?" Eddied shrugged. Steven had told Eddie all about those killings when the two had talked last Saturday.

"On the day before our big meeting at your ranch, Eddie, I was having lunch with North Anderson and Beth Barker . . . and she said that she and her husband, Francisco Montes, had just gotten back from Las Vegas."

Eddie was looking at Steven, eyes wide open.

"I think Beth is the ringer . . . and part of the assassination contract on me, you, and North."

"OMG!" Eddie got up abruptly and started out of the office in a rush. "Let's go, Steven; my car is outside."

Running past reception, Steven yelled, "Marce, lock the door behind us and stay by the phone until I call."

Eddie's cruiser was parked right by the outside door. Eddie jumped in and Steven went around on the passenger side. Eddie pulled out on Sun Bowl Drive and headed downtown.

———

They were flying down Mesa, lights flashing, at ninety miles per hour, speeding downtown.

Eddie hit the radio: "Samson, call me on my cell, over." Eddie pulled out his cell and waited. In seconds, it buzzed. "I'm on Mesa toward downtown, flasher on, no siren. Listen . . . no radio use. We got us a situation . . . immediately secure the courthouse without alerting anyone. Then, secure the seventh floor . . . all entries and exits. Have a swat team ready, got it? I'm ten minutes away . . . out!" Eddie clicked off and to Steven, "It's three thirty . . . any idea where she might be?"

"I'm not sure . . . I know she was in trial yesterday, but she could be either in Judge Marguez's court or in her office . . . I guess."

Eddie clicked his cell again. "Samson, we need a net around ADA Beth Barker. She's either in Marguez's court on three or in her office . . . still no radios . . . or tip offs. She can't know anything is up." He clicked off again and continued flying down Mesa towards downtown.

In seconds, Eddie drove into the courthouse parking garage, up the ramp to the third floor. Two other cruisers were there waiting. Samson, by one of the cruisers, was waiving.

Eddie parked by the cars and looked at Steven again. "You want to come with us, Steven?" He was smiling as he got out.

"You bet! Wouldn't miss it for the world! But I sure hope my hunch is right, or it's gonna' be pretty embarrassing!" Steven, now with a smile on his face as well, followed Eddie.

Samson said, "Chief, she's in her office. Marguez's jury is in the jury room deliberating."

Eddie nodded and asked, "Seventh floor all tight?"

Samson nodded. "Air tight! Swat's in place in the public restroom, locked and loaded."

"Let's go! Steven, you hang back, okay?" Eddie led the way, with Samson and three other officers following.

"Gotcha," Steven said and followed, last in line. They walked across the skywalk, past security to the elevators where another officer was holding the elevator doors open.

When all were in the elevator, it rose to seven in seconds. Eddie led them all out, Steven last. They were met by two more officers.

Eddie said to one, "Swat ready?"

The officer answered, pointing, "In the restroom."

Eddie motioned to Steven and said to the group around him, "This is how we'll do it. It'll be just me and Steven going in to see Ernie, like we've done before a hundred times. We'll act normal and see if Beth is in, so we can discuss some things about the special prosecution. Once we know she's in, I'll call you to stand by and follow us in." Steven joined Eddie, and the two walked in the district attorney's office, through massive, wooden double doors encased in bullet-proof glass. All officers stayed put.

Eddie walked right in, with Steven behind, and up to another bullet-proof glass enclosure. The woman behind the glass saw Eddie smiling and waving, and the door buzzed open immediately. Eddie opened the door for Steven, and they walked through to a reception desk, behind which sat a matronly woman with white hair and thick coke bottle glasses. She looked up. "Chief Egen, how are—"

Eddie interrupted her, an index finger to his mouth directing her to be quiet, and said, "Need to see the boss. Is he in?"

She shook her head.

Eddie asked quietly, "Ms. Barker in her private office?"

She nodded yes.

"Is she alone?"

She nodded yes again and whispered, "She's on the phone."

Eddie pulled out his cell. When his call was answered, he said, almost whispering, "She's in her office, alone, on the phone . . . we're by the door to the hallway offices. You know the setup . . . come on in to back us up. We're going in. I'm leading, and Steven is with me. Beth's office is third down on the left . . . I'll count to ten. Ready? One . . . two . . . three."

Eddie drew his Glock, chambered a round, full auto, locked and loaded. "Four . . . five . . . six . . . seven."

Eddie grabbed the door handle and eased the hall door open, still counting, "Eight . . . nine."

The swat team came behind them slowly as Eddie went into the hallway, Steven right behind. They walked slowly down the hall to the target office. Eddie grabbed the handle and threw open the door. Over Eddie's shoulder, Steven could see Beth on the phone. She swung around, startled with wide-eyed astonishment.

Beth dropped the phone in disbelief as Eddie and Steven barged in. She went for the top drawer of her desk, and in a flash, she had a gun in her hand, raising it up.

Eddie fired first—bam, bam, bam—three shots, hitting her center. Beth thought, *How do they know?* She dropped the gun. Her beautiful, startled sapphire eyes were wide open as she sank back into her desk chair and died. Her head slumped to her right, and the gun fell to the parquet wood floor and clattered.

Eddie went around the desk and checked her pulse. "She's dead; call the coroner." He picked up the gun, held it up, and said, "It's a 9mm Beretta with a silencer."

As the other officers filed in, Steven looked around the large, elegant, and opulent private office: plush leather couches and wing back chairs, cherry desk, and expensive Tiffany and Cartier lamps all sat on highly polished blush parquet floor covered by a two-inch-thick, colorful oriental rug. Steven estimated the rug was likely worth twenty-five thousand dollars.

Steven was drawn to one corner of Beth's office. He eased over to a magnificent oil painting in one corner, lit by a directional light shining on it. A hauntingly beautiful, yet terrifying, jet-black spider, the size of a dinner plate, was grasping and protecting three large, tan fetal bubbles. The spider had an unmistakable, blood-red hourglass tattoo on her shiny jet-black marble back: a terrifyingly beautiful black widow spider.

———————

On Sunday evening, Steven and Vanessa sat on the balcony of Vanessa's apartment, looking down on the parking lot where Vanessa had been abducted three days earlier. Caspurr and Harley hovered around her.

Vanessa was well, having recovered from the trauma of the abduction and was thankful for the good Lord's grace and for His designated angels, the officers of the El Paso Police Department. Their swift action in rescuing her meant she was now safe and well.

Steven was well also, having recovered from the abject terror, despair, anguish, and desperation he had felt as he watched the abduction from the balcony. He turned to look at Vanessa. "My precious angel, I thought at that moment that I had lost you." Tears formed in Steven's eyes as he continued, "And I thought I lost all that we had . . . our lives and future together as one, us . . . all gone." He hugged the love of his life, who was crying herself.

She drew away, wiped her eyes with a tissue, and directed her dazzling sunshine smile at Steven. "So, Beth Barker was the evil ringer in El Paso, right inside the special prosecution team itself?"

"Yes, ma'am," Steven said composing himself. "She was a ruthless killer. The ballistics report established her gun was the weapon that killed the two Royal Canadian Mounted Police officers at the border crossing . . . and, as Courtney told me, the license plate on the car that the Mountie put down in his log book was that of a rental from McCarran International Airport, obtained with a false driver's license."

"Tell me what happened . . . how did you figure it out?"

"Well, my love, I had a really bad feeling about her from the get-go!"

So, Steven told her about Christina's betrayal and that her contact was a woman. Also, that when Steven met with North Anderson and Beth Barker for lunch, prior to their strategy meeting on Eddie's ranch, he heard Beth remark in small talk that she and Francisco, her toy-boy husband, had just returned from a weekend in Las Vegas.

"Then, after we got back from the Thanksgiving raft trip, and my house was almost destroyed, Beth suggested a guy as possible help for the law office. I had Courtney check him out, and he said the report was not good at all. Also, the black Suburban used to abduct you was impounded, had stolen Alaska plates and Russian markings. But the clincher, I guess, was when I recently talked to Courtney, and he told me about the border guards in Canada could've been killed by a woman, that the rental car was from the McCarran International Airport in Las Vegas. And when Christina said her contact was a woman, I suddenly guessed that Beth Barker was a part of the contract hit all the time that she was working on the special prosecution team."

"OMG," is all Vanessa could say.

"And after Eddie killed 'Black Widow Beth'—as we started calling her—he got a search warrant for Beth's house from Judge Carbon and went out with a swat team to arrest her husband, Francisco Montes. They surrounded the house, broke down the door, and found Francisco dead in their upstairs bedroom. The coroner said he died from three gunshots in the back of his head, 9mm. They were from Beth's Beretta, the one from her desk drawer, when Eddie killed her downtown. Also, at Beth's home, the swat team found a complete layout of my house from the county clerk, a sketch of this apartment and visitor parking right below, and a complete diagram of the Chico Gringo Ranch. I also think that guy Beth wanted me to interview, I forget his name, was in cahoots with her. Beth didn't know I had a CIA source to check him out and didn't know that I'd heard from you!"

Vanessa asked, "So she had an unknown partner as well?"

"Yes, that's my gut feeling! Beth Barker was, in fact, the El Paso plant that led the whole assassination team. They found fresh DNA evidence at the hunting lodge in Manitoba, which is fifty-three miles from the border check point, where Beth murdered the two Canadian officers. Forensics found that the same gun used in that double murder matched Beth's 9 mm she died with. This confirms that she was there when they all received their instructions to kill me and the whole prosecution team. But I saved the best for last." Steven smiled and continued, "They also found unidentified DNA in semen stains in Beth's bedroom sheets, which were found in the laundry room. The DNA was recent, like within the last three days . . . and it was *not* the DNA of her husband, Francisco!" Steven was finished with Black Widow Beth Barker. "Enough of them—it's over! So, to that end, Vanessa, you're my life and my love, and you're going to be my wife!"

She stood and again directed her dazzling sunshine smile at Steven. "Why, Steven Josef Vandorol, is that a proposal?"

CHAPTER 28

Steven Vandorol, special prosecutor and deputy district attorney of the 65th Judicial District stood before a podium in the grand jury room at the El Paso County Courthouse in downtown El Paso to give his opening remarks: "Ladies and gentlemen of the grand jury, Chief El Paso District Judge Kathy Carbon." Steven paused, looked over to the judge sitting on the elevated bench of her district court, nodded, and said, "Good morning, Your Honor."

She nodded back in acknowledgement as Steven continued, "Chief Judge Carbon has empaneled you, ladies and gentlemen, as the secret grand jury of the 65th Judicial District Court to hear all the evidence to be presented and then, upon your majority vote, either to issue the superseded bill of indictment or decline to issue by 'no bill to issue.' Do you all understand your office and duty as grand jurors?"

All were nodding in the affirmative as Steven continued, "If anyone does not understand my question or is unwilling to serve as a grand juror, please let me and the court know right now as all further proceedings will be under oath and taken down by a certified court reporter." Steven paused, again nodded at Judge Carbon, and said, "Ladies and gentlemen of the grand jury, would you please rise and raise your right hand?"

The entire grand jury panel, all thirty-five grand jurors, El Paso County, Texas, residents and owners of real estate in El Paso County, rose from their seats in Judge Carbon's courtroom gallery and raised their right hands. Steven looked over the gallery to make sure all were standing. He paused a moment and then looked over to the judge, nodded, and said, "Your Honor."

Judge Carbon looked as pretty as ever; Steven noted. Wearing a full black robe, she rose from her seat, raised her right hand, and said, "Ladies and gentlemen of this special El Paso County and great state of Texas grand jury, please all raise your hands. Do you solemnly swear to discharge your duties as grand jurors . . . so help you God? Your answer will be in the affirmative, 'I do.'"

In unison, all said, "I do!"

Still standing, the judge addressed the panel: "You have all now been sworn and empaneled as a secret grand jury, and from this moment forward, you are not to discuss these proceedings with anyone else whatsoever except those in this courtroom right now. You may all be seated." Judge Carbon then looked to Steven. "Mr. Vandorol?" She smiled and sat down.

Steven smiled right back, rose from his chair, walked back to the podium, grabbed both sides with his hands, surveyed the seated panel, paused a moment, looked at the judge, and said, "Thank you, Your Honor, I'm privileged to be here before you . . . I'd like to first introduce my co-counsel, Mr. North Anderson, first assistant district attorney to the district attorney, 65th district, Mr. Ernesto Luis Martinez." He looked over to the counsel table and gestured to where North Anderson sat with his hands folded before him. "North, would you please stand?"

North Anderson rose from his chair, looked at Steven, smiled, nodded, looked at Judge Carbon, and nodded toward her as well. He looked out at the grand jury, smiled again, raised his right hand, and sat back down.

Steven, still standing at the podium, said, "Thank you, Mr. Anderson. I would also like to introduce my law partner, Vanessa Carson, seated next to Mr. Anderson, also my co-counsel in this momentous case, as Ms. Beth Barker, a former member of our prosecution team, is unable to further participate. Would you please stand, Ms. Carson?"

Vanessa, also beautiful as ever, stood, smiled her radiant smile at the jurors, nodded to Judge Carbon, and sat back down.

Steven continued, "I also want to acknowledge and introduce my good friend, Major G. Jack Reacher who joined the special prosecution as the prosecution team's liason with Major General John Nicholson, Texas Adjutant General, the Texas Attorney General's and Governor's office."

"In that position, Major Reacher coordinates the security of the Texas-Mexico border with our own Texas Rangers, the Texas National Guard and federal forces at Fort Bliss and Biggs Army Air Field. Major Reacher is also currently the brigade commander of 3rd Cavalry's Apache helicopter group. As such, Major Reacher will be our district attorney, Mr. Ernesto Luis

Martinez's and this special prosecutions' military enforcement arm under direct command of our Texas governor, the Honorable Greg Abbott."

Steven looked to the counsel table. "Major Reacher, would you please stand?"

Major G. Jack Reacher stood and nodded to Judge Carbon, then looked at the grand jurors, smiled, raised his right hand, and sat back down.

The major was in full formal army dress uniform. He was an imposing figure that looked like he could have been a running back for the Dallas Cowboys. Tall, about six four, two hundred and thirty pounds, handsome, with piercing blue eyes, Major Reacher looked like a young Roger Staubach, the Heisman Trophy winner at the Naval Academy and later all-time most prolific quarterback with the Dallas Cowboys.

Major Reacher had played football at West Point where he *was* an All-American quarterback, and remembered Steven as a freshman cadet running back whose knee injury ended his football playing days.

Steven smiled at Major Reacher, nodded at Judge Carbon, turned to the grand jury panel, and began, "Ladies and gentlemen of the grand jury, you are entrusted at this moment in the history of our beloved United States of America, and our beloved great state of Texas to guard and save our Constitution and the rule of law, which is separating all of us from another civil war . . . a second civil war . . . this one against our own federal government based in Washington, DC, Denver, Los Angeles, New York City, and Chicago."

Steven paused, looked around the room, and continued: "A federal government that has been infiltrated by radical Muslim Islamist terrorists and communists, encouraged, allowed, appointed by, and aided and abetted by the president of the United States himself . . . Barack Hussein Obama." Steven paused again, glanced at his co-counsel North Anderson—who nodded in agreement—took a deep breath, and continued: "We will show you all the evidence that has been accumulated over the last year since the original indictment was issued against the Alvarado defendants, father, Alberto, and his son, Ricardo Alvarado, and other co-defendants and co-conspirators related to the sale of fraudulent insurance annuities, which is the largest fraud prosecution in Texas history."

Steven looked out over the grand jury panel and took a drink from a bottle of water before continuing: "However, the evil and criminal activities of the Alvarado defendants, father, Alberto, and his son, Ricardo Alvarado, and other co-defendants, pale in comparison to those who have committed treason against our, *your* United States of America."

The entire courtroom was totally quiet and very still. Dead silence. You could have heard a pin drop.

Steven replaced the lid on the bottle and put it on the lectern. "My co-counsel and I will present evidence to you, irrefutable evidence of treason by the president of the United States, the former attorney general, and the former secretary of state *and* current nominee for president of the Democratic Party.

"In this special prosecution and by the superseded indictment, you, the grand jury representing the people of the great state of Texas, will enforce the rule of law of this land and the Constitution that provides that it will be treason, under Article 3, Section 3 of the Constitution of the United States, which provides, and I'm reading verbatim, 'Treason against the United States, shall consist only in levying War against them, or in adhering to their Enemies, *giving them Aid and Comfort*. No Person shall be convicted of Treason unless on the Testimony of two Witnesses to the same overt Act, or on Confession in open Court.'

"Under the Constitution of the United States of America, you will indict all the defendants, including the president, for *treason* as defined in our Constitution, the ultimate law of our land, and for conspiracy to commit treason, for giving our sworn enemies—Muslim radical terrorists, both foreign nationals and those in our own government, aid, comfort, money, and financing. All the defendants, especially the president, have, as the Constitution provides, 'Adhered to our sworn enemies, *giving our sworn enemies aid and comfort*' . . . and financing, money, as the Alvarado family, father, Alberto, and son, Roberto Alvarado, have done . . . and can and will *prove* to this grand jury, you all, ladies and gentlemen of this panel, by several credible secret testimony, irrefutable documentary and forensic evidence, *and* the testimony of our surprise witness—the Judas in the White House.

"Ladies and gentlemen of the grand jury, let me simplify this prosecution for you! Ms. Carson and Mr. Anderson are now providing you with the fifty-seven-page superseded and amended indictment for your information and review. Please don't be frightened by this massive document . . . our prosecution team has worked on it for months, and it's a revision and amendment of a previous indictment filed almost three years ago.

"Well, ladies and gentlemen of the grand jury, please don't be mad at me, or our prosecution team for providing you with this massive document filled with legalese and verbiage that sometimes even we lawyers don't understand! Goodness knows our own legal assistants are upset at us for all this legal mumbo-jumbo!"

Most in the grand jury panel were nodding and smiling as Steven continued, "Briefly, the essence of this special prosecution is as follows: First, there were the Alvarados, father, Alberto, and his son, Ricardo Alvarado, two of the richest men in both the United States of America and the Federal Republic of Mexico—the original corruptors, I'll call them—because all the money they had accumulated through their worldly activities wasn't enough!

"The two men became addicted to money and the lust, power, and control that money brought. It was their aphrodisiac! Their addiction! So, the two men devised a scheme to make even more money—the sale of fraudulent insurance annuities—a giant Ponzi scheme—and corrupted a legitimate power and electric company and two law firms to do their evil bidding.

"This corruption reached all the way into the current admistration and White House, which willingly participated in that evil and eventually even furthered it. All this ended in treason by 'adhering to our sworn enemies and giving them aid and comfort.'

"You now have before you a fifty-seven-page indictment that alleges 153 separate counts and criminal violations among all defendants and co-conspirators, both named and unnamed, alleging criminal acts, including fraud, money laundering, drug and weapons smuggling and trafficking, white slavery, aiding and abetting Muslim Islamic terrorism, and the most egregious and evil count—treason—against our United States of America, the Constitution of our sovereign republic, and you, ladies and gentlemen, us, me, and all the people of our great country!"

"Ladies and gentlemen of the grand jury, Mr. North Anderson will now review the evidence accumulated in over four years of extensive investigation by our El Paso Police Department, Chief of Police Edward Egen, and our own Texas Rangers." Steven paused, looked over to North Anderson, and said, "Mr. Anderson?"

North Anderson rose again and walked to the podium, passing Steven as he walked to the counsel table. He faced the grand jury panel, squared his shoulders, took a deep breath, and looked over all seated in the courtroom. North Anderson was an imposing sight as he stood tall behind the podium. At almost six foot four inches and around two hundred and forty pounds, with broad shoulders and muscular arms, he was dressed impeccably in a charcoal gray suit, snow white shirt, and red, white, and blue stripped tie. *North resembles ESPN football announcer Lynn Swan*, Steven thought as he passed North going to his seat.

North made his remarks: "In addition to the corruption and crimes perpetrated by the Alvarados and various defendants, we face a radical Muslim terrorist threat and war unlike anything we've ever faced in our history . . . or in the history of Western civilization. "First, let's examine a few basics: When did the threat to us start?"

North Anderson paused, looked around the panel, and continued, "Many will say September 11, 2001. The answer, as far as the United States is concerned, is 1979, twenty-two years prior to September 2001, with *all* the attacks made by Muslim men in their twenties or thirties: Embassy hostages, 1979; Beirut, Lebanon Embassy, 1983; Beirut, Lebanon Marine

Barracks, 1983; Lockerbie, Scotland, Pan-Am flight to New York, 1988; first New York Trade Center attack, 1993; Dharan, Saudi Arabia, Khobar Towers Military Complex, 1996; Nairobi, Kenya, US Embassy, 1998; Dares Salaam, Tanzania, US Embassy, 1998; Aden, Yemen, USS Cole, 2000; New York World Trade Center, 2001; the "field" in Pennsylvania, 2001; and the Pentagon, 2001."

North Anderson paused again, glanced at Steven, then at the judge, and looked straight at the grand jury panel seated before him as he continued, "During the period from 1981 to 2001, there were 7,581 Muslim terrorist attacks worldwide . . . and on September 11, 2001, almost 3,000 Americans died as a result of four hijacked airliners; 25,000 of our fellow Americans were injured as two airliners destroyed the Twin Towers World Trade Center in New York City, which were the two tallest sky scrapers in the world. The third slammed into the Pentagon in Washington, DC, while the fourth was downed in a Pennsylvania field when brave passengers retook the plane from the hijackers with the now famous saying, 'Let's roll,' by American hero, Todd Beamer . . . God rest his soul!"

North Anderson paused, solemn, and closed his eyes for a moment. He opened them again, looked up, and then said, "God Bless them all . . . may they all rest in peace."

North paused again, wiped his eyes, and continued, "The September 11, 2001, attack was carried out by nineteen Muslim men in their twenties and thirties."

North paused again for the third time, looked around to the fresco behind Judge Carbon of the blindfolded statue of justice, holding a sword in one hand and the balanced scale of reason in the other. He swept his right hand over it and continued, "As the blindfolded statue of the archangel Gabriel shows, his right hand has the sword of righteousness . . . and this prosecution and your true bill of indictment is the people's sword of righteousness."

CHAPTER 29

"You and your team of incompetents have failed once again," Gravelly Voice said on the speaker to four assassins slouched around the table. Two were still sipping Stolichnaya, the best Russian vodka, while another was on his third shot of the best tequila in Mexico, Hornitos, and the fourth, as always, drank hot tea from his gold-inlaid china cup sitting on an even more delicate, scrolled saucer.

The four at the table said nothing as Gravelly Voice continued, his hushed voice seething with anger: "You, Colonel Lemev, as the leader of the assassination team, have been paid millions but have failed miserably, the superseded bill of indictment was issued and arrest warrants are likely forthcoming."

The four still said nothing.

General Wang Xiangsui, sitting comfortably in the big leather easy chair holding a folded newspaper in his lap and drinking from a large bottle of distilled mineral water, unfolded the newspaper very dramatically, so all could see as Gravelly Voice continued: "This hit contract is now withdrawn and terminated." Gravelly Voice paused a beat and then continued, "And this cell number is dead." As was the line.

Total silence.

"I'm glad the Muslim *pryamaya kishka* didn't ask for a refund," Colonel Lemev laughed as all in the room broke out in laughter as well. Even the two usually serious Chinese Communists wore amused smiles as Lemev continued, "And we can talk freely now as all our Muslim *friends* left to join all the other cockroaches assembling in Mexico."

Ward Powell, sitting on Lemev's right, said, "So, Lemev, how much more did you get from the Alvarados?" He glanced at Uri, also sitting at the table across from him, who nodded so imperceptibly that only the general noticed.

"Up yours, Powell!" Lemev answered.

"Gentlemen, gentlemen, please," General Xiangsui said. "Our moment in the history of the world is upon us." He paused for dramatic effect, and his ugly, fat tongue flicked out as he continued, "The superseded indictment bill, published in the Wednesday, August third edition of the *Dallas Morning Clarion*, will not only unite the American people against their own government, but against *all* Muslims in America. As far as the Muslim cockroaches are concerned, the old Chinese proverb that the enemy of my enemy is my friend, no longer applies." He chuckled and burped.

Powell was still slurring his words, his nose still bandaged. "So, General, when is *our* big moment in history?"

The general interrupted, "Mr. Powell, let me remind you that I predicted September 11, 2001, when almost five thousand of your countrymen died, in *my* book *Unrestricted Warfare: China's Master Plan to Destroy America*, which I co-authored with my partner Colonel Liang." The general paused, looked around the room, and continued, "Who do you think was behind it and orchestrated that carnage, Mr. Powell?"

All remained silent.

General Xiangsui, with some effort, raised his obese body from the recliner, straightened his oversized jacket that had ridden up past his large stomach, threw the folded newspaper in the middle of the table, and said, "Colonel Liang, my friend, are you ready for a relaxing dinner at Café Central? My driver will take us."

As the two were strolling out, arm in arm, Colonel Lemev unfolded the newspaper, and, together, those remaining read the headline news article...

The Dallas Morning Clarion

Dallas's Leading Newspaper, $3.00[1]
Dallas, Texas, Wednesday, August 3, 2016

State of Texas v. Washington, DC
Texas Declares War on Federal Government

El Paso, TX. The State of Texas has declared war on the federal government of the United States of America based in Washington, District of Columbia, by superseded bill of indictment in Cause No. 123456, and filed this past Monday in the District Court of El Paso County, State of Texas.

This amended indictment supersedes the indictment previously filed on October 21, 2014, against the Alvarado family: Mexican national multi-billionaire Alberto Alvarado, father, and son, billionaire El Paso resident, Ricardo Alvarado, primary defendants; El Paso Power and Electric, LLC; Henderson Lane, Washington, DC, law firm; and various other defendants, but it now expands to indict the president of the United States, Barack Hussein Obama, his administration, former attorney general of the United States, the Obama Justice Department, and a list of several Muslim terrorist organizations and individual Muslims, both American citizens and foreign nationals, who financed, aided, and abetted radical Muslims nationally and internationally, all listed on the State Department's list of terrorist organizations, including the Muslim Brotherhood, Hamas, Hezbollah, the Holy Land Foundation for Relief and

---

1   See Author's Note—Appendix of this novel

Development, Council on American-Islamic Relations (CAIR), and other named individual and entity defendants.

The superseded bill of indictment names President Barack Hussein Obama, former Attorney General Eric Holder, Obama-appointed Czars, and Obama administration appointees, the heads of AFT and Homeland Security, as indicted co-conspirators in aiding and abetting radical Muslim terrorist activities and worldwide Islamic terrorism and Muslim Caliphate.

Most prominent in the non-federal government defendants listed in the indictment are the Alvarado family, Mexican national multi-billionaire Alberto Alvarado, father, and son, multi-billionaire El Paso resident, Ricardo Alvarado, who along with an unindicted co-conspirator, George Soros, are alleged to have committed treason by aiding, abetting, and financing radical terrorist Muslim Jihad, or Holy War, against the national security of the United States and further conspiracy with the other defendants herein in the 157 separate counts and criminal violations, as stated in the indictment, which has been sealed by the presiding judge, the Honorable Kathy Carbon, chief district judge.

The superseded bill of indictment now charges all the defendants named with now 157 separate counts and criminal violations among all defendants, named co-conspirators and various unnamed co-conspirators, with criminal violations including fraud; money laundering; drug and weapons violations; smuggling and trafficking; white slavery; aiding and abetting and financing Muslim Islamic radical terrorism activities; and treason and conspiring to commit treason against the national security of the United States and the states of Texas, Arizona, New Mexico, and Oklahoma.

In related news to the special prosecution and superseded bill of indictment, 65th District Attorney Ernesto Martinez told the *Dallas Morning Clarion* that arrest warrants were likely to be issued for all defendants named in the superseded bill of indictment in the four state jurisdictions of the states of Texas, New Mexico, Arizona, and Oklahoma that joined the state of Texas in the filing of this El Paso County, Texas, criminal indictment.

The warrants, District Attorney Ernie Martinez said, would be executed in Texas by officers of the Texas Rangers and Texas National Guard upon such defendants that are apprehended in Texas, all to be incarcerated in the Texas correctional facilities at Huntsville, all units; La Tuna Federal Prison, outside of El Paso; and Ft. Bliss Military Reservation Prison. All defendants receiving death penalties will be executed at the Allan B. Pollunsky Unit, Texas's men's death row.

"I am also saddened to report that Ms. Beth Barker, assistant district attorney leading our drug enforcement unit and valuable member of the special prosecution, was found dead in her office last week of self-inflicted gunshot wounds that were classified as a suicide," Martinez said. She is survived by her husband, El Paso real estate developer Francisco Montes.

"Above all, we will maintain the integrity of our borders with Mexico and enforce the Constitution of the United States and all our laws regarding our sovereignty," said El Paso Police Chief Edward "Eddie" Egen.

District Attorney Martinez also reported that a preliminary injunction to close the border of Texas to the Republic of Mexico has been granted. The Texas-Mexico border is forthwith closed and sealed as of 12:01 a.m., Monday, August 1st, 2016.

A full hearing on the merits of the injunction will likely be set in January, 2017, by Chief Judge Kathy Carbon, due to a very crowded hearing docket, Angie Timmons, El Paso County District Court clerk said yesterday.

General John Nicholas, commanding officer of the Texas National Guard, said that his command would carry out the orders of the governor of the state of Texas. When contacted by the *Dallas Morning Clarion*, the governor's chief of staff had no comment.

Representatives of the Muslim organizations and individuals named in the superseded bill of indictment could be not be reached.

All other federal government defendants named in the superseded bill of indictment refused to acknowledge Texas jurisdiction and the president's chief of staff stated that the solicitor general of the United States would be travelling to El Paso to contest Texas's jurisdiction over duly elected or appointed federal government officials or employees.

When contacted by the *Dallas Morning Clarion*, spokeswoman for Democratic presidential candidate Hillary Clinton, Huma Amadin, had no comment to this Texas superseded bill of indictment.

Due to the momentous nature and consequences of this criminal prosecution as a result of the superseded bill of indictment, it is reproduced in this news story verbatim and only those portions regarding criminal acts were allowed to be published by chief judge of the 65th District Court of El Paso County, State of Texas, the Honorable Kathy Carbon, district judge presiding. All that follows is verbatim.

The superseded bill of indictment has been redacted, in that portions of it are not shown in the best interests of national security of the United States, District Attorney Ernesto Martinez said yesterday at his press conference in El Paso.

The superseded bill of indictment follows with redacted portions not shown.

CHAPTER 30

"Shall we summarize, my angel?" Steven asked the love of his life.

Steven Vandorol and Vanessa Carson were standing in the sand, barefoot, facing each other and holding hands on the shore of the Rio Grande flowing gently south in Santa Elena Canyon.

Ten feet away from the couple stood Eddie and Andi Egen and Major G. Jack Reacher and Joan Reacher, the witnesses. They were all standing barefoot in the sand in the late afternoon in Santa Elena Canyon of Big Bend. High Sierra Ponce limestone walls jutted straight up from the Rio Grande, providing majestic walls to the good Lord's East Texas Cathedral.

"Sure, it's already in our hearts and minds, isn't it?" Vanessa answered, smiling her sunshine smile, looking directly into Steven's eyes. She looked astonishingly beautiful in her white cotton dress that flattered her figure.

She was stunning as Steven gaped at her. Goodness clearly shone on her precious face, which had just a hint of makeup. Her honey-blonde hair was pinned up with delicate white posies. Her perfect lips, with soft pink lipstick, were in a sensual pout. Her eyes were open wide: trusting, loving, perfect mirrors of her good heart and soul. She was radiant and fully in sunshine-mode, even at dusk at the shore as the sun set slowly behind the horizon. Both her eyes twinkled mischievously, reflecting her wonderful humor, serenity, peace, happiness, and joy. Her eyes reflected perfectly in Steven's own eyes, like mirrors, as he gazed upon her lovingly.

"I will love you forever and always, my princess, my angel bride, Vanessa. And I will remain absolutely vigilant against any rest of the world intrusion or interference, especially from my own addictions, or demons. And I will never take anything for granted in our upward progression, till death do us part. Then we will be joined forever in paradise with the Father, our Lord, and the Son, our Savior, Jesus Christ, who gave His earthly life so that we may live."

The brilliant yellow-orange sun was just setting. It was a spectacular Texas sunset, the colors magnificent, brilliant oranges, reds, and golden yellows, all sparkling on billowing clouds in the vast azure blue sky.

And under the sunset sky, with the good Lord and Jesus Christ above and in their hearts, Steven and Vanessa held each other's hands and looked directly in each other's eyes.

As she looked up into his eyes, Steven made his vow and commitment to her: "My promise and commitment to you, my angel bride, is that I, Steven, with the good Lord in my heart, saved by the Lord and by the blood of Jesus Christ for this day, having survived on this earth only by His grace, take you, Vanessa Rose, to be my earthly wedded wife, partner, and friend. I do so with pride, passion, respect, trust, and tenderness . . . to grow in that love, growing each and every day in my heart in our upward progression, in all humility, honestly sharing truth with you all the time, till death do us part. Then I'll join with you in faith and spirit in the Lord and Christ's presence." Steven took the ring from his pocket, still holding her left hand, and placed the simple white gold band on her ring finger and lightly kissed her hand.

Steven wore white linen slacks and a long-sleeved, tan linen shirt, sleeves rolled casually to his forearms. Holding her hands, smiling broadly, and looking directly into her beautiful hazel eyes, Steven listened as Vanessa made her vows: "My promise and commitment to you, Steven, my love, is that I, Vanessa Rose, with the good Lord in my heart, also saved for this day by the Lord and by the blood of the Lamb, Jesus Christ, and having survived on this earth only by His grace, take you, Steven Josef, to be my earthly wedded husband, partner, and friend. I do so with pride, passion, respect, trust, and tenderness . . . to grow in that love, growing each and every day in my heart in our upward progression, in all humility, honestly sharing truth with you all the time, till death do us part. Then I'll join with you in faith and spirit in the Lord and Christ's presence." She then placed her father's gold wedding ring on Steven's left hand.

And in that moment, with the good Lord above and in their hearts, the high limestone walls jutting up from the water to their right, and the deep blue Madera and Carmen Mountains to the left, Steven Vandorol and Vanessa Carson became husband and wife. Their labor of love and individual transformation was complete, their individual prayers answered. They were one.

The good Lord was in their hearts and blessing their union as partners. They were just as the two dolphins in the picture swimming in perfect synchronicity ahead of the tramp steamer, which symbolizes a world of chaos, conflict, turmoil, and death.

And then their friends, Eddie and Andi, and G. Jack and Joan, joined them, and all holding hands in a small circle together, said the Lord's Prayer in unison.

As they finished, Steven Vandorol looked at his wife. "Mrs. Vandorol, I love you always and am your Steven forever." And then he kissed his bride.

Eddie was already holding a flute of champagne. "Here's to Mr. and Mrs. Vandorol, Steven and Vanessa." Jack handed flutes to the happy couple and their guests.

And all toasted the newlyweds.

Following the toast and congratulations, three couples walked toward the clearing in the canyon. Some fifty yards away sat an AH-64D Apache Longbow attack helicopter, the United States' most advanced attack helicopter. *Airship Genesis* was stenciled on both sides of the elegant and majestic giant dragonfly. And in white shoe polish lettering was the phrase "Just Married."

CHAPTER 31

Vanessa and Steven were taking time just for themselves. It was their honeymoon. After a perfect lunch of huevos rancheros, chorizo, menudo, and flour tortillas, the two newlyweds took a drive to the Wyler Aerial Tramway at Franklin Mountain State Park to ride the tram up to Ranger Peak. Their marriage before the good Lord above and their upward progression of love gave them peace, serenity, happiness, and joy, and they were celebrating their love on their honeymoon.

Steven and Vanessa, holding hands and sitting side by side on the aerial cable car, rode to the top of the peak on a 2,600-foot steel cable. The chain was clickety clacking like steel tank tracks on pavement.

The view of El Paso and Juarez was breathtaking. The Santo Christo Mountains of Mexico, hulking colossuses like huge, dead dinosaurs, black, gray, brown, and purple, stood in the distance as giant sentinels around the pass to the north, in Spanish, "El Paso Del Norte," Steven told his bride. The largest hulk towering above all the others had graffiti markings, not unlike the Hollywood sign over Los Angeles. This graffiti, in Spanish, said, "Juarez La Bibilia es la verdad viela," translated to "Juarez City, the Bible is the truth."

To the north was Fort Bliss, and into New Mexico the panorama was endless, with downtown El Paso just like a multi-colored Lego city scattered randomly on a silvery blanket. The colors were truly God's, the Ultimate Artist's palette of colors, as they shined by the sparkling Texas sunshine.

"Steven, this is our heaven on earth!" Vanessa said, drawing closer yet to Steven. "Let's always remember this moment in time, okay?" Vanessa's sunshine smile was more dazzling to Steven than the spectacular views and brilliant colors all around them as they rose to the top of Ranger Peak. "What a truly amazing view."

"Just wait till we get to the top," Steven said. "It's 5,632 feet—more than a mile high above sea level—and you can see the view of seven thousand square miles encompassing three states and two nations, a perfect vista of the vastness and stark beauty of the American Southwest!"

"Steven, you are such a dreamer . . . and artist. I just love your lyrical descriptions." Vanessa was still smiling at him.

"But all of it pales in comparison to your smile . . . and I'm full of bull, too, with a lot of really useless information." Steven laughed as the aerial car was drawing near the peak.

The ride up had been magnificent as Steven and Vanessa cuddled close, totally awed by the view. The cable car lurched to a stop, and the cabin attendant walked to the door. Steven and Vanessa, still holding hands, also rose and followed her.

"It'll be just a minute before the door will open," the cabin attendant said. "The door lock monitoring system has to be turned off at the base station."

"How does that work?" Practical Vanessa, ever curious, turned her dazzling smile to the attendant.

She was glad to answer. "Well, the double doors open outward once the system is turned off with the main controls at the base station below," she said, as the door made a loud click. "Then it just swings outward." The attendant gave it a hard push, and the double doors swung out over the concrete platform. "Watch your step." The attendant motioned for them to exit the cable car.

But Vanessa wasn't quite done: "So, once the system is turned off at the base station below, anybody can just shove it open with a hard push?"

"Yes, ma'am," she answered. "We're all about safety and a quick and easy exit once we get here to the top!" The attendant was smiling proudly back at Vanessa.

Vanessa had the last word: "As long as the system is not turned off at the base station below while the cable car is mid-air, right?"

"Right!" Steven answered for the attendant as he stepped off and held his hand out for the love of his life.

"Thank you for the explanation," Vanessa said to the attendant. The newlyweds stepped off the cable car, both smiling brightly. The attendant waved, smiling also, as Vanessa hugged Steven.

"Wow, that was so much fun!" Vanessa exclaimed.

Steven agreed as he led Vanessa on the accessible ramp and concrete walkway that led to the paved grounds of the observation deck where they could have a three-hundred-sixty-degree view of the panorama below.

Vanessa, dragging Steven by the hand, said, "Let's check out the high-power binoculars." She was so excited.

They dropped in quarters, and the binoculars came to focus. With their eyes on the lenses, both looked around in awe, speechless. After several minutes of negotiating the 'binoculars, Vanessa said, "This is heaven, Steven. The good Lord's grace is on us right now." She was tearing up as her bright hazel eyes glistened with moisture.

Steven walked slowly to her, hugged her, and said, "I love you, Vanessa Rose, forever and always, with all my heart, body, mind, and soul. I am your Steven forever." He kissed Vanessa Vandorol, his forever and always bride, with the good Lord above and all of El Paso, Texas, spread out below.

———

A black limousine slowly pulled up to the entrance of the Café Central restaurant in downtown El Paso. The limo stopped. It was a black Mercedes limousine with all the chrome painted black. All that black, and the black one-way glass of the windows, gave the car a sinister look. The doorman, dressed like a four-star general, stepped to the curb and opened the door. Steven told Charlie, their driver, to be back in a couple of hours.

Vanessa Vandorol stepped out on the sidewalk and said to the doorman, "How are you, Louie?" She was smiling brightly.

The doorman knew Vanessa very well. "Fine, Mrs. Vandorol." He was smiling from ear-to-ear as well. "And how are you, Mr. Vandorol?"

Steven followed his bride. "Great, Louie! Couldn't be better!"

The front of the restaurant was magnificent, like a dream of times long ago in the early 1940s. The awning, extending to the main entrance, was a black inverted half-moon with ocean wave fringes to the entrance. Large, white block numerals adorned the front with "4444" in Broadway Elite, a popular pre-war Art Deco style to indicate 4444 North Oregon Street. The entire building, two stories, was light pink with pre-war architecture. Surrounding the building was a one-foot-high pink wall holding a moat of desert flowers and dwarf palm trees. The words "Café Central" appeared in huge black script, and above that, in hot-pink neon on a glistening chrome background, the words "El Paso" were written in the same style as the numerals.

Steven put his arm around his bride's shoulder and led her to the restaurant's huge double doors. The smiling doorman held one door open to let the happy couple in, ushering them into the magnificent dining room. An explosion of beautiful colors flooded the immense room. It was a sensual delight, with soft, subdued lights and shimmering tans, yellows, greens, and pinks.

The couple took in marvelous palm trees, marble columns, and thick carpets—all plush pink. Sparkling white linens were on the tables, all altars to crystal glasses, sterling silver settings, and gold vases, with live, luscious flowers of every color of the spectrum. Tuxedoed waiters and bus boys in starched shirts, black bow ties, skin-tight black slacks, and black cummerbunds scurried about. The aromas, especially of chile peppers and garlic, flooded the senses.

Steven was all eyes. "My love, this place looks like a scene from the old movie *Casablanca*."

"You got it!" Vanessa smiled brightly. "The piano player's name should be Sam."

Steven laughed. Tonight especially, he felt like a silly teenager. "And Louie should be Sidney Greenstreet, the fat guy in *Casablanca*."

Although the room was immense, the myriad of columns and palm trees made each table a private party. Tony, their favorite waiter, was now the maître d' and led Steven and Vanessa to their favorite table for two.

"My, you look wonderful, Mrs. Vandorol," Tony said to Vanessa, seating her at their favorite table. "Congratulations to the newlyweds, Mr. and Mrs. Vandorol . . . Ustedes son Señor y Señora Esteban Vandorol, novios casados."

Vanessa smiled. "Thank you, Tony. You're so sweet, especially when you say it in Spanish."

"Absolutely stunning, Mrs. Vandorol!" Steven said as he admired his angel bride. Vanessa directed her dazzling sunshine smile his way as she sat down.

She looked more brilliant than the first time Steven saw her in his office in El Paso almost nine months ago. In this moment, he fell in love with Vanessa all over again. But this time, Vanessa was his forever and always friend, partner, wife, and soul mate. Steven continued to admire his bride. She was wearing a red silk strapless cocktail dress cut to her knees. It fit her like a glove and enhanced her tiny, perfect figure.

"Thank you, my husband and law partner."

"The usual, Mr. and Mrs. Vandorol?" Tony was beaming, standing tall in his black tuxedo. "Or champagne cocktails?"

"Champagne cocktails, absolutely, Tony!" Steven was wearing his navy-blue sport coat, starched, snow white button-down shirt, and red, white, and blue stripped tie with tailored tan slacks and his favorite boots.

"Very good," Tony said. "Your waiter this evening will be Jorge."

"Thank you, Tony."

Steven looked at his bride and said, "I think I'll call you 'Sigh' tonight."

"Why 'Sigh'?"

"Because you are so beautiful, it makes me sigh."

"You can call me 'Sigh' tonight. I like it. Especially the way you say it, Steven. But I really like 'Mrs. Vandorol' much better." She paused a beat, then continued, "How do you say, 'Congratulations to the newlyweds,' in Spanish, my Steven?"

Steven answered in Spanish immediately, "Como se dice, felicitacion a los recien casodos, en espanol, mi Esteban."

Vanessa laughed out loud at the very literal translation of her question. She fanned herself with her right hand and said, "It makes me hot when you talk in Spanish!"

———

The evening whizzed by way too fast. A lush feast of exceptional food, drink, jokes, and boisterous laughter gave way to subdued conversation and ended with dessert: three layered ice cream cake with a cherry right on top.

Vanessa and Steven paid no attention to anyone except each other. They were at a private party all their own. They played and flirted more and more as the evening wore on. Steven had not noticed, but the restaurant had thinned out. The tuxedoed waiters were serving after-dinner drinks. The couple still sat close, almost as one, their heads leaning closer and closer.

Vanessa put her warm little hand gently on Steven's leg and asked innocently, "Why don't we go to our room for after-dinner drinks?" The newlyweds had a suite at the El Paso Del Norte Hotel in downtown El Paso, not far from the restaurant—a mere block away.

"I was just about to suggest that," Steven answered and quickly signed the check. He placed his left hand on hers, gathered it up, and rose, still holding her hand. His excitement was building.

She had another dazzling smile for him. She rose and slid close to his side. Holding hands, together they ambled to the entrance, oblivious of all.

Louie asked, "Everything in order, Mr. Vandorol?"

"Couldn't be better, Louie." Steven smiled and winked. "Everything was wonderful and getting better!"

Louie straightened his shoulders and replied, "Excellent. Excellent. Please come back soon." He went ahead and led them to the door.

"We will, very soon," Steven said, walking out and squeezing the tiny hand in his palm. Vanessa squeezed back.

The four-star general opened the door. They walked out under the black awning and back into the present, to the warm El Paso air, the smells and traffic noises of horns honking, gasoline and garbage odors lingering.

As they walked out of the restaurant holding hands and laughing, Charlie was standing by the rear door of the limo. The sinister black Mercedes limo was at the curb, motor idling. He let go of Vanessa's hand and slid his arm around her waist. Hers slid around his, but neither said anything. Both were smiling. The two walked leisurely to the limo. Charlie opened the door for them, "Good evening, Mr. and Mrs. Vandorol. I hope you enjoyed your dinner."

"Why yes, Charlie, it was delicious," Vanessa answered and slipped in. Steven followed. It was quiet again and dark. Only the quiet hum of the air conditioner could be heard.

It was a very sumptuous limo. There was a bottle of champagne on ice and two crystal flutes and two silver vases by the rear window, each holding one yellow rose.

Charlie turned back and asked, "Where to, Mr. and Mrs. Vandorol?"

"Oh, just drive around and show us the sights of El Paso," Steven answered, winking at Vanessa, who smiled brightly back at him...

"Sure thing." He replied.

Vanessa was giggling under her breath. "Oh, so you want to see the sights," she whispered with a glint in her eye." She pressed a button on the panel to her left. A whirring sound emitted as the opaque glass partition between the front and back seats slowly rose. With another button and a quiet buzz, a black velour curtain slid all the way across. The two were completely alone. They could look out, but no one could look in. They were completely alone in a quiet ocean of black velvet. Now, with dark tinted windows and the divider up, it was like Vanessa and Steven were invisible to the whole world.

After pouring the champagne, Steven handed Vanessa hers, and together they toasted to their future "peace, serenity, happiness, and joy." The champagne was excellent, and they downed their champagne and set the glasses to the side. Vanessa kicked off her red high heels, revealing her very small, wonderfully milky white feet.

Steven took Vanessa's hand. "I love you with all my heart and soul. Forever and always." So, with love in his heart and passion in his eyes, he moved toward her for that very special kiss.

———

Almost an hour later, Vanessa lowered the divider and said, "Charlie, I think it's time to head to the hotel. We've seen enough." They laughed quietly to each other.

In mere minutes, the limo stopped. Charlie got out, came around, and opened their door. "Did you enjoy the sights, Mr. and Mrs. Vandorol?"

Steven winked. "Immensely!" His arm entwined his bride, and they walked to the hotel entrance, through the front door, and into the lobby. It was completely deserted. Steven saw the large clock with the roman numerals right above the elevator doors: 12:40 a.m.

"This truly is a beautiful hotel!" Vanessa said as they walked arm in arm.

"Yes, I agree completely, and just wait until you see the suite." Two smiling faces hurried to the elevators with urgency. The door opened, and they stepped in. Their honeymoon suite was on the fifteenth floor of the high-rise hotel. In seconds, the door opened, and two newlyweds walked out from the elevator and down the hall.

Steven said, "Well, my love, here we are, the honeymoon suite!" He took out the key card and handed it to Vanessa. Almost without a pause, he lifted her into his arms. "Mrs. Vandorol, would you please open the door, so I can carry my bride over the threshold?"

Vanessa was smiling so brightly it nearly took Steven's breath away. She put the card in the slot, and Steven, carrying her with his back to the door, walked into their honeymoon suite.

The lights were dim and the view out the huge picture window of downtown El Paso and Juarez—the millions of sparkling, shimmering multicolored lights—was breathtaking! The bed had been turned down, plush robes were laid out, and champagne, Godiva chocolates, and two red roses in a crystal vase were on the table, compliments of the El Paso Del Norte Hotel.

Steven, still holding Vanessa in his arms, gently let her feet touch the floor. They embraced and kissed lightly. Steven gently put his hands on her shoulders and turned Vanessa around and began to slowly unzip her beautiful red dress . . .

———————

The next morning, a really bright sun woke them, and they felt like they were in El Paso heaven.

"Did you have a good sleep, my love?" Vanessa asked Steven.

"The sleep was great, and so was everything that came before!"

Vanessa blushed, but said, "Everything about last night was a dream come true. Now I'm hungry, and we have champagne, so why don't you order room service, with orange juice, and we'll have mimosas with our breakfast!" Vanessa jumped from the bed, grabbed one of the robes left out by the hotel staff, wrapped herself in it, and dashed to the bathroom.

Steven smiled and thanked the Lord that He had brought her into his life. Picking up the phone, he dialed the front desk. "Room Service, we would like a big jug of orange juice, a carafe of coffee, two Eggs Benedicts with lots of bacon, and a basket of pastries."

CHAPTER 32

"So, where have you been, Ward?" asked Colonel Lemev after he found Powell sitting in the kitchen of the safe house in Sunland Park. Powell was petting Ubiytsa laying by his feet, like a huge bale of hay, but with a big red tongue out, panting from the heat. "Have you just returned from almost a month of debauchery, drinking, and eating? I swear, Ward, I can't understand how you do it!"

"It's the big three: stamina, stamina, stamina!" Powell laughed, a lecherous smirk on his once again handsome face, as the bandage was off his nose and bruises healed. "And prodigious amounts of the products of the great American free enterprise system gone wrong: Viagra, Cialis, and Levitra for me . . . and coke, meth, trazodone, Rohypnol, ecstasy, crack, and heroin for the ladies." He was lying as usual. He wasn't about to tell Lemev that he got beaten up by a smaller Mexican, because he got caught in a compromising position with the man's' wife, that his two thugs he paid to abduct Vanessa were still in the hospital, and that his main 'secret source' on the inside of the prosecution was dead. *I'm gonna miss her, though, she was really a lot of fun . . . and so hot when she was on,* Powell thought, a wistful look in his glazed over eyes.

Colonel Lemev noticed, knew Powell was lying, but said, "Really, I thought you said you didn't need any of that stuff." Colonel Lemev paused, smiled. "It sounds like you're just another American addict!" Colonel Lemev was done with that subject. "What about the one contact you said was on *your* side?" Lemev paused and swallowed. He looked like he had just swallowed something rancid. "Will she betray Vandorol?" Lemev was lying. He knew that Beth Barker, whom he had recruited himself, was dead and that she had been the insider on the special prosecution team all along. *Ward Powell doesn't' know about all the fun I had with her, before he got there with our reinforcements, in the rustic cabin hidden in the dense forest near the US-Canadian border,* Lemev remembered most fondly.

"She already has!" Powell replied, lying again, a smug look on his handsome face. "She is an insider, and Vandorol is still distracted with his two main Achilles' heels, major whore dog that he and his buddy were in DC. He's still doing someone else's bidding, but this time for Eddie Egen, the police chief, just like he used to do for his older brother all his early life . . . and for his buddy in Washington, DC."

"Oh, yeah?" Lemev interrupted, tiring of Ward's droning. He wasn't making any sense. "What about Vandorol's new media stardom as the hero of all the American conservatives? He is like a fricking superhero in the Southwest, especially in Texas, with all the conservative media coverage and hype he is getting." Lemev paused again, looking at Powell. "Did you see the article they did about some book Steven wrote about his huge rise and fall back in the early 90s in the Sunbelt, Ward?"

"Yeah, I did! But it's just a bunch of meaningless hype!" Powell paused, his face now contorted into an ugly snarl. But he's nothing. I'm still going to have fun and watch him die a slow and ugly death."

Ward Powell, eyes shining and on fire, looked like Lucifer himself, Lemev thought.

"You better not underestimate him, Ward," Colonel Lemev said. "Steven Vandorol is the ultimate survivor. Just as the Chinese Commies say—" Changing the subject, he asked, "What about the ranch? Are we set with *our* plan?"

"Well, that Mexican on the Egen Ranch was really easy to turn. He is just another Mexican that money and drugs could buy." *Just like the two I turned to kidnap Vanessa,* he thought. "For that, he would betray his own mother! But he's a good actor. We, I, completely turned him, and everybody on the ranch, including Eddie Egen, are all completely clueless." Powell was really proud of himself.

Powell thought this would be the perfect time to appease General Xiangsui, who was throwing his massive weight around the whole assassination team and giving him a lot of crap. "Colonel Lemev, what would you think about asking Colonel Liang to lead the assassination team for the raid and killing spree that we're planning for the Egen ranch? After all, the stupid Muslims that made you a rich man beyond your wildest dreams, and your Washington, DC contacts, who actually ordered the hit, don't even know about Colonel Liang or General Xiangsui being right here in El Paso and running the whole show." Powell quickly winked at Lemev twice, imitating the fat Chinese general.

Colonel Lemev was thoughtful. "I don't know, Ward . . . I've got superiors in the KGB and Putin's buddies, who are all watching me." Lemev had a large ego and wanted to be a hero of Mother Russia, besides being a multi-millionaire. Lemev was frowning, thoughtful.

Ward Powell thought it was time to let Lemev know his place and set him straight: "They're my superiors as well, Lemev! But *my* contacts are right in there with Vladimir's own inner circle, as you know."

Lemev looked like a deflated gorilla, slumped shoulders, looking down, still frowning.

"Hey, Lemev, I didn't mean to hurt your feelings. After all, once we're done here in El Paso, we're gonna kill all the Chinese and Muslims anyway!"

Colonel Lemev cheered up at the killing part. "Okay, Ward, I'll ask Liang to lead the raid, okay?" Lemev *was* enjoying all the benefits Powell was providing and wanted to keep those benefits coming unabated. *And the cool ten million US dollars that were just deposited in my offshore account was really nice as well*, Lemev thought to himself.

"That ought to really please the two 'partner' co-authors," Powell said.

Both were laughing now.

CHAPTER 33

It was exactly two o'clock on the moonless, black morning. All buildings on the Chico Gringo Ranch compound were dark and shapeless, except the main house, which stood brilliantly lit against a pitch-black background, like a cruise ship on a completely dark ocean.

On the over twenty-five-hundred-acre ranch, the compound was over forty acres by itself. The back entrance to the compound was gated and had three dense rows of concertina barbed wire around the main house, with regular barbed wire on the fences surrounding the forty-acre tract.

To the east lay Fort Bliss military range, and to the west open pasture land all the way to New Mexico. To the north, scrub desert burned hot all the way to Fort Bliss Military Reservation, some five miles away.

The compound was surrounded by several tall oak, mesquite, and acacia trees, neatly spaced and windrowed. The main entrance on the south ran to the two-lane road, from which another paved road split the eighty acres, lined on both sides with tall oaks and ranch fencing that kept in the ranch's almost two-thousand-head cattle herd on the pasture land.

To the right and left of the back entrance stood two huge barns—one for horses, the other for cattle and milking—and two large tool sheds, with horse equipment, tractors, and other machinery, plus two bunkhouses for cowboys and other employees of the ranch.

The main house had a circular drive in front and two guest houses, with two bedrooms in each, on either side. The swimming pool, with landscaped deck, and pool house, with bar and dressing room, were all in the back of the main house.

The house was the only designed farm house of Frank Lloyd Wright. It was a contemporary three-story, with eight bedrooms, four baths, dining, living, den, and recreation areas, and a magnificent full-service kitchen and pantry.

Both bunkhouses were also full service for cowboys and all employees alike, with kitchen, dining, and sleeping areas, plus storage and pantry facilities. Both had racks of Winchester repeaters, ammo, and belts of Colt 45 repeaters in holsters for their cowboys to protect the herd from all desert predators: coyotes, rattlesnakes, and pumas.

Security was very tight. The main house itself was bathed in light from directional flood lights aimed up and into the trees and landscaping all around the house. Motion detectors surrounded the house and both guest houses. Armed horsemen patrolled the fenced main compound, and armed guards patrolled inside and around the buildings.

It was almost September 11, 2016, the fifteenth anniversary of the devastation of the Twin Towers of the World Trade Center in New York City.

Steven Vandorol was spending the weekend with Eddie and Andi, staying in one of the guest houses with Vanessa, who was on her way there from the office where she had worked all day catching up after their honeymoon weekend. Steven was working late in the guest house, getting ready for the temporary restraining order hearing on Monday before Judge Carbon, who had issued arrest warrants to all defendants named in the superseded new indictment.

Eddie had left him around midnight, and it was almost one thirty. Steven was still wearing the clothes he wore to work that day: dark slacks, long-sleeve button-down blue shirt—now unbuttoned—white T-shirt, and his favorite maroon Tony Lama boots. His navy-blue blazer was draped on the back of a chair. Rommel lay on the bed, sleeping soundly.

Steven picked up his cell phone, dialed, and waited.

"Hello, sweet Steven," Vanessa answered.

"I'm done for the day, my angel! Waiting on you. Are you about ready?"

"Yes, my love. I'm almost ready to head your way." Vanessa paused, then continued, "Is Eddie still with you?"

Steven said, "No, he went to bed about midnight."

"Okay, sweetie. I'm on the way. I'll need some wine. I love you, my Steven."

"I love you, my angel." Steven clicked off, poured two glasses of wine, turned on Celine Dion, *Power of Love*, his favorite album, and sat down to wait for the love of his life.

The unexpected, tremendous explosion was deafening. A violent fireball blazed through and smashed the paneled bedroom window to bits in an ear-splittingly loud roar. The impact shock blasted Steven out of the chair and showered him with glass and debris. He rolled and was up in a flash, going to the dresser to get his Glock. He chambered a round as the door exploded into another shower of wood and splinters. He fired three times, then total blackness.

———

When Steven woke, groggy and in intense pain, he was sitting bound with zip ties, arms laced around steel pipes. He was bleeding from his nose, ears, and gash on his neck. Rommel quietly sat by Steven, chained to a concrete abutment with a heavy chain, snout on his front legs.

Steven and Rommel were caught. He shook his head, and the cobwebs cleared a bit. He had no idea how long he had been unconscious. He still had ringing in his ears from the explosion.

Ward Powell and Colonel Stanislav Lemev sat in chairs smiling, watching him intently. Both were in full Spetsnaz Russian Special Forces dress uniforms.

Steven remembered that when his door exploded in a shower of wood and splinters, two men in black came blasting in, both with stun guns. A third intruder blasted through the window in another shower of glass.

Steven saw the one coming through the window first, so he aimed and shot him through the heart. The intruder fell to the floor dead. He turned to the door, where the two entering fired twice, after which he felt a sharp, knife-like pain in the back of his neck, and then total black oblivion.

Ward Powell spoke first. "So, the conservative media star is waking up?" he asked. "Well, let me introduce you to my buddy and former hero of the former Soviet Union . . . ta da!" He swept his arm dramatically toward Lemev and slammed the sap across Steven's face like a whip, drawing blood.

"Colonel Stanislav Lemev," Powell continued as he whipped the sap across Steven's face again, drawing blood again on the backhand swing. "Colonel Lemev, do you have a few words for the American conservative media star?" He whipped Steven again. Powell was really enjoying himself. Rommel wasn't.

Rommel was up on all fours, alert, ears sticking straight up, a menacing roar of a growl coming deep from his throat. So, Powell wielded the sap once more, slapping the dog across his snout, and Rommel's regal head snapped. No sound at all came out, but his eyes were huge, blood-red marbles of light.

Colonel Lemev straightened his shoulders to his full height and sneered. "We finally meet, Mr. Vandorol. I've heard and read so much about you." He took the sap from Ward and slapped it across Steven's face several times, back and forth, back and forth.

Hurting badly, blood flowing from his mouth and nose, Steven said nothing.

Colonel Lemev continued, "Our hit contract is fulfilled—or will be once you're dead . . . and that will come shortly . . . but it's going to be very slow and extremely painful . . . dat vesel'ye." (Enjoyable)

Powell interrupted, "And you're going to watch me take your little new wife, Vandorol."

Are the two married? Lemev thought as he interrupted Ward, "Correction, *my little* buddy! When *we both* take your little wife . . . that you've been showing around."

Powell couldn't contain his excitement. He interrupted again, almost breathless, "And for killing our assassination team leader, Ms. Baker, I'm going to let my dog have a taste as well."

"Ward, let's quit messing around here," Lemev sneered, looking at Steven. "I'm ready for some action."

"Okay . . . okay," Powell answered, looking at Rommel, who was tensing on his chain with his tail tucked between his legs in attack mode. "But first we'll get rid of the dog." He was going to hit Rommel again but hesitated when he looked at the gleaming, blood-filled eyes, barred white teeth, and massive jaw. Powell looked at Lemev, who was nodding, so he stopped short and looked back at Steven.

"Now, Mr. Media Star, you'll get to watch your stupid dog die!" He slowly walked to the door, opened it, and let a huge dog into the room, a beast from hell. "Mr. Steven 'Conservative Media Star' Vandorol, meet my little puppy dog, Ubiytsa! In case you don't know . . . in Russian that means 'Killer.' Steven watched the dog slowly amble into the room, look all around the basement, and fix his eyes on Rommel.

Two ferocious, snarling dogs, one almost the size of a timber wolf, the other of a small pony, faced each other, sharp teeth bared under vice-like massive jaws. Both let forth growls like rolling thunder. Twenty-five feet apart, with mere slits for eyes, the massive dogs sized each other up in a face-off. It was the lull before the storm. Rommel was up on all fours, straining and taunt, still chained to the support pole.

Ubiytsa looks like a demon gargoyle, Steven thought.

A lower moan, like a howl from hell itself, and the demon dog lunged. It seemed as if the massive animal were in an old-time movie in slow motion. One frame at a time, but accelerating, pure evil flew at Rommel.

Rommel was standing tall, elegant, almost regal, with his legs braced on the floor. The slow-motion movie continued as "Killer" leapt at him. In a flash, Rommel uncoiled like a steel whip and lunged, pulling and ripping the chain from the pole, deftly side-stepped Ubiytsa as the gargoyle flew past Rommel, colliding with the wall like a freight train.

The slow-motion movie ended as Killer crumpled and slid off the wall to the floor in a disorganized heap. Rommel stood perfectly still, legs braced on the floor, growling softly. The dog knew that evil would be coming again.

Killer was disoriented. He shook his head, once, twice, three times, a huge mop shaking, and stared at the magnificent Apollo of all dogs, standing like a granite statue, waiting.

Killer shook his head again. Apparently, some of the daze dissipated. Killer rose to all fours, shook his whole body—tremors like an earthquake surged from head to tail. He inhaled once, twice, and exploded toward Rommel. No more old-time movie or slow motion. Evil moved as quickly as a black panther in a dead run at the perfectly still statue.

In an instant, Rommel and Killer clashed like two armored spearheads in battle, both rearing up as two mountain rams butting horned heads. Both were thrown backward from their crash into each other. A split second more and both lunged again. This time Killer's sharp canines gashed Rommel's powerful shoulder, drawing blood. The two giants were in a massive tangle, snarling, screaming, jaws snapping, all in a tangle of legs, paws, snarling and biting.

Both were tiring as the furious battle to the death continued; the growling dogs tore at each other's throats. Both dogs were well-trained: one in evil, the other in goodness. Both were in good shape, well fed, and well-conditioned, but one hated and the other loved. But the climate of Texas was the difference. Killer was tiring faster, the debauchery and evil in El Paso now and throughout the dog's previous life were taking effect. Killer lurched forward again, rich crimson blood now flowing in two places.

With every ounce of strength in his massive shoulders concentrated at the height of his lunge, Rommel hit Killer like a battering ram and exploded like a cannon shot at Killer's throat. He hit his bullseye, and his jaws closed like a steel trap. As Rommel shook, he ripped his foe's throat completely out, leaving a gaping hole. Killer dropped to the ground, jugular pumping blood in a fountain of red, pooling. Killer was dead. The battle was over. Ward and Lemev looked at the dead dog in frozen disbelief.

Steven, hurting badly and still groggy, watched Rommel ease out the open basement door, unnoticed by either Powell or Colonel Lemev.

First, still sitting in the chair, Steven was mercilessly beaten again by Powell and Lemev, who took turns, laughing, snarling like jackals, and drawing blood until Steven was in oblivion and blackness again. Before the blackness, he heard Powell say, "Oh, by the way, we got your little wife, and she betrayed you big time . . ."

And Steven Vandorol, battered and bleeding, quietly prayed to his Lord and Savior, Jesus Christ.

CHAPTER 34

Powell boarded the Wyler Aerial Tramway gondola dragging a blindfolded Vanessa behind him, her arms held together at her delicate wrists with zip ties. He was holding an Uzi in his left hand, and still in his dress uniform.

The aerial cable car was at the tramway dock, both double doors wide open.

Right behind them, Colonel Lemev, also in uniform, pulled Steven. Steven's left hand was handcuffed with silver handcuffs to Colonel Lemev's right hand, while Lemev held an AK-47 in his left hand. He dragged Steven into the cable car right behind Powell and Vanessa, exactly where, just a few short weeks ago, Steven and Vanessa had been in heaven on earth on their honeymoon.

Steven's face was swollen, his nose broken once again and eyes almost swollen shut. Blood oozed slowly from his right ear and large bruises marked his face and neck. The blue long-sleeved shirt he was still wearing was torn on the side and soaked with blood. Steven was completely off balance and stumbling badly, having absorbed the savage beating at the hands of Lemev and Powell.

"Well, Vanessa, get yourself prepared to have the time of your life," Powell said, smiling lecherously. "Are you ready to feel what it's like to be with a real man?"

Steven gritted his teeth but said nothing, as Colonel Lemev dragged him along into the cable car. Lemev was also smiling sardonically, a mirror image of his new buddy, Ward Powell. Colonel Lemev was really enjoying himself and looking forward to watching Powell take Vanessa at the top of the peak and then becoming a member of the "mile high club" himself. After all, the Ranger Peak of Franklin Mountain was 5,632 feet above sea level—more than a mile high.

Colonel Lemev was totally distracted in anticipation of that event, but he continued smiling. *The women in El Paso are plentiful and really luscious,* he thought to himself, *but watching Vanessa get it will be even better.*

Steven was completely silent, watching everything as anger, which he thought he had cured, was raging and seething inside him once more. He remained silent and watchful, though he hurt intensely.

Steven still said nothing as Powell pulled a blindfolded Vanessa through the door of the aerial cable car. "All aboard," Ward said with a lascivious look. He pulled Vanessa in and kissed her on the neck. Colonel Lemev likewise pulled Steven right behind him, as both stepped into the gondola. Lemev was giggling like a pubescent school boy.

Steven still said nothing.

After the beating, Colonel Lemev had searched Steven thoroughly. But Lemev had made two big mistakes. Hand cuffing only Steven's left hand to his own right hand, he had forgotten to check Steven's favorite Tony Lama handmade sea turtle boots. Lemev had taken away Steven's Glock and his 22-caliber Derringer, but didn't check Steven's boots for the throwing knife, which remained perfectly hidden in the soft sheath in the right boot.

The cable car door slammed shut behind them as Powell sat down and dragged blindfolded Vanessa down beside him. "Don't you wish you still had your 25-caliber little sissy gun that you tried to kill me with, Vanessa?" Powell kissed her slim, snow white neck again.

Vanessa jerked away sharply. She recognized the voice. She had heard that voice before, but she was still blindfolded. "Why don't you take off my blindfold so I can see your face, you little coward!"

"I'll tell you what I'm going to do. First, I'm gonna untie your wrists." Powell, using his knife, sliced through the zip ties as the cable car lurched upward and her hands came loose. "And then I'm going to start removing your clothes so we can all see your sweet little body all the way up to the peak. How does that sound?" Powell paused and, still looking at her, took off his own uniform field jacket.

Vanessa said nothing, as she rubbed her slim wrists with her hands, then removed the blindfold, blinked twice, and stared at Ward Powell. "Bob Le Mont!" she screamed.

As soon she saw Ward's face, she recognized him being Bob La Mont, who had apparently disguised himself in Lubbock, but she knew at once that he and his buddy had been the ones who drugged and raped her. She looked at him with complete, utter contempt. If looks could kill, her look would have killed Powell instantly.

"I'm going to kill you for what you did!" she screamed.

Ward Powell actually laughed out loud, now holding her by her throat. "Real brave now aren't you, Vanessa?

Steven, now seething with burning rage, still said nothing.

Beside him, a totally distracted Colonel Lemev sat, eyes wide open, enjoying himself immensely at the prospect of watching Powell start to remove her clothes. Smiling like an idiot, Colonel Lemev's eyes were glazed over in abject lust, and he had a twisted grin on his ugly face. He seemed to be almost in a trance, mouth partially open, as he watched Vanessa.

The cable car continued to climb, clickety clacking like tire chains on dry pavement. Powell put his right arm around Vanessa, almost choking her, and with his left hand, he unbuttoned her silk, pale pink blouse, starting at the top. "You're going to enjoy this!" He paused, looking directly at Steven, and added, "You, too, Vandorol! Enjoy it while you can 'cause at the peak you're going to die . . . a very slow and painful death." He continued unbuttoning slowly.

Colonel Lemev, smiling as well, said, "Hurry up, Ward!" Lemev's eyes were glossy with excitement. "I get her next!" Colonel Lemev was almost salivating like a very ugly dog.

Steven remained outwardly calm, seemingly dazed and hurt, but he was recovering fast, and his seething anger was growing exponentially. Lemev was on his left. He had handcuffed his scorpion-tattooed right hand to Steven's left hand—the second of Lemev's mistakes.

Steven glanced again at the massive steel guardrail immediately to his right and calculated the distance between the steel rail and Lemev's ugly face to be about three feet. He slowly looked back at Vanessa, and their eyes locked. Her eyes widened; eyebrows raised; her hazel eyes were sparkling. Vanessa had Steven's undivided attention as the cable car was almost halfway up the peak, another thousand feet up.

Steven inhaled slowly so as not to attract either Powell's or the colonel's attention and let it out very slowly. Vanessa's hands twitched, signing to Steven, "Door lock monitoring system off." Her sweet, small hands were just two butterflies dancing for an instant that went completely unnoticed by both killers, but was very much noticed by her husband.

Steven thought, *Bless her. Somehow, she managed to turn off the door lock monitoring system at the base controls of the tramway station below.* He acknowledged Vanessa's signing with his eyes, blinking twice. The cable car soared now almost a thousand feet above a vast canyon 240 feet deep that had thousands of cacti and jagged, razor-sharp rock formations at its bottom.

Steven slowly moved his left leg against the seat brace below the seat and hooked his left boot under the steel pipe, creating the fulcrum of a lever for maximum leverage. He braced his right leg against another seat brace below. Steven's right index finger slowly inched his right pant leg up.

Powell had unbuttoned the last button on Vanessa's silk blouse, exposing her breasts in her lace bra. Powell inhaled deeply, touched the top of her breasts roughly, and moaned with animal lust. Powell's eyes were glazed over, as if he were in a trance. Powell started to unzip Vanessa's skirt.

Ugly Lemev was reaching the peak in excitement and lust as he stared at her breasts and watched Powell undress her. He seemed to be in a trance as well, completely oblivious of Steven's slight movements.

Steven braced his legs and inhaled. In one swift move, with all the strength and might his battered body could muster, he grabbed the colonel's arm with both hands and jerked him across his own body. Lemev's forehead exploded into the steel brace on Steven's right with an ugly, hollow crunch like his head was hit with a baseball bat.

As Lemev slid to the floor like a tattered rag doll, Steven was on his feet. With his right hand, he pulled out the throwing knife, flipped it in the air, caught it by its razor-sharp point, and in one smooth motion, he threw it right at Ward Powell.

Startled by the commotion across the aisle, Powell stood up, although still in a lust-filled haze. With hardly enough time for surprise to register on his handsome face, the razor-sharp knife sliced into his throat, severed his carotid artery, and exited the back of his neck, its tip bloody.

Powell gurgled a lone tubercular cough, loud and horrific, as bright red blood foamed from his mouth. He bled out instantly as blood sprayed from the wound like a fire hose nozzle turned on. For several moments, Powell stayed upright, just a guy leaning on a rail, and then everything gave way for him at once. Vanessa, all five foot one and less than one hundred pounds, shoulder down like the tiny football player she had always wanted to be, hit Ward Powell like a cannonball. The double doors flung open and outward, sending Ward Powell into the canyon abyss. Vanessa caught herself by the door brace and held on.

"Bon voyage, you evil snake!" she screamed as Powell plummeted into a thousand cacti and razor-sharp, jagged rock formations 240 feet below. He hit like a bag of evil excrement and splattered on the rocks and vegetation.

Vanessa stepped away from the door, steadied herself, and collapsed on the cabin floor to her knees. She covered her face with both hands and cried, tears streaming through her slim fingers. Steven quickly searched the pile of dirty laundry at his feet to find the handcuff keys in Lemev's left pocket. He took the cuffs off his shackled left hand and looked down at the pile of garbage at his feet.

In the tall tales told by firelight around the old campfire, in the old Western movies Steven, and now Vanessa, loved to watch, there was always conversation. The bad guy had to be told why he had to die. The reference to the injured parties—Vanessa and Steven, and those who may have perished on the ranch—gave the bad guys the chance to either repent or snarl further defiance. Either response could turn a story into a classic, depending on the hero's pithy reply.

But tall tales were tall tales and old movies were just movies. Neither were real in the world, the real ROW.

Steven said nothing at all.

Steven quietly dragged the 270-pound ugly colonel to the open cable car doors and unceremoniously kicked him out with his sea turtle boot into the same abyss Powell had plummeted just moments before. Like a huge bag of garbage, Colonel Lemev screamed for a thousand feet and also exploded against the cacti and jagged rocks below.

Steven didn't watch the very messy and bloody puddle Colonel Lemev probably became. Instead, he turned to Vanessa, picked her up off the cabin floor, and held her tightly as the cable car hooked into the platform at Ranger Peak, 5,632 feet above sea level.

Steven held Vanessa, sobbing on his shoulder. Steven said nothing but continued to hold her as tightly as possible, allowing the storm in her heart, body, mind, and soul to slowly dissipate.

Vanessa finally sighed deeply, once, twice, and drew away a bit, still holding Steven close. "Thank you for saving my life, my Steven!" She paused, wiped the tears from her eyes, and said, "I love you with all my heart and soul and will forever and always." And she smiled her radiant smile once again, brilliant and shining. Steven fell in love with her all over again.

"And I thank you, Vanessa, the love of *my* life, for saving mine! We did this together, as one." Dreamer Steven then became the practical one. "Angel, we better make this look good . . . for the three thugs still holding the tramway station below, okay?" Steven let her go as she nodded. "And I love you forever and always and am yours forever."

Steven pushed the already open door wide open, gathered up Ward's Uzi and field jacket, and Lemev's AK-47, and took Vanessa by the hand. Both stepped off on the concrete platform, slammed the doors, and the cable car started back down, chain chattering, clickety clack, like tank tracks on pavement.

CHAPTER 35

As Steven and Vanessa held each other on the peak, having saved each other, Ward Powell and Colonel Stanislav Lemev lay dead and disemboweled on the canyon floor.

Then the jackals of hell were unleashed on El Paso, Texas, on September 11, 2016, a perfectly bright, sunny, cloudless, and cool day. As the two watched, all hell broke loose in downtown El Paso and Ciudad Juarez right below.

Simultaneous explosions rocked downtown El Paso in at least a dozen places that Steven and Vanessa could see, just like tornadoes touching down out of the dark clouds, rocking and shuddering the mountain like an earthquake. The two survivors also saw fires starting, as if by spontaneous combustion, all over the downtown landscape below, as they watched from their expansive vantage point above.

Within seconds, the entire downtown was a fireball whirlwind of chaos and destruction, belching flames with smoke rising to the sky. The sounds were deafening, the ground trembling and shuddering. A few more minutes of chaos, and the mushroom clouds reaching skyward were joined by a thousand wailing sirens all enhancing the tumultuous din below.

Steven and Vanessa, holding each other even closer, watched the spectacle below in shock and awe, eyes open wide in anticipation. A stream of fire trucks and emergency vehicles flooded onto elevated Interstate I-10 from the east and west, all headed downtown, cars and trucks stopping or pulling over to the shoulders en masse.

The entire downtown was soon on fire, white mushroom clouds rising skyward.

Steven looked to the bridge from Juarez into El Paso and said, "Vanessa . . . look there." He pointed. In the distant haze below, on the El Paso-Juarez bridge into downtown El Paso, cars were exploding, flipping, and falling like tinker toys into the Rio Grande below as ten massive battle tanks moved forward, advancing in a straight line.

Steven quickly counted five tanks on each side of the concrete north-south divider, all firing at the vehicles on the bridge, turrets swinging their main guns back and forth, blowing and exploding cars out of their way.

They're all Chinese Communist T-99 main battle tanks, Steven, the tank buff, thought. *T-99s in Mexico?* "The tanks are clearing the bridge . . . oh my God . . . look behind the tanks, Vanessa."

Vanessa looked and saw that following the tanks were what seemed like dozens and dozens of Humvees, armored personal carriers, tracked vehicles, and jeeps. Then, squinting to see, in the far distance, right behind the mass of vehicles, they saw thousands of black uniformed soldiers carrying weapons and black flags, waving and shimmering in the midday Texas sky. They could hardly be seen in the smoke and haze. The troops were moving slowly, like a giant prehistoric black millipede, throbbing, moving into El Paso from Juarez.

The lead tanks were almost to the El Paso side of the bridge when suddenly several more explosions simultaneously rocked downtown again, sending another round of flames and smoke into the downtown sky. Several more downtown buildings completely disappeared in immense clouds of smoke and firestorm. Steven thought, *The municipal building just went up in smoke!*

"Steven, look over there," Vanessa said, pointing east toward Fort Bliss.

Steven looked and now saw five M1A2 Abrams main battle tanks leaving the Key Gate of Fort Bliss, heading down Airway Boulevard toward Interstate I-10 and moving fast.

As the couple watched from their mile-high vantage point, they saw about twenty Bradley fighting vehicles right behind the tanks, all moving at full speed. The tanks were almost flying, the fifty-five-ton monsters almost going airborne down Airway Boulevard, heading straight to elevated I-10 as well.

Steven and Vanessa were both stunned, awed, frightened and excited by the spectacle of powerful vehicles headed toward the interstate like a massive freight train rushing full speed down a track.

"Look, Vanessa, behind the Bradleys." Steven pointed again.

"Wow, what are those vehicles?"

"Striker armored Humvees . . . see on top sticking up? Those are rocket launchers." Another line of about twenty vehicles rocketed past the Bradley fighting vehicles to catch up with the battle tanks like another giant very fast centipede—this one with antennae on its armor-plated back.

Back to the east, the ten Communist Chinese enemy battle tanks, now on the bridge, were almost into downtown El Paso. The bridge was now completely covered with armored vehicles and thousands of black-clad soldiers, all streaming onto the bridge like cockroaches. Steven and Vanessa continued to watch.

It was like they were watching a tennis match, their heads looking east, then west, back and forth, all in rapt awe and horror.

To the west, the Abrams battle tanks were now on the elevated interstate, heading west toward downtown, followed by the Bradleys, Striker armored vehicles, and Humvees, almost flying. All looked like miniature toys on a giant stage below.

On the other side of the interstate, the four lanes going east were also filled with a line of tanks, Striker armored vehicles, and personnel carriers. Both sides of I-10 were moving forward, all at once, toward downtown El Paso, which was completely engulfed in flames and smoke. Several dark, billowing mushroom clouds reached for the sky above as two giant centipedes moved in from opposite directions.

Never letting go of each other, Steven and Vanessa watched hell unfolding below. Together they prayed, "Our Father, who art in heaven, hallowed be thy name, thy Kingdom come, thy will be done, on earth as it is in heaven."

Their prayer was interrupted by the deafening sound of jet engines and rotors, like billions of swarming, angry bees suddenly rising from Biggs Army Airfield to their left. Steven and Vanessa continued to pray, "Give us this day our daily bread and forgive us of our debts, as we forgive our debtors." Both now looked to the east.

Rising skyward from Biggs Army Airfield were some fifty AH-64D Apache attack helicopters, like a swarm of giant dragonflies. When they reached Steven and Vanessa's eye level in the distance, they lifted up skyward, all at once, dipped down, and swarmed in toward downtown El Paso like a tornado funnel cloud. Steven and Vanessa continued to pray: "And lead us not into temptation, but deliver us from evil."

Downtown El Paso was now shrouded in smoke and fire. Even the El Paso Camino Real Hotel, the tallest building in downtown El Paso, where they spent their honeymoon just a few weeks ago, was barely visible.

It was as if a sparkling, pulsating black cloud now covered downtown El Paso, the bridge across the Rio Grande, and Juarez. The black cloud sat astride the once magnificent view like a giant black mushroom.

"For thine is the Kingdom and glory and the power in Jesus Christ's holy name."

Together, Steven and Vanessa said, "Amen," as the tornado cloud of Apache attack helicopters, like a giant buzz saw, swept into the immense cloud hanging over downtown El Paso. Holding each other even more tightly, they watched the giant black coffin cloud below in complete silence and awe, from more than one mile up. Both were seated by the coin-operated binoculars, which they didn't need, as the destruction was vast and apparent.

The giant black mushroom was pulsating with a million lights blinking inside, like a massive Fourth of July fireworks display. The battle for downtown El Paso raged for what seemed like hours to Steven and Vanessa. The two still held the weapons they took from the tram at the ready.

When the fireworks show ended abruptly, the giant black cloud sat there stationary -a immense, black, rotting pumpkin.

Steven and Vanessa had ringside seats to the hell below but kept their eyes fixed on the tram station, which had been under the control of Powell and Colonel Lemev's men.

Yet, they never came.

The sun slowly set in the western sky with one last explosion of multicolored neon purple, orange, and yellow light over the Monte Christo

Mountains of northern Mexico, until all was quiet. Steven and Vanessa held each other as darkness descended, along with complete silence and eerie stillness—only a few lights could be seen all the way to the horizon.

Vanessa looked at Steven and said, "Did you hear what I said that Ward Powell was Bob Le Mont, who, with his friend, raped me in Lubbock?"

"Yes, my angel, and nothing further need be said." He picked up Powell's army field jacket and gently put it around her shoulders. They lay entwined in each other's arms in the darkness, nestling in each other's warmth until exhaustion overtook them.

Sunrise was totally brilliant on Ranger Peak as Steven and Vanessa huddled in each other's arms. They opened their eyes at the same time to absolute silence and stillness. They looked at each other, both groggy, but smiling brightly.

"Oh my God, Steven, you're hurt! I hardly noticed last night! I was so scared!"

"Your warmth overnight was the best healer after our horrific day. We're still alive, still in one piece." Steven smiled and kissed her on the forehead. "All by the grace of our Lord."

"Steven Vandorol, my husband, we became one on this mountain, and by the grace of God and our Savior, Jesus Christ, we have survived as one," Vanessa smiled her sunshine smile.

"Vanessa, my love, I am reminded of a posting I saw once that said, 'One day someone is going to hug you so tightly that all of your broken pieces will stick back together again.' And this is that time."

The long-silent gondola pulley started cranking again – like tank tracks, sticking, clicking and clacking on pavement - startling both.

Steven and Vanessa prayed the Lord's Prayer again, both grasping their weapons, the Uzi and AK-47.

After an eternal moment in time, the tank track ticking on pavement endlessly like a rain storm stopped at the docking station below the observation deck. Steven and Vanessa strained to look, holding each other and their weapons ready.

"I love you, Vanessa, love of my life, forever and always, and I am your Steven forever," Steven said, cocking the AK-47, holding it over the concrete abutment.

"I love you, Steven Vandorol, and I'll see you before our Lord." Vanessa paused, tears streaming down her beautiful face. She cocked the Uzi. "We are one, Steven."

CHAPTER 36

Eddie Egen and Ray Ortega were riding the gondola up to Ranger Peak.

Eddie's ranch had been a battleground, and the ranch compound was in shambles. The surprise attack was devastating and completely successful. The beautiful Egen home was completely destroyed, only the basement remained intact. The attackers were themselves destroyed by three Bradley armored personnel carriers under command of Major G. Jack Reacher, arriving just after Steven and Vanessa were abducted by Ward Powell and Colonel Lemev. The carriers were still holding the ranch compound area, though leveled and destroyed completely.

Eddie Egen and Ray Ortega were both armed with AR-15s, locked and loaded. Both were somber, sad, and silent and had nothing to say. The Chico Gringo was in ruins, the herds of cattle and horses scattered. Simultaneous explosions had rocked the main house and two guesthouses. The destruction was complete. The bunkhouse and arsenal inside were also destroyed and leveled.

Some two dozen killers had swarmed the compound all at once from all four sides, killing all police officers and Texas Rangers who comprised the protective shield; more than two dozen were dead. It was a well-planned, well-organized killing. They had insider information and intelligence. Eddie and Ray knew that someone in their midst had betrayed them all.

Right before the guesthouse exploded, and Steven and Rommel were captured, Steven had managed to text Ray to put their contingency security plan in place. Ray immediately called in Major G. Jack Reacher's Apache attack helicopter command and three Bradley fighting vehicles, fully armed and manned, which were all standing by at Fort Bliss five miles from the Chico Gringo. The vehicles were immediately dispatched and rolling within minutes, arriving when the killers were mopping up the compound. The massive detonations had already destroyed the entire compound.

By the grace of the Lord, Eddie Egen, unable to sleep, had walked out to sit by the pool and was there enjoying the quiet when the attack began. When the main house exploded, Eddie locked himself in the pool house where he kept an AR-15 handy. He fought off the attackers until the Bradleys from Fort Bliss arrived.

Downtown El Paso was in ruins as well, the three bridges into Juarez completely destroyed, and the Camino Real Hotel gutted. It would take weeks before both cities' interrupted power grid, electricity, and mobile communications could be fully restored.

Both the El Paso County Courthouse and Federal Courthouse were saved, and Texas Rangers killed all Muslim infiltrators based on intelligence previously gathered from the special prosecution witnesses.

As the grand jury had previously issued the superseded indictments back in August, District Attorney Ernie Martinez and First Assistant North Anderson issued the arrest warrants for all defendants, signed by District Judge Kathy Carbon.

Defendants Alberto Alvarado, father, and Roberto Alvarado, son, were arrested almost immediately at their luxurious westside El Paso homes and were in custody at Fort Bliss.

El Paso was all clear and secure as the 3rd Armored Cavalry had secured the bridges into Juarez and repulsed an ISIS and Communist Chinese invasion. The ten imported Communist Chinese T-99 main battle tanks were no match for the firepower of the five A1M1 Abrams tanks, along with the AH-64D Apache attack helicopters. They wreaked havoc and devastated all enemy armored vehicles.

Ray screamed out loud, "Eddie, look down there!"

Eddie looked down. Some four hundred feet below lay the former Ward Powell, still in his full 'Spetsnaz Russian Special Forces dress uniform, minus the field jacket, but in tatters. He was barely recognizable as just a mass of bloody flesh, arms, and legs. He looked like an extra on the *Walking Dead* television show.

Eddie adjusted his binoculars until they focused. "Oh my God, Ray, that's Steven's knife that we used to tease him about. It's sticking out . . . only its handle is showing in Powell's throat, bloody point coming out the other side. And get this, Ray . . . a huge, black buzzard is feasting on Powell's eyes while another is plucking on his balls!" Eddie smiled. "That's a great resting place for Steven's knife," he said as he aimed and fired a volley, totally disintegrating the lifeless body and the feasting buzzards until the clip was completely empty. "Dust to dust, piece of garbage. Burn in hell!" Eddie ejected the clip and replaced it with another.

The gondola continued to climb, the chains clattering, shifting, and clanking upward on the massive cables that held it suspended. Then it was Ray's turn. Almost one hundred yards from where Powell remained just a grease spot, Colonel Stanislav Lemev lay completely disemboweled, also in a shredded Spetsnaz Russian Special Forces dress uniform. The buzzards had almost devoured all his entrails before the volley that disintegrated Powell had scared them away; only a skeleton remained. The buzzards were still circling above, waiting for dessert, when Ray opened fire, turning the former hero of the Soviet Union into dog food as well.

The gondola continued to rise, clattering and rambling; the chains moaned, sounding like a sad funeral dirge.

"I pray that Steven and Vanessa are okay." Eddie again was sobbing. "That evil maniac, Powell, killed my Andi."

After the compound was secure, Eddie called Ray, who shared his suspicion, and together they confronted Jesus Chavez, who Ray and Steven had suspected since the meeting with General Nicholas, at the strategy meeting on Eddie's ranch, back in September of last year. He confessed to being the insider for the assassination team that Colonel Lemev and Ward Powell led, and that Ward Powell himself had paid him very well.

Under extreme interrogation pressure, Jesus told Eddie where they had taken Vanessa and Steven after their abduction from the ranch. Complete dossiers on both Ward Powell and Colonel Lemev provided immediately by local FBI AIC Jack Reynolds to El Paso PD and Texas Rangers completed the intelligence.

"Andi's with the Lord now, Eddie," is all Ray could say as the gondola rumbled and clattered to a stop at the concrete docking station on Ranger Peak. The observation deck was about fifty yards away.

Eddie threw open the double doors, and Ray and Eddie ran toward the stairs and saw weapons, an Uzi and AK-47 propped against the wall ledge, muzzles pointed toward the docking station.

"There, up there, Ray, two guns . . . I think," Eddie yelled.

Ray screamed, "Steven, Vanessa, don't shoot! It's us, Eddie and Ray. We won! We won!"

Silence. Complete silence. The two continued running and met silence as they reached the summit and the two propped-up weapons. They were not there. Steven Vandorol and Vanessa Vandorol had disappeared.

Gone.

Nothing.

The Dallas Morning Clarion

Dallas's Leading Newspaper, $3.00
Dallas, Texas, Wednesday, October 12, 2016

Texas Blocks President

The president's policy of deferring the deportation of millions of undocumented immigrants was stricken by El Paso County District Judge Kathy Carbon as it applied to the State of Texas.

Judge Carbon also signed and issued Texas arrest warrants for the arrests of all defendants named in the warrants, for failure to appear in her court to show cause why the temporary injunction granted by the judge to close the entire border with Mexico along the Rio Grande River should not become a permanent injunction, and the superseded bill of indictment filed in El Paso County District Court on August 1, 2016, should not be heard and tried in the 210th District Court on the merits.

In a fifty plus page opinion handed down late Monday, Judge Kathy Carbon ruled that the Department of Homeland Security was enjoined from implementing the president's executive actions. Judge Carbon further issued a preliminary injunction blocking the administration from implementing the deferred deportation program.

Texas Gov. Greg Abbott, a Republican, filed suit in December on behalf of Texas and twenty-six other states opposing executive

---

2   See Author's Note—Appendix of this novel

actions proposed by the president prior to the November national elections. The temporary injunction halts the administration's actions on immigration—moves that would have protected up to five million undocumented immigrants from deportation—as the state's lawsuit moves forward.

"The president abdicated his responsibility to uphold the United States Constitution when he attempted to circumvent the laws passed by Congress, via executive fiat, and Judge Carbon's decision rightly stops the president's overreach in its tracks," Abbott said in a statement. "We live in a nation governed by a system of checks and balances, and the president's attempt to bypass the will of the American people was successfully checked today."

The injunction is related to a program known as Deferred Action for Parents of Americans and Lawful Permanent Residents, or DAPA. The program allowed undocumented parents of lawful US citizens or permanent residents to defer deportation and seek job benefits.

Part of the program was set to go into effect on Wednesday; it would have expanded deportation protections for people who were brought into the country illegally when they were children. Protections for parents of US citizens and permanent residents were expected to start in May.

Judge Carbon wrote, "Once these services are provided, there will be no effective way of putting the toothpaste back in the tube should plaintiffs ultimately prevail on the merits."

In news related to the indictment, the attack and bombings that occurred in El Paso on September 11, 2016, were blamed on Mexican drug cartel violence which the Washington, DC, FBI is currently investigating. An FBI spokesman said yesterday that no particular group or Juarez cartel has taken responsibility. Damage to downtown El Paso appears to be minimal, federal government representatives stated.

Judge Kathy Carbon had issued an order for all defendants named in the special prosecution pending in El Paso County to show cause as to why the permanent injunctions should not be issued, yet defendants did not appear, after having been duly served with due process of law, either in person or by counsel.

Judge Kathy Carbon also signed and issued Texas state warrants for the immediate arrest of all the defendants named in the grand jury true bill of superseded indictment, including the president of the United States and other members of the administration and the leading Democratic Party candidate for the president.

Judge Carbon's office issued her statement yesterday: "These warrants for arrest are valid within the borders of our great state and will thereby be fully executed and enforced." Carbon, a district judge sitting in El Paso, Texas, was nominated by President George W. Bush in 2002.

The arrest warrant is shown in its entirety below.

Steven and Vanessa walked along in the gentle surf, holding hands, on the deserted Cape Carmel beach on the Mediterranean Sea as the brilliant orange and crimson sun was slowly sinking into the horizon.

"Cute little toes, Mrs. Vandorol!" Steven said to his wife, best friend, lover, and soul mate. "We've done it with the grace of our Lord and our Savior, Jesus Christ."

"And have done that together as one!" Vanessa added. "Saving each other by hugging each other so tightly that all the broken pieces in each of us are back together again."

And now the two were one.

Hand in hand, Steven Vandorol and his wife, Vanessa Vandorol, now married before their Lord and Savior, Jesus Christ, in their minds, hearts, and souls for almost four years, slowly walked in the gentle foam of the surf, the warm waters on the eastern shore of the Mediterranean Sea gently lapping at their bare feet. The air was clear and dry and they could smell the salt of the gentle surf and sea.

Vanessa looked like an angel to Steven. As he always would say to her, "Look at yourself through my eyes, my love, and you'll see an angel."

She wore a loose-fitting T-shirt, extra-large to cover the fifth-month swelling of her precious little tummy, that went down almost to her knees, still revealing her strong legs down to her cute little feet. She was carrying Steven's favorite sandals for her in her left hand. With hair cut short, no makeup on, and the same sparkling hazel eyes, she directed her radiant sunshine smile at her husband, walking beside her.

Steven looked down at the love of his life and smiled as well. "Remember when I first walked into my office with a burger and coke, and you dazzled me with your sunshine smile?"

"The five years since we met in El Paso just flew by in a blink of our eyes, my Steven."

They both wore T-shirts with *Atlas Shrugged* written across the front. Steven and Vanessa had become John Galt and Mrs. John Galt, dropping out of the ROW, just like the two characters in Ayn Rand's famous 1958 epic novel. They were living on a beach in a simple cottage among the palm, olive, and fig tree orchards. A vineyard sat right behind their small cottage, some fifty yards away.

As they walked by their small house, they saw their cat, Caspurr, lounging in the front windows, and their two dogs, Rommel and little Harley, cavorting on the shaded front porch as Caspurr watched them nonchalantly.

Coming the other way and walking toward them, a man and a woman appeared, led by a beautiful German Shepherd. He, a large man, and she, a beautiful, small woman, were also barefoot, walking toward them and smiling brightly.

"Major Reacher and Mrs. Reacher, will you join us for cocktails this fine evening?" Steven said to the couple.

"We'd be delighted," former United States Army Major G. Jack Reacher answered as the sun was setting into the perfectly calm, sparkling Mediterranean Sea on the western horizon.

———

Back in El Paso, Texas, four years ago on Ranger Peak of the Franklin Mountains, Steven and Vanessa held their weapons all alone on the observation deck anticipating attackers. They prayed the Lord's Prayer and waited, straining to look.

Suddenly, on the other side of Ranger Peak rose a giant, elegant dragonfly with the brilliant sun as the back drop. It was an AH-64 Apache Longbow attack helicopter, the United States Army's most advanced. The helicopter, named *Airship Genesis,* was piloted by Army Ranger Major G. Jack Reacher with flight helmet on and in the pilot's seat all alone. He was waving to Steven and Vanessa, smiling broadly.

With Steven and Vanessa Vandorol on board, grinning like two happy teenagers and holding each other tightly, the helicopter landed in a remote area of the Fort Bliss Army Reservation, right by a well-camouflaged large travel trailer.

After a long rest and much needed medical attention, especially for Steven, he and Vanessa, his two kids, Josef and Karina, Major G. Jack Reacher and Mrs. Joan Reacher, their large German Shepherd, Fritz, huge Rommel, tiny Harley, and a silly cat, Caspurr, embarked on a well-supplied AH-64D Apache Longbow attack helicopter. Stripped of all armaments, but equipped with extra fuel tanks, the helicopter disappeared into the sunset, heading west around the world to a brand-new life with their Lord and Savior, Jesus Christ.

They learned later on from the internet and social media that while the initial invasion from Mexico into El Paso and Juarez failed, the United States was still under attack from the north, through Canada, by invading

Russians, Communist Chinese, and Muslim Jihadist terrorists. America's free territory was shrinking accordingly.

In November, the US presidential elections quelled the rising tide of evil temporarily with the election of Donald Trump. Even still, the insidious corruption of government, education, religion, family, and culture by Muslims, illegals, communists, Latin American criminals, leftist progressives, and the American Democratic Party—fueled by a propaganda leftist fake news media—subverted all that was good and turned all into abject evil. The tyranny and soft bigotry of lowered expectations was slowly killing America, and would continue in the rest of the world unabated until the coming of our Lord and Savior.

But the Vandorols and Reachers no longer cared. While there is no salvation for humanity as a whole, there was survival for them as individuals, with the good Lord in their hearts.

Steven and Vanessa were one, in heart, mind, spirit, and soul. With the grace of the Lord, the two had survived. Two dolphins had out distanced the tramp steamer of the ROW and swam into forever and always together. Their upward progression of love culminated at the small beach home on the Mediterranean Sea halfway around the world. It was an oasis on Cape Carmel, a few miles from Nazareth, the birth place of Jesus Christ, and it was soon to be the birthplace of their first little one, amidst the rest of the world's most violent territory: Israel, the Middle East, and the Holy Land, 11,905 kilometers, 7,397 miles, or 6,428 nautical miles from El Paso, Texas.

As the four walked together toward the small house, Steven turned to Major Reacher and said, "Well, Jack, are you ready to tell Vanessa and I what the *G* in your name stands for?"

The former West Point graduate, former army ranger major, and veteran of the war in Iraq and Afghanistan smiled at Steven and Vanessa and said just one word:

"Gabriel."

THE END

AUTHOR'S NOTE AND APPENDIX TO THIS NOVEL

What follows this author's note is the fictionalized, redacted, simplified, and shortened version of footnote No. 1 - the actual indictment and factual background from Steve Emerson's The Investigative Project on Terrorism (IPT), especially the use of the indictment and the federal conspiracy prosecution and proceedings in the 2014 Federal District Court case in Dallas, Texas, that resulted in Hamas, The Council on American-Islamic Relations (CAIR), and other terror organizations being placed on the State Department's list of active terrorist organizations.

Also, following the superseded and amended indictment, is the fictionalized warrant for the arrest and detention of all the fictionalized defendants named referred to in footnote No. 2, Epilogue, page 202.

Chinese Communists Colonel Qiao Liang and Colonel Wang Xiangsui are in fact the real co-authors of *Unrestricted Warfare: China's Master Plan to Destroy America* (Translated from original Communist Chinese documents with an introduction by Al Santoli), Pan American Publishing Company, 2002 (ISBN 0-9716807-2-8). For the purposes of *El Paso Sunrise* and this continuation novel, *El Paso Sunset,* both Liang and Xiangsui are in the public domain worldwide. They have both been fictionalized as characters in a work of fiction, and their characterizations are also products of my imagination.[3]

---

3   Note below and hereafter—and portions redacted and shortened for the reader's convenience are shown with the following four astericks: * * * *

IN THE DISTRICT COURT OF EL PASO COUNTY
THE STATE OF TEXAS

§
§   No. 123456
§

v.

Alberto Alvarado   §
Ricardo Alvarado   §
Henderson and Lane   §
Holy Land Foundation for   §
Relief and Development (1)   §
    also known as the "HLF"   §   Superseded Bill of Indictment
Shukri Abu-Baker (2) §   Returned on August 1, 2016
Mohammad ElMezain (3)   §
Ghassan Elashi (4)   §
Haitham Maghawri (5)   §
Akram Mishal (6)   §
Mufid Abdulqader (7) §
Abdulrahman Odeh (8)   §
Barack Hussein Obama, 44th *President of the United States of America* (9) §
Eric Holder, Attorney General of the United States (10)   §
Valerie Jarrett, White House Chief of Staff (11)   §
Michelle Obama (12) §
Hillary Clinton (13)   §

SUPERSEDED BILL OF INDICTMENT

The Grand Jury also charges: THE MUSLIM BROTHERHOOD, THE ISLAMIC STATE LEVANT, THE ISLAMIC STATE UNINDICTED COCONSPIRATORS, AND ALL CAPTIONED DEFENDANTS, ALL AS FOLLOWS:

INTRODUCTION

At all times material herein:

1. The Harakat AlMuqawamah alIslamiya is Arabic for "The Islamic Resistance Movement" and is known by the acronym Hamas. Hamas, which is sometimes referred to by its followers as "The Movement," is a terrorist organization based in the West Bank and Gaza Strip (Gaza). Hamas was founded in 1987 by Sheikh Ahmed Yassin as an outgrowth of the Palestinian branch of the Muslim Brotherhood. The Muslim Brotherhood is an international Islamic organization founded in Egypt in 1928 and is committed to the globalization of Islam through social engineering and violent *jihad* (holy war). Hamas' published charter states that Hamas' purpose is to create an Islamic Palestinian state throughout Israel by eliminating the State of Israel through violent *jihad.*

2. Hamas achieves its goals through a military wing, known as the Izz elDin al Qassam Brigades, and a social wing, known as *Dawa* ("preaching" or "calling").

* * * *

3. Hamas' military wing is responsible for carrying out suicide bombings and other terrorist attacks within Israel, the West Bank, and Gaza. These attacks have targeted civilians and resulted in the death and injury of hundreds of individuals, including American citizens.

4. Hamas' social services are, in large part, administered by local Hamas-affiliated zakat committees and other ostensibly charitable organizations. "Zakat," or "alms giving," is one of the pillars of Islam and is an act incumbent on all practicing Muslims.

* * * * *

Such uses include the provision of weapons, explosives, transportation services, safe houses, and job salaries for operatives.

5. Hamas' Political Bureau sits above the social and military wings and serves as the highest-ranking leadership body in the Hamas organization.

* * * *

6. The International Emergency Economic Powers Act (IEEPA) confers upon the President of the United States the authority to deal with threats to

the national security or foreign policy of the United States. On January 23, 1995, pursuant to this authority, President William Jefferson Clinton issued Executive Order 12947, which declared a national emergency resulting from the grave acts of violence committed by foreign terrorists designed to disrupt the Middle East Peace Process.

* * * *

Any dealings in those funds after the designation date, or any attempt to avoid acknowledgment of the funds, is unlawful.

7. To implement Executive Order 12947, the United States Department of Treasury, through the Office of Foreign Assets Control, promulgated the Terrorism Sanctions Regulations [for]… (d) any conspiracy formed for the purpose of engaging in a prohibited transaction. A willful violation of any of these provisions is a criminal offense.

* * * *

8. On October 8, 1997, by publication in the Federal Register, the United States Secretary of State Madeleine Albright designated Hamas as a Foreign Terrorist Organization pursuant to Section 219 of the Immigration and Nationality Act (INA), as added by the Antiterrorism and Effective Death Penalty Act of 1996

9. The Muslim Brotherhood (Hamas' parent organization) has maintained a presence in the United States since at least the early 1980s. During the times relevant to this Indictment, the Muslim Brotherhood in the United States had approximately ten to fifteen working committees, including a Palestinian Committee whose designed purpose was to support Hamas. The Palestinian Committee had authority over several organizations, each with a specific purpose in its mandate to support Hamas, such as propaganda, community relations, and fundraising.

10. In or around 1988, shortly after the founding of Hamas, the Holy Land Foundation for Relief and Development ("HLF") was created by the defendants, Shukri AbuBaker, Mohammad ElMezain, and Ghassan Elashi, to fulfill the fundraising component of the Palestinian Committee.

11. The Islamic Association for Palestine (IAP) was the propaganda organization of the Palestinian Committee. It had offices in several cities throughout the United States, including Dallas and Chicago.

12. The defendant Shukri Abu-Baker was the President, Secretary, and Chief Executive Officer of the HLF. The defendant Shukri Abu-Baker's brother is Jamal Abu-Baker, aka Jamal Issa, the former Hamas leader in the Sudan and the current Hamas leader in Yemen.

13. The defendant Mohammad ElMezain was the original Chairman of the Board until in or about 1999, when he became Director of Endowments for the HLF. The defendant Mohammad ElMezain is a cousin of Hamas Deputy Political Chief and Specially Designated Terrorist Mousa Mohammed Abu Marzook.

14. The defendant Ghassan Elashi was the original Treasurer and became the Chairman of the Board of the HLF in 1999. He was also an incorporator of the IAP. The defendant Ghassan Elashi is related by marriage to Hamas Deputy Political Bureau Specially Designated Terrorist Mousa Mohammed Abu Marzook.

15. The defendant Haitham Maghawri was the Executive Director of the HLF.

16. The defendant Akram Mishal was the Project and Grants Director for the HLF. The defendant Akram Mishal is a cousin of Hamas Political Bureau Chief and Specially Designated Global Terrorist Khalid Mishal.

17. The defendant Mufid Abdulqader was a top fundraiser for the HLF. The defendant Mufid Abdulqader is the halfbrother of Hamas Political Bureau Chief and Specially Designated Global Terrorist Khalid Mishal.

18. The defendant Abdulrahman Odeh was the New Jersey representative of the HLF.

The HLF's Relationship with Hamas

19. During Hamas' and the HLF's beginnings, and in furtherance of their designed objective, the HLF provided significant financial resources to Hamas leaders and key strategists.

* * * *

20. As previously described, the HLF was deeply involved with a network of Muslim Brotherhood organizations dedicated to furthering the radical violent agenda espoused by Hamas * * * * violent dramatic skits depicting the killing of Jewish people.

21. In October 1993, in response to a United States sponsored Middle East peace initiative between the Israeli government and the Palestinian Liberation Organization, known as the Oslo Accords * * * *

22. In 1994, a dispute arose between the HLF and another Hamas fundraising entity in the United States. Then Hamas Political Chief Mousa Mohammed Abu Marzook resolved the dispute and determined that the HLF would be the primary fundraising organization for Hamas in the United States.

* * * *

23. The HLF supported Hamas by subsidizing 'its vital recruitment and reward efforts in the West Bank and Gaza.

* * * *

24. In 1992, the Government of Israel deported over 400 members of Hamas and other Islamic terrorist organizations to southern Lebanon in response to a surge in violence by Hamas militants against Israeli soldiers, police, and civilians. The HLF provided financial assistance to the deportees and publicly lauded itself for its response to the deportation. Deceased Hamas leader Sheik Abdel Aziz Rantisi was one of the deportees whose family received financial assistance from the HLF.

* * * *

25. In furtherance of a worldwide Muslim Caliphate, the President of the United States of America, Barack Hussein Obama, has by executive orders appointed the following Muslims in his administration:
• John Brennan, current head of CIA
• Valerie Jarrett, White House Chief of Staff
• Arif Alikhan, Assistant Secretary for Policy Development for Homeland Security
• Mohamed Elibiary, Homeland Security Advisor

Conspiracy to Provide Material Support to a Foreign Terrorist Organization

(18 U.S.C. § 2339B (a) (I))

26. Paragraphs one (1) through twentyfive (25) of the Introduction to this Indictment are hereby realleged and incorporated by reference as though fully set forth herein.

27. Beginning on or about October 8, 1997, and continuing until the date of the indictment, in the Dallas Division of the Northern District of Texas and elsewhere, the defendants Holy Land Foundation for Relief and Development (HLF), Shukri Abu-Baker, Mohammad El-Mezain, Ghassan Elashi, Haitham Maghawri, Akram Mishal, Mufid Abdulqader, and Abdulrahman Odeh, and others known and unknown to the Grand Jury, knowingly conspired to provide material support and resources, as those terms are defined in Title 18, United States Code, Section 2339A(b), to wit, currency and monetary instruments, to Hamas, a designated foreign terrorist organization, in violation of Title 18, United States Code, section 2339B(a)(1).

28. Beginning from January 17, 2007, since his inauguration as President of the United States of America, in furtherance of worldwide Caliphate and in support of the Muslim Brotherhood and the Islamic State of Levant, Barack Hussein Obama has committed treason in violation of Title 18, United States Code, section 2339B(a), and the Constitution of the United States of America.

MANNER AND MEANS OF THE CONSPIRACY

3. – 10. Redacted

Overt acts against all defendants follow and are not reproduced.

COUNT THIRTY-SEVEN ALSO FOLLOWS.

COUNT THIRTY-SEVEN

TREASON

(26 USC § 72077401)

1. The allegations of all previous paragraphs one (1) through thirty-six (36) are hereby realleged and incorporated by reference as though fully set forth herein.

2. The defendants, Barack Hussein Obama, Eric Holder, Hillary Clinton, Valerie Jarrett, and Michelle Obama have committed acts of treason against the United States of America and the people of the United States and the states of Texas, Oklahoma, Arizona, New Mexico, Kansas, Colorado, Idaho, and Montana, by opening the southern border of the United States and conspiring with the Muslim Brotherhood and Islamic State to infiltrate the country and government in Washington, DC, Denver, CO, New York City, NY, Los Angeles, CA, and Seattle, WA, and the government of Iran.

COUNT THIRTY-EIGHT
VIOLATION OF THE CONSTITUTION OF THE UNITED STATES

1. The allegations of all previous paragraphs one (1) through thirty-eight (38) are hereby re-alleged and incorporated by reference as though fully set forth herein.

3. The defendants, Barack Hussein Obama, Eric Holder, Valerie Jarrett, and Michelle Obama have violated and/or conspired to violate the Constitution of the United States by illegal and unconstitutional executive orders against illegal immigration, thus opening our southern border to Muslim terrorists of the Muslim Brotherhood and Islamic State terrorists.
SUPERSEDED BILL OF INDICTMENT ENTERED:

_____
Grand Jury Foreperson

August 1, 2016
Date

Kathy Carbon

_____
CHIEF JUDGE OF THE DISTRICT COURT

EL PASO COUNTY, STATE OF TEXAS
APPROVED AS TO FORM:
ERNESTO L. MARTINEZ, DISTRICT ATTORNEY
65TH JUDICIAL DISTRICT, STATE OF TEXAS
BY_____
STEVEN J. VANDOROL, Special Prosecutor and Deputy District Attorney
AND
BY_____
NORTH G. ANDERSON, First Assistant District Attorney and Trial Attorney
El Paso County Courthouse
1800 Texas Street, 5th Floor
El Paso, Texas 75242[4]

WARRANT FOR THE ARREST OF DEFENDANTS
IN THE DISTRICT COURT OF EL PASO COUNTY, STATE OF TEXAS
EL PASO DIVISION - STATE OF TEXAS - CRIMINAL NO. B-14-254
Alberto Alvarado
Ricardo Alvarado
Henderson and Lane
Holy Land Foundation for Relief and Development (1) also known as the "HLF"
Shukri Abu-Baker (2)
Mohammad ElMezain (3)
Ghassan Elashi (4)
Haitham Maghawri (5)
Akram Mishal (6)
Mufid Abdulqader (7)
Abdulrahman Odeh (8)
Barack Hussein Obama, 44th President of the United States of America (9)
Eric Holder, Former Attorney General of the United States (10)
Valerie Jarrett, White House Chief of Staff (11)
Michelle Obama (12)
Hillary Clinton (13), Candidate and Nominee for the Democratic Party for President (Former Secretary of State)

---

4   See Author's Note and Appendix

ORDER ISSUING WARRANTS TO ARREST DEFENDANTS

The court, having found that the state of Texas has satisfied all the necessary elements of the superseding indictment to obtain and issue a temporary injunction and arrest warrants for their immediate arrest within this jurisdiction and for their failure to appear, after being duly served, forthwith, and hereby grants the motion for temporary injunction and hereby issues warrants for the hereinabove specifically named defendants in the indictment for the stated crimes against the state of Texas as follows: the President of the United States, Barack Hussein Obama; Valerie Jarrett, White House Chief of Staff; Jeh Johnson, Secretary of the Department of Homeland Security; R. Gil Kerlikowske, Commissioner of United States Customs and Border Protection; Ronald D. Vitiello, Deputy Chief of United States Border Patrol, United States Customs and Border Protection; Thomas S. Winkowski, acting Director of Untied States Immigration and Customs Enforcement; Leon Rodriguez, Director of United States Citizenship and Immigration Services; and Eric Holder, former Attorney General of the United States. All are hereby enjoined from implementing any and all aspects or phases of the Deferred Action for Parents of American and Lawful Permanent Residents (DAPA) program as set out in the Secretary of Homeland Security, Jeh Johnson's, memorandum dated November 20, 2014 ("DAPA Memorandum"), pending a final resolution of the merits of this case or until a further order of this court, the United States Court of Appeals for the Fifth Circuit, or the United States Supreme Court. The reasons for this injunction are set out in detail in the accompanying Memorandum Opinion and Order, but to summarize, it is due to the failure of the defendants to comply with the Administrative Procedure Act. All the above are named defendants, having stubbornly and contemptuously disregarded this court's prior order to show cause, although duly served and notified. Therefore, they should be held in contempt and arrested and apprehended by any and all law enforcement in the state of Texas and within its jurisdiction for failure to appear and show cause as to why the temporary injunction should not be made permanent.

For similar reasons, the United States of America, its departments, agencies, officers, agents, and employees and Jeh Johnson, Secretary of the Department of Homeland Security; R. Gil Kerlikowske, Commissioner of United States Customs and Border Protection; Ronald D. Vitiello, Deputy Chief of United States Border Patrol, United States Customs and Border Protection; Thomas S. Winkowski, acting Director of United States Immigration and Customs Enforcement; and Leon Rodriguez, Director of United States Citizenship and Immigration Services are further enjoined from implementing any and all aspects or phases of the expansions (including any and all changes) to the Deferred Action for Childhood Arrivals (DACA) program as outlined in the DACA Memorandum pending a trial on the merits of this case or until a further order of this court, the Fifth Circuit Court of Appeals, or the United States Supreme Court.

Further, warrants for the arrest, to be exercised and served within the borders of the state of Texas, are hereby ordered against the following defendants for their crimes and misdemeanors:

Barack Hussein Obama: conspiracy to commit treason; TREASON;

Eric Holder: conspiracy to commit treason; TREASON;

Valerie Jarrett: conspiracy to commit treason; TREASON;

Michelle Obama: conspiracy to commit treason; TREASON; and

Hillary Clinton: conspiracy to commit treason; TREASON.

And for the above-named individual defendants, in their individual capacities, for conspiracy to commit treason and TREASON, LET WARRANTS FOR THEIR ARREST BE ISSUED AND ALL SAID DEFENDANTS GOVERN THEMSELVES ACCORDINGLY.

Arrest Warrant and Return

To: Any authorized law enforcement officer in the state of Texas, YOU ARE COMMANDED to arrest and bring before the district judge without unnecessary delay all defendants named in the superseding indictment true bill for the offenses fully stated therein.

Signed this 11th day of September, 2016.

Kathy Carbon, Chief District Judge
El Paso County, State of Texas

ABOUT THE AUTHOR

Louis Bodnar, also the author of *El Paso Sunrise, a Novel,* published in 2019 by Morgan James Publishing, and *Sunbelt, a Novel* (1986), by Quadrangle Press, is a retired attorney living in Broken Arrow, Oklahoma, with his wife, Joan. A naturalized American citizen, he was born in Vilshofen, Germany, as his Hungarian parents fled from Budapest, Hungary, at the end of World War II. Upon the death of his father, Dr. Steven Bodnar, the  former Hungarian Minister of the Interior and one of the leaders of the Hungarian National Socialist Party, Arrow Cross, and The Earl of Legeney, Louis emigrated to Brazil with his mother and brother.

He spent eight years in Brazil with his mother, Angela, and older brother, Steven, three years of which he lived on a Brazilian ranch, known as a *fazenda,* and the remainder in a Sao Paulo emigrant slum known as Villa Anastacio.

In 1958, through the efforts of his Aunt Ilona, a war bride of an American soldier she met in Germany, he and his mother emigrated to the United States to join their family in South Bronx, New York City. In March of 1958, his mother died of cancer and his aunt and uncle became his guardians. As the uncle, Ted Lewis, was career military in the US Army, his next military assignment was overseas to Tokyo for three years. Louis attended a military dependents' high school the first two years. Thereafter, Ted Lewis was assigned to Fort Sill, Lawton, Oklahoma, where Louis graduated from Lawton Senior High School.

Louis received an undergraduate degree from Oklahoma State University, a Juris Doctorate from the University of Oklahoma, and was a candidate for an LLM in International and Comparative Law at Georgetown University Law Center in Washington, DC. He has practiced law in the Southwest since

1972 in Oklahoma, Washington DC, Dallas and El Paso, Texas, and is a retired attorney currently in education and living with his wife, Joan, and their rescue beagle mix dog, G. Reacher, in Broken Arrow, Oklahoma. He has a son, Joey, and his wife, Missy, living in Waco, Texas, with two grandsons, Jacob and Logan. He also has a daughter, Angela Timmons, and son-in-law, Andrew, and two grandchildren, Bailey and Brady, living in Jenks, Oklahoma, as well as a stepson, Devin Dorney, living in Tulsa, Oklahoma.

While actively practicing law in El Paso, Texas, from 1987 to 2002, Louis was an associate municipal judge for the City of El Paso and a special prosecutor in the *State of Texas v. Maury Kemp, et. al* insurance fraud case, which was the single largest insurance fraud case in Texas at that time.

AVAILABLE NOW

EL PASO SUNRISE, A NOVEL, by Louis Bodnar

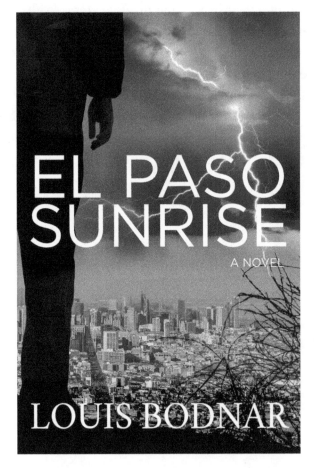

MORGAN JAMES PUBLISHING

(New York – London – Nashville – Melbourne – Vancouver)

Published and Lauched September 2019 in El Paso, Texas

AVAILABLE IMMEDIATELY AT REDUCED PRICE (POSTAGE INCLUDED) AT AUTHOR'S WEBSITE:

www.LouisBodnar.com

CPSIA information can be obtained
at www.ICGtesting.com
Printed in the USA
JSHW041609230321
12824JS00006BA/97